PENGUIN MODERN CLASSICS

The House in Paris

Elizabeth Bowen was born in Dublin in 1899, the only child of an Irish lawyer and landowner. She was educated at Downe House School, Kent. Her book *Bowen Court* is the history of her family and their house in County Cork and *Seven Winters* contains reminiscences of her Dublin childhood. In 1923 she married Alan Cameron who held an appointment with the B.B.C. and died in 1952. She travelled a great deal and divided a good deal of her time between London and Bowen Court, which she inherited.

She is considered by many to be one of the most distinguished novelists of the present age. She saw the object of a novel as 'the non-poetic statement of a poetic truth' and said that 'no statement of it can be final'. Six of her books have previously been published by Penguin. These are *The Demon Lover and Other Stories*, *The Death of the Heart*, *The Heat of the Day*, *The Hotel*, *The Last September*, *Friends and Relations* and *To the North*. Her other novels include *A Time In Rome*, *A Day in the Dark* and her last book, *Eva Trout*. She wrote six volumes of short stories including *Encounters* and *Look At All those Roses*; and two volumes of essays, *Collected Impressions* and *After-Thought*.

She was awarded the C.B.E. in 1948 and received the honorary degree of Doctor of Letters from Trinity College, Dublin, in 1948 and from Oxford University in 1956. In the same year she was appointed Lacy Martin Donnelly Fellow at Bryn Mawr Women's College in the United States. In 1965 she was made a Companion of Literature by the Royal Society of Literature. She died in 1973.

The House in Paris

Elizabeth Bowen

with an Introduction by A. S. Byatt

Penguin Books

Penguin Books Ltd, Harmondsworth, Middlesex, England
Penguin Books Inc., 7110 Ambassador Road, Baltimore, Maryland 21207, U.S.A.
Penguin Books Australia Ltd, Ringwood, Victoria, Australia
Penguin Books Canada Ltd, 41 Steelcase Road West, Markham, Ontario, Canada
Penguin Books (N.Z.) Ltd, 182–190 Wairau Road, Auckland 10, New Zealand

—

First published 1935
Published in Penguin Books 1946
Reissued in Penguin Modern Classics, with an Introduction by A. S. Byatt, 1976

—

Copyright © the Estate of Elizabeth Bowen, 1935
Introduction copyright © A. S. Byatt, 1976

—

Made and printed in Great Britain by
Cox & Wyman Ltd,
London, Reading and Fakenham
Set in Intertype Baskerville

Contents

Introduction

My relationship with *The House in Paris* has been odd, continuous and shifting, for roughly thirty years. It has had a disproportionate influence, both good and bad, on my ideas about the writing of novels and, indeed, about the nature of fiction. It seems proper to begin by explaining this since I do now believe it to be both the best of Elizabeth Bowen's novels, and a very good novel by any critical standards. But the reading process behind these judgements has been complicated.

I was given *The House in Paris* by my father when I was quite a small child, maybe ten or eleven, roughly the age of Henrietta in the novel itself. My father was under the impression that the book was a historical novel, having mistaken Elizabeth Bowen for the historical writer, Marjorie Bowen. I began the book, a compulsive reader, having already worked my way through most of Scott and much of Dickens, expecting to find a powerful plot, another world to inhabit, love, danger. I found instead my first experience of a wrought, formalized 'modern' novel, a novel which played tricks with time and point of view. A novel, also (and this I remember clearly as being supremely important), which clarified, or would have clarified if I had been clever enough to focus it, the obscure, complex and alarming relationships between children, sex and love. There were powerful phrases which lodged in my mind and have stayed there. 'Years before sex had power to touch his feeling it had forced itself into view as an awkward tangle of motives.' Or, 'The mystery about sex comes from confusion and terror: to a mind on which these have not yet settled there is nothing you cannot tell.' Or, 'There is no end to the violations committed by children on children, quietly talking alone.' I finished the book, deeply uncertain about what was happening, deeply

7

troubled about how to judge the relative weight of any of the events or people. I read it, in fact, with a social, sexual and narrative innocence which was the equivalent of Henrietta's own. I learned, from that reading, two things. First, that 'the modern novel' was difficult: it stopped and analysed little things, when you wanted to get on with big things – it made it clear to you that you did not understand events, or other people. And, more important, more durable, I learned that Elizabeth Bowen had *got Henrietta right*. Adult readers are too given to saying, of children like Henrietta, that 'real' children are not so sophisticated, so articulate, so thoughtful. What I remember with absolute clarity from this reading was a feeling that the private analyses I made to myself of things were vindicated, the confusions I was aware of were real, and presumably important and interesting, since here they were described. There is a sense in which Henrietta, and indeed Leopold, are more subtle images of the innocent or immature perception of adult behaviour than James's Maisie, in *What Maisie Knew*. Maisie is a *tour de force*, a brilliant creation, a vehicle both for James's technical mastery and for his moral commentary. But Leopold, and still more Henrietta, are children equipped with the language of the secret thoughts of intelligent children, with no more and no less than that. They make Maisie seem very much a creature of adult artifice.

After this innocent reading I put the book away for some years. In my late teens I read it again, several times; focused now much more on Karen and the central section of the novel, on love, passion, the breaking of convention, the moment of truth, the definition of identity. At that stage I think I saw the novel very strongly as a model of good writing, an example of how to be precise about thought, emotion, passion and character. To me then the restaurant scene in Boulogne, the bedroom scene in Hythe, seemed to be the central scenes, remarkable for concentrating so much passion in so few words, for the violence of life one looked for in books and feared to miss in reality.

Later still I came to think less well of the novel, dismissing

8

it as too much a work of 'fine-drawn sensibility'. It seemed too much the novel-as-object, inexorably shaped and limited by its own internal laws. I had by then read James, Forster, Woolf, Ford: 'modernism' no longer shocked or confused me. I became a discriminating reader and saw merits in the heavy, broad, open-ended Victorian novels, admired by Dr Leavis and Iris Murdoch, which made Elizabeth Bowen's precise distinctions, her craftsmanship, appear minor virtues, and her world, so economically, so selectively presented, appear shadowy. And then, recently, I read the novel again and saw that it is one of those books that grow in the mind, in time. As it is impossible at Henrietta's age to realize the nature of sex, however aware one is of its presence, so at the age when one is necessarily interested in imperative passion, the identity of the character stripped for action, decisive or disastrous, it is impossible to *realize* that sex has a history, that children are the result of sex, that children are people, produced by other people's sexual behaviour, and that with children, as with lovers and husbands, relationships of some complexity exist. One may think as a child reader, as a young reader, that one is aware of the relationship of Leopold to the plot of the book. But to recognize the full emotional force of his existence one has simply and necessarily to have lived through a certain amount of time. As with Henrietta, I came to realize that Elizabeth Bowen had got Leopold right. His claims on the reader's attention, on the other characters' attention, are justified morally and artistically.

I have described this reading and re-reading at such length because it is at the least an indication of some imaginative force in Elizabeth Bowen, but also because it was, with this novel, a peculiarly valuable way into its themes and subject matter. *The House in Paris* is a novel about sex, time, and the discovery of identity. That my readings of it in some way reflected the process it was dealing with was, in the end, my good luck.

'Plot might seem to be a matter of choice. It is not. The

particular plot is something the novelist is driven to: it is what is left after the whittling-away of alternatives.' Elizabeth Bowen opened her *Notes on Writing a Novel* (1945, reprinted in *Collected Impressions,* Longmans, Green & Co., 1950) with this statement. I think, finally, it is in the simple brilliance of the plot that the power of *The House in Paris* lies. It is a plot of considerable primitive force – child in search of unknown parents, parents in search of unknown child, love and death as identical moments of extremity. It works by playing these powerful emotions and events off against the confusions, the limitations, the continuities created by a particular civilization, a particular time and culture. Thus in the first part, 'The Present', Leopold and Henrietta are both attempting to define, or assert, their own identities, which are thrown into relief by the alien quality of the enclosing Anglo-French house in Paris inhabited by adult passions, and equally by adult social conventions, with which they are not used to dealing. Leopold is in a state of disaster and crisis: Henrietta is a normal little girl, trying to deal with tragedy through a set of responses formed only for controlled social situations.

'Today was to do much to disintegrate Henrietta's character, which, built up by herself, for herself, out of admonitions and axioms (under the growing stress of: If I am Henrietta, then what is *Henrietta*?) was a mosaic of all possible kinds of prejudice. She was anxious to be someone, and, no one having ever voiced a prejudice in her hearing without impressing her, had come to associate prejudice with identity. You could not be a someone without disliking things ... Now she sat biting precisely into her half of roll, wondering how one could bear to eat soppy bread' (pages 25–6). Henrietta 'longed already to occupy people's fancies, speculations, and thoughts'. Whereas Leopold, brought up by his adopted parents, was 'over understood ... He knew too well these people found him remarkable ... Where he came from, kindness thickened the air and sentiment fattened on the mystery of his birth. Years before sex had power to touch his feeling it had forced itself into view as an awkward tangle of motives. There was no one he could ask frankly: "Just how odd *is* all this?" The disengaged Henrietta had been his first looking-glass' (pages 34–5). Leopold's situation of extremity and indefiniteness is emphasized by the letter he reads from the adopted parents, with its complete ignorance of his nature and needs, its grotesque emphasis on his dangerous heredity and possible digestive upsets.

We do not consider him ripe for direct sex-instruction yet, though my husband is working towards this through botany and mythology. When the revelation regarding himself must come, what better prototypes could he find than the Greek and other heroes, we feel. His religious sense seems still to be dormant. We are educating him on broad undenominational lines such as God is Love.

We have of course no idea *what* revelations Leopold's mother may see fit to make, but we do trust you will beg her to be discreet and have regard for his temperament and the fact that he has not yet received direct sex-instruction. Almost any fact she might mention seems to us still unsuitable (page 41).

Leopold's reading of this letter, at a point when the reader is as unaware as he is of the possible nature of his mother's 'revelations' and indeed of his mother, is a brilliant piece of plotting. So is the transition from Leopold's quest for self in Part I to Karen's quest for self in Part II, 'The Past'. The transition from Leopold's mother's non-appearance to the account she did not give him of how he had come to be is masterly. It is not simply authorial sleight-of-hand that gives Elizabeth Bowen the authority to open her fictional account of Leopold's origins with a claim that an *imaginary* mother, like a work of art, can tell the truth because she is not encumbered by either time or conventions. 'The mother who did not come to meet Leopold that afternoon remained his creature, able to speak the truth ... He did not have to hear out with grave discriminating intelligence that grown-up falsified view of what had been once that she, coming in actually, might have given him. She, in the flesh, could have offered him only that in reply to the questions he had kept waiting so long for her: 'Why am I? What made me be?'

And Elizabeth Bowen adds that 'the meeting he had projected could take place only in Heaven – call it Heaven; on the plane of potential not merely likely behaviour. Or call it art, with truth and imagination informing every word' (page 67).

Elizabeth Bowen's definition of the object of a novel is directly relevant here. It is also as good a statement of the complex relations of truth and fiction as I know. 'Plot must further the novel towards its object. What object? The non-poetic statement of a poetic truth ... Have not all poetic truths already been stated? The essence of a poetic truth is that no statement of it can be final.' Earlier in the same essay she said that plot, as well as being story, 'is also "a story" in the nursery sense = lie. The novel lies, in saying something happened, that did not. It must, therefore, contain uncontradictable truth to warrant the original lie.' Thus Leopold's projected talk with Karen is a lie, as Elizabeth Bowen's novel is a lie, but both are charged with 'poetic truth' and related to each other. And there is a sense, one of the real achievements of the book, in which the following flashback to Karen's love for Max carries the plot forward. The 'poetic truth' of this novel, as I see it, is about the discovery of identity, and in this sense the woman, Karen, and the man, Max, are continuations of the children Leopold and Henrietta, although they are also means to the re-definition, the restatement, of the child Leopold, in the light of our knowledge of them. That is, the reader moves forward from childhood to young adult love, although the narrative time shifts backwards.

Karen, like the children, defines herself by plotting extremity, disaster, against convention. Her family is happily, successfully conventional in a way nothing in the house in Paris is. They have an 'unconscious sereneness behind their living and letting live' which 'Karen's hungry or angry friends could not tolerate'. 'Nowadays such people rarely appear in books; their way of life, though pleasant to share, makes tame reading ... Karen saw this inherited world enough from the outside to see that it might not last, but for that reason, obstinately stood by it.' (pages 70–71). Ray, whom she is to marry, is of it. Max, like his son, powerful and over-sensitive, has no available conventions, so has to define himself. 'Intellect, feeling, force were written all over him; he did in fact cut ice.' Mrs Michaelis, Karen's mother, sees that Karen is shaken by him, and makes one of those generalizations, true and inadequate, that together make the tone of this book: careful definition, re-definition, judgement, further judgement.

'She thought, young girls like the excess of any quality. Without knowing, they want to suffer, to suffer they must exaggerate; they like to have loud chords struck on them. Loving art better than life they need men to be actors; only an actor moves them, with his telling smile, undomestic, out of touch with the everyday that they dread. They love to enjoy love as a system of doubts and shocks. They are right: not seeking husbands yet, they have no need to see love socially' (page 107). Karen's dying Aunt Violet, held even when dying by the everyday, the continuous, the social, sees Karen wistfully as a woman of 'character' who could and should have 'an interesting life'. Karen, in bed with Max, contemplating the possibility of Leopold, thinks that Leopold would be disaster and realizes that Aunt Violet 'saw Ray was my mother: did she want this for me? I saw her wondering what disaster could be like. The child would be disaster.'

Karen's reflections on the impossible disaster represented by the possible Leopold are the next stage in the movement of the plot around the themes of death, sex, identity, time, violence and convention. Imagined Leopold is the imagined, improbable future. 'If a child were going to be born, there would still be something that had to be ... I should see the hour in the child, I should not have rushed on to nothing.' Karen is afraid that her act has been unreal, will come to seem unreal because it has no past or future. In fact, disaster, Leopold's birth, Max's death, are reality, the real future; they are what is, and not what is imagined.

In Part II Karen and Max, who have no shared past, and

do not know that they share a future, talk about history (page 143). We are told 'side by side in the emptying restaurant, they surrounded themselves with wars, treaties, persecutions, strategic marriages, campaigns, reforms, successions and violent deaths. History is unpainful, memory does not cloud it; you join the emphatic lives of the long dead. May we give the future something to talk about.' In Part III it is Ray Forrestier and Leopold together who engineer a continuity, a movement from past through present to future which is on Leopold's part dramatic, and on Ray's the product of a profound sense of the saving value of convention, of love as seen by Karen's dead mother (who 'died of Leopold'), as protective, practical, normal. Leopold is told by Madame Fisher that he is in a story whose plot has the necessity of fairy-tale. 'No doubt you do not care for fairy-tales, Leopold? An enchanted wood full of dumb people would offend you; you are not the young man with the sword who goes jumping his way through. Fairy-tales always made me impatient also. But unfortunately there is no doubt that in life such things exist . . .' (page 200). Ray, described as looking like 'any of these tall Englishmen who stand back in train corridors unobtrusively to let foreigners pass to meals or the lavatory . . . was the Englishman's age: about thirty-six . . . He had exchanged the career he once projected for business, which makes for a more private private life' (pages 212–13). Ray, that is, appears to be anonymous. But Karen's dramatic act has changed him too; he is in a fairy-tale, and his wife sees him as a fanatic. He is aware that he and Karen are not alone, are not two – they are haunted, as Max and Karen, momentarily, were not – by the absent third, Leopold. Ray, mystically according to Karen, practically according to himself, sets out to rectify the situation. And when Ray meets Leopold, the identities of both are defined, in action. Elizabeth Bowen's description of this action is a marvellous continuation of the fairy-story metaphor and the practical detail of the 'non-poetic' novel working together. Leopold is both the prince and the cross, bewildered, egotistical little boy, clearly seen and taken in hand. The story has moved, in our minds, from innocence, through violence, to insight, from the child's eye, through the obsessive eye of love and the momentary act, to the extraordinary and I think unpredictable ending, where expectations are more than fulfilled and the disparate elements of plot and vision are brought together.

There is much more that could be said. This is both a very elegant and a very melodramatic novel. Again in the *Notes on Writing a Novel*, Elizabeth Bowen discusses the concept of 'relevance' which she declares is 'imperative'. Everything, she concludes, Character, Scene, Dialogue, must be strictly relevant to the Plot. The elegance of this novel bears witness to her triumphant skill in this field. Not a dialogue in the book does not turn in some way on the central problems and forces it deals with. No situation is described which does not illuminate others. (Consider Mme Fisher's marriage, as it is presented by Mme Fisher to Henrietta, and its relation both to Leopold's idea of love and marriage and to Henrietta's own.) Images recur: mirrors, and eyes as mirrors of identity, Leopold as a growing tree. There are times when such formal elegance, such energetic pursuit of total relevance, can seem narrowing, or claustrophobic, or detracting from our sense of reality and importance. Elizabeth Bowen learned much from James, and much from Virginia Woolf. One of the things she learned was James's respect for developed form in fiction, his sense that one could achieve subtleties unavailable to the creators of the 'loose, baggy monsters' of the nineteenth century. In her weaker works this preoccupation can create a sense of strain, contrivance, even fuss, which diminish the force of the poetic truth. In this novel her priorities seem to me vindicated by the power of the plot. She writes, for all her elegance, with a harshness that is unusual and pleasing. There are moments of vision and metaphor, akin both to James and to Virginia Woolf, but recognizably Elizabeth Bowen's own. As when Naomi's 'sudden tragic importance made her look doubtful, as though a great dark plumed hat had been clapped aslant on her head'. Or Henrietta who, 'feeling like a kaleidoscope often and quickly shaken, badly wanted some place in which not to think'. But the characteristic tone is the author's cool judgement of the power of events, the true nature of events, of the Plot, as she sees it. As a child, I thought I was learning sensibility and fine discrimination from this novel. Now, more importantly, I feel that Elizabeth Bowen's description of Ivy Compton-Burnett's quality applied also to her own work. She wrote of her in 1941: 'Elizabethan implacability, tonic plainness of speaking, are not so strange to us as they were. This is a time for *hard* writers – and here is one.'

A. S. BYATT

Part 1

The Present

I

IN A TAXI skidding away from the Gare du Nord, one dark
greasy February morning before the shutters were down,
Henrietta sat beside Miss Fisher. She embraced with one
arm a plush toy monkey with limp limbs; a paper-leather
dispatch case lay at her feet. Miss Fisher and she still both
wore, pinned to their coats, the cerise cockades which had
led them to claim one another, just now, on the platform:
they had not met before. For the lady in whose charge Henrietta had made the journey from London, Miss Fisher's
cockade, however, had not been enough; she had insisted on
seeing Mrs Arbuthnot's letter which Miss Fisher said she had
in her bag. The lady had been fussy; she took every pre-
caution before handing over a little girl to a stranger at such
a sinister hour and place. Miss Fisher had looked hurt. Henrietta, mortified and embarrassed, wanted to tell her that the
suspicious lady was not a relation, only a friend's friend.
Henrietta's trunk was registered straight through to Mentone, so there had been no further trouble about that.

There was just enough light to see. Henrietta, though
dazed after her night journey, sat up straight in the taxi,
looking out of the window. She had not left England before.
She said to herself: This is Paris. The same streets, with
implacably shut shops and running into each other at odd
angles, seemed to unreel past again and again. She thought
she saw the same kiosks. Cafés were lit inside, chairs stacked
on the tables: they were swabbing the floors. Men stood at a
steamy counter drinking coffee. A woman came out with a
tray of mimosa and the raw daylight fell on the yellow
pollen: but for that there might have been no sky. These
indifferent streets and early morning faces oppressed Hen-

rietta, who was expecting to find Paris more gay and kind.

'A Hundred Thousand Shirts,' she read aloud, suddenly.

Miss Fisher put Mrs Arbuthnot's letter away with a sigh, snapping the clasp of her handbag, then leaned rigidly back in the taxi beside Henrietta as though all this had been an effort and she still could not relax. She wore black gloves with white-stitched seams that twisted round on her fingers, and black furs that gave out a camphory smell. At the Gare du Nord, as she stood under the lamps, her hat had cast a deep shadow, in which her eyes in dark sockets moved, melancholy and anxious. Her olive-green coat and skirt, absorbing what light there was, had looked black. She looked like a Frenchwoman with all the animation gone. Her manner had been emotional from the first; there was something emotional now about her tense way of sitting. Henrietta, nervous, tried to make evident, by looking steadily out of the window on her side, that she did not expect to be spoken to. She had been brought up to think it rude to interrupt thought.

But Miss Fisher, making an effort, now touched one of the monkey's stitched felt paws. 'You must be fond of your monkey. You play with him, I expect?'

'Not nowadays much,' said Henrietta politely. 'I just always seem to take him about.'

'For company,' said Miss Fisher, turning upon the monkey a brooding, absent look.

'I like to think he enjoys things.'

'Ah, then you do play with him!'

It was not in Henrietta's power to say: 'We really cannot go into all that now.' Re-crossing her feet, she lightly kicked the dispatch case, which contained what she would want for two night journeys and during the day in Paris: washing things, reading matter, one or two things to eat. Turning away again to look at the street, she was glad to see shutters taken down from one shop: a woman in felt slippers was doing this. A paper-kiosk opened to take its stock in; a lady in deep mourning attempted to stop a bus: the frightening

18

cardboard city was waking up at last. Violent skidding traffic foreignly hooted, and Henrietta wished there were more light.

'Is this a boulevard?'

'Yes. You know, there are many.'

'My father told me there would be.'

'We cross the river soon.'

'How soon will it be daylight?'

Miss Fisher sighed. 'The mornings are still so late. How happy you are to be going south, Henrietta. If I were a swallow you would not find *me* here!'

Henrietta did not know what to say.

'However,' Miss Fisher continued, smiling, 'to have been met by a swallow would not help you much. It would have been a great disappointment to me to fail your grandmother. Fortunately, my mother is better this morning: she slept better last night.'

'I'm sorry your mother is ill,' said Henrietta, who had forgotten Miss Fisher had a mother.

'She is constantly ill, but wonderfully full of spirit. She is most anxious to see you, and also hopes to see Leopold.'

Miss Fisher's mother was French and they lived in Paris: this accounted, perhaps, for Miss Fisher's peculiar idiom, which made Henrietta giddy. Often when she spoke she seemed to be translating, and translating rustily. No phrase she used was what anyone could quite mean; they were doubtful, as though she hoped they would do. Her state of mind seemed to be foreign also, not able to be explained however much English you had ... This illness made her mother sound most forbidding: Henrietta had a dread of sick-rooms.

Leopold? thought Henrietta. The thought that Miss Fisher might have taken the liberty of re-christening her monkey, whose name was Charles, made her look round askance. She said: 'Who is Leopold?'

'Oh, he's a little boy,' Miss Fisher said with a strikingly reserved air.

'A little boy where?'

'Today he is at our house.'

'French?' pursued Henrietta.

'Oh, hardly French: not really. You will see for yourself. You will think,' Miss Fisher said, with the anxious smile again, 'that we have a depôt for young people crossing Paris, but that is not so: this is quite a coincidence. Leopold is not crossing Paris, either; he came to us late last night by the train from Spezia, and will return, we expect, tomorrow or the day after. He is in Paris for family reasons; he has someone to meet.'

'Where's Spezia?'

'On the Italian coast.'

'Oh! Then he's Italian?'

'No, he is not Italian ... I have been wanting to ask you, Henrietta, to be a little considerate with Leopold when you meet him this morning: you may find him agitated and shy' — *her* agitation came on at the very idea, making her knit her gloved fingers, twisting the seams round further.

'Why? Do journeys upset him?'

'No, no; it is not that. I think I had better explain to you, Henrietta — it is Leopold's mother he is going to meet. And he has not met her before — that is, since he can remember. The circumstances are very strange and sad ... I am only telling you this much, Henrietta, in order that you may not ask any more. I beg you will not ask more, and I specially beg you to ask Leopold nothing. Simply play with him naturally. No doubt you will find some game you can both play. He is in an excited state and I do not wish him to talk. It is for the morning only: his mother will be arriving early this afternoon and before that, naturally, I shall take you out. I did not anticipate this when I promised your grandmother that you should spend the day here between your trains. Leopold's coming to us was arranged since that, very suddenly, and I was most anxious not to disappoint your dear grandmother when she had been at such pains to arrange everything. I believe she will not blame me for the coincidence. It appeared impossible that Leopold's mother should be in Paris on any other day — I was equally anxious not to put *her* out, for you can see what importance she must attach to this meeting. It has all been very difficult. Tomorrow, I am intending to write to your grandmother, explaining the matter to her as far as I may. I feel sure she will not blame me. But I feel sure she would not wish you to ask Leopold questions; it is all sad, and she might not wish you to know. By questioning him you would only distress yourself and agitate him: there is much, as a matter of fact, that Leopold does *not* know. I know how much above the world your grandmother is in her thoughts, but I should not like to upset her, or feel she might misunderstand.'

Henrietta, who had listened to most of this pretty blankly, said: 'I don't suppose she would bother. Where *does* Leopold live, then?'

'Oh, you see, near Spezia, with a most charming family who have a villa there – You must show him your monkey: I am sure he will like that.'

'I never ask people things,' said Henrietta coldly.

Miss Fisher went on looking wretchedly undecided. One of her troubles was, quite clearly, being unaccustomed to children. Henrietta had the advantage of her, for, as almost an only child – she had one married sister – she was only too well accustomed to grown-ups. 'Perhaps,' Miss Fisher plunged on, 'I should not have told you so much. It is hard to know what is best: it is all difficult for me, when my mother is too ill to consult.'

Henrietta regretted that Leopold was not a girl: she did not like boys much. Last night's shaken broken sleep, now the stress of being in Paris, made her thoughts over-clear, and everything had echoes. Tossing her longish fair hair back she exclaimed: 'I expect that will be all right.'

They crossed the river while Miss Fisher was speaking. In a sort of slow flash, Henrietta had her first open view of Paris – watery sky, wet light, light water, frigid, dark, inky buildings, spans of bridges, trees. This open light gash across Paris faded at each end. It was not exactly raining. Then, passing long grinding trams, their taxi darted uphill: the boulevard was wide, in summer there would be shade here. They swerved right, round the dark railings of a statuey leafless garden – 'Look, Henrietta, the Luxembourg!' – then engaged in a complex of deep streets, fissures in the crazy gloomy height. Windows with strong grilles looked ready for an immediate attack (Henrietta had heard how much blood had been shed in Paris); doors had grim iron patterns across their glass; dust-grey shutters were almost all bolted fast . . . Miss Fisher, by reaching down for Henrietta's case, made it clear that they were arriving. The taxi stopped; Miss Fisher got out and paid; Henrietta got out and looked up and down the street.

The Fishers' house, opposite which the taxi stopped, looked miniature, like a doll's house: it stood clamped to the flank of a six-storied building with balconies. On its other side was a wall, with branches that in summer would toss gaily showing over the top. Up and down the narrow uphill street the houses were all heights: none so small as the Fishers'. At each end, the street bent out of sight: it was exceedingly quiet and seemed, though charged with meaning, to lead nowhere. Unbright light struck between the flanks of the houses, making their inequality odder still: some were trim and bright, some faded, crazy or sad. Henrietta's exact snobbishness could not 'place' this street – was it mean or grand? – in the unsmiling light it had unity. She saw spaces of wall, with shut grey gates and tree-tops, over which towered buildings in other streets. It was exceedingly silent, though you heard in the distance Paris still going on; the height all round would have made it darkish at any hour. A maid was shaking a mat out of one window; elsewhere, shutters were unwakingly shut. In fact, it was early for people to be about – there were no shops, nothing to get to work. But it would not really have surprised Henrietta if no one had ever walked down that street again.

The Fishers' house looked small because of its narrowness. It was three stories high, and also, stepping back, Henrietta saw another couple of windows, mansard windows, peering down from above. Its cream front was a strip marbled with fine dark cracks; it just held, below the mansards, five wide-awake windows with grey shutters fixed back; two, then two, then a window beside the door – around these pairs of windows the house made a thin frame. Miss Fisher put her latch-key into the door, which was grained brown and had a knob in the middle. Henrietta thought: Perhaps it is not really so small inside? Or perhaps it stretches back ... The house, with its clean tight blinds across inside darkness, managed to look as proud as any in the street; there was nothing 'bijou' about it; it looked stern. Henrietta heard later that the site was valuable; Mme Fisher was, in spite of her poverty, most obstinate in refusing to sell.

Miss Fisher's key turned and she pushed the door open. Henrietta took a last look at the outside of the house, which she never saw in daylight again. Shifting Charles up her arm, she followed Miss Fisher in.

The hall was dark, it had a clean close smell. Miss Fisher switched on the light, showing a red flock wallpaper; indoors, her manner became more assured and commanding. 'Now, dear,' she said, 'I expect you would like a bath.'

'No, thank you,' said Henrietta, who did not want to undress here.

Miss Fisher was disappointed. 'Oh, dear,' she said, 'I had the bath heated specially. Don't you think, Henrietta, your grandmother would like you to?'

As a matter of fact, Henrietta's grandmother, Mrs Arbuthnot, seldom looked beyond her finger-nails, except once or twice when she had peered into her ears to see if they could be waxy; when Henrietta did not at once answer a question or reply to an observation, kindness led her to think that the child must be getting deaf. Henrietta, though already a little vain, did not yet like washing; she repeated firmly: 'No, thank you; I feel too sleepy to have a bath.'

'Poor Henrietta – look, you shall go to bed!'

'No, thank you, I'm too sleepy to have a bath but not sleepy enough to sleep,' Henrietta explained – glancing, meanwhile, at the shut doors, then up the staircase, wondering where Leopold might be. Was he, with some excitement, hearing her arrive? It made her jealous to think his unknown mother must be most in his thoughts, if he *were* awake, so that her own arrival must mean less. If he woke up excited, the cause would not be Henrietta; he might be thinking about her without curiosity, or perhaps not even thinking about her at all. Already, she longed to occupy people's fancies, speculations and thoughts.

It was agreed by Miss Fisher, after some more discussion, that Henrietta should wash as much as she liked, then come down to the salon for coffee, rolls and butter, then lie on the salon sofa to sleep or not, as she wished. She should be quiet in there, nobody should disturb her. Turning warningly at the foot of the steep stairs Miss Fisher put a finger to her lips, to remind Henrietta someone was ill somewhere. So up they crept like thieves. You saw no windows; the hall and stairs were undraughty, lit by electric light. The inside of this house – with its shallow door-panels, lozenge door-knobs, polished brass ball on the end of the banisters, stuffy red matt paper with stripes so artfully shadowed as to appear bars – was more than simply novel to Henrietta, it was antagonistic, as though it had been invented to put her out. She felt the house was acting, nothing seemed to be natural; objects did not wait to be seen but came crowding in on her, each with what amounted to its aggressive cry. Bumped all over the senses by these impressions, Henrietta thought: If *this* is being abroad ...

They went through Miss Fisher's room, where the bed was not yet made and which smelled of Miss Fisher and eau-de-Cologne, into her *cabinet de toilette*. Here a window opened on steep roofs; raw town air came in. The *cabinet* with its unexpected fittings enchanted Henrietta, who thereupon decided that Miss Fisher's humility could have nothing to do with money; she was clearly well off. Henrietta had once crossed London with a 'distressed lady' and had not failed to observe her jotting down what she spent in a little pocket-book as they went along. Miss Fisher, more lordly, had omitted to do this ... Henrietta chased a cake of sandal-wood soap in the foreign water, feeling it lap her wrists. Rubbing round the rim of her face with a fringed towel she thought: I am washing in Paris ...

24

Behind one of those landing doors, the sick French lady lay. And which would be Leopold's? Or was he a floor higher? Hearing china clink, Henrietta went downstairs, to follow the fragrance of coffee into the salon. Here at a round table Miss Fisher sat pouring out, moving cups in a placid, settled way. Now she had her hat off, daylight through the white window-blind showed up her face in its true proportion and character. Her hair was dark, with a dullish gloss on it; she wore it bound round her head in two plain bands. Her rather fine forehead added sense and solidity to the rest of her over-mobile face: agitation must count for less than had first appeared. In bony sockets still full of brown shadow her eyes had an incalculable depth. Her prominent, not beautiful mouth had lines round it that looked patient, not grim or ironic. She was thin all over. She enjoyed pouring out coffee: when she was calm she was perfectly calm. She had led Henrietta to think her a greater fool than she was. Henrietta had no way of estimating her age, which turned out later to be about thirty-nine.

'My mother still feels well,' she said as Henrietta sat down. 'She had been asleep again.'

'I hope I didn't wake her?'

'No, she was ready to wake. When she woke, she asked at once if you had come.'

Henrietta's heart sank slightly: she felt like a meal being fattened up for a lion. However, she buttered a roll and ate: Miss Fisher, meanwhile, broke a *croissant* in two and dipped it with perfect naturalness into her coffee, smiling away to herself for some interior reason and not observing Henrietta's surprise. Henrietta was sure you did not do this with bread: travel had still to do much for her priggishness about table manners. Today was to do much to disintegrate Henrietta's character, which, built up by herself, for herself, out of admonitions and axioms (under the growing stress of: If I am Henrietta, then what is *Henrietta*?) was a mosaic of all possible kinds of prejudice. She was anxious to be someone, and no one having ever voiced a prejudice in her hearing without impressing her, had come to associate prejudice with identity. You could not be a someone without disliking things ... Now she sat biting precisely into her half of roll, wondering how one could bear to eat soppy bread.

The tight-scrolled crimson sofa backed on the wall opposite the window, having its head to the door. The room had a satiny paper, striped yellow and grey, and a scrolled grey marble mantelpiece with an iron shutter pulled down inside: any heat in here came from hot water pipes. Against the wall opposite the mantelpiece stood a chiffonier with gilt beadings and marble ornaments; next to the window, facing the sofa, a consol table with no mirror behind. There were four green velvet armchairs, like doll's-house furniture magnified, and the round centre table on which the tray stood. Any space round the walls was filled up with upright chairs. The curtains draped stiffly round the muslin-masked window clearly did not draw. The parquet was bare and waxed: the room smelled of this.

When breakfast was over, Miss Fisher spread a sheet of *Le Matin* across the end of the sofa for Henrietta's feet, then Henrietta lay down with her feet on the newspaper. A small satin bolster, hard as a Japanese head-rest, supported her head; she lay stretched straight out in alarmed passivity, as though on an operating table. Miss Fisher having carried away the coffee tray, everything immobilized in the salon but the clock's pendulum, which Henrietta watched.

Miss Fisher looked back to say: 'Can you sleep in daylight?'

'There's not much light,' Henrietta said in a faraway voice. The room, at the back of the house, looked on to a courtyard like a well between walls, with one tree whose outline showed through the blind.

'Then try to sleep, Henrietta,' said Miss Fisher. 'Remember, you will be travelling again tonight.'

'I want to go out soon.'

'Paris won't run away,' said Miss Fisher. Her voice trailed off; she melted out of the room.

That image of streets in furtive chaotic flight, and of the Seine panorama being rolled up, was frightening for the first minute; then a lassitude in which reedy fantasies wavered began like smoke to fill Henrietta's brain. She relaxed more on the sofa, shutting her eyes. But she could not hear the clock without seeing the pendulum, with that bright hypnotic disc at its tip, which set the beat of her thoughts till they were not thoughts. Steps crossed the ceiling and stopped somewhere: was Miss Fisher standing by her sick mother's bed? She can't be dying, she wants to know about me. The stern dying go on out without looking back; sleepers go out a short way, never not hearing the vibrations of Paris, a sea-like stirring, horns, echoes indoors, electric bells making stars in the grey swinging silence that never perfectly settles in volutions of streets and empty courts of stone.

Henrietta, waking, opened her eyes.

Leopold said, 'I didn't know you were in here.'

He had come well into the room, and might have been there some time. He was still part of the dream she had not quite had.

'Have I been asleep long?'

'I don't know when you went to sleep.'

'Soon after I came here.'

'Yes, I heard you come. About three hours ago.'

'Then where did you think I was?'

'I thought I would find out.'

Going back to shut the door, which was open, Leopold added, 'As a matter of fact, she told me not to come in here.'

Having shut the door, Leopold walked across to the mantelpiece, which he stood with his back to, looking at Henrietta with no signs of shyness, in a considering way. He had a nervous manner, but was clearly too much taken up with himself to be frightened of anyone. She saw a dark-eyed, very slight little boy who looked either French or Jewish; his nose had a high, fine bridge and his hair grew up in a crest, then lay down again; he had the stately waxen impersonal air of a royal child in a picture centuries old. He wore a bunchy stiff dark blue sailor blouse, blue knickerbockers and

27

rather ugly black socks ... Henrietta, sitting up on the sofa, pushed into place more firmly the semi-circular comb that held back her hair.

<h2 style="text-align:center">2</h2>

Henrietta, composedly sitting up on the sofa, pushing the curved comb back, made Leopold think of a little girl he had once seen in a lithograph, bowling a hoop in a park with her hair tied on the top of her head in an old-fashioned way. His own inner excitement was so great that nothing outside, in this house, struck him as odd at all. But he had seen, from the way she had lain stretched on the sofa before waking, that even in sleep Henrietta was being exposed to unfamiliar sensation. She had lain, hair hanging down, like someone in a new element, a conjurer's little girl levitated, rigid on air, her very sleep wary. But now she woke, her manner at once took on a touch of clear-sighted, over-riding good sense, like Alice's throughout Wonderland. She might marvel, but nothing, thought Leopold, would ever really happen to her.

He said: 'Miss Fisher says you're here for the day.'

'I'm just crossing Paris,' Henrietta said with cosmopolitan ease.

'Is that your monkey?'

'Yes. I've had him ever since I was born.'

'Oh,' said Leopold, looking at Charles vaguely.

'How old are you?' Henrietta inquired.

'Nine.'

'Oh, I'm eleven.'

'Miss Fisher's mother is very ill,' said Leopold. He sat down in an armchair with his knees crossed and, bending forward, studied a cut on one knee. The four velvet armchairs, each pulled out a little way from a corner, faced in on the round table that reflected the window and had in its centre a tufted chenille mat. He added, wrinkling his forehead: 'So Mariette says, at least.'

'Who is Mariette?'

'Their maid. She wanted to help me dress.'

'Do you think she is going to die?' said Henrietta.

'I don't expect so. I shall be out, anyway.'

'That would be awful,' said Henrietta, shocked.

'I suppose it would. But I don't know Mme Fisher.'

It is never natural for children to smile at each other: Henrietta and Leopold kept their natural formality. She said: 'You see, I'd been hoping Miss Fisher was going to take me out.'

Leopold, looking about the salon, said: 'Yes, *this* must be a rather funny way to see Paris.' But he spoke with detachment; it did not matter to him.

'I don't feel as if I was anywhere,' Henrietta complained.

Leopold got up and strolled away to the window. With his back turned to Henrietta, looking out at the tree, he said in an off-hand voice: 'My mother's coming today, so she and I will go out.'

'What will you do?'

'Oh – have tea at a *patisserie*.'

'My grandmother's gone to live at Mentone.'

'Oh. Is that why you're going there?'

'Yes; did Miss Fisher tell you?' said Henrietta, gratified.

'I suppose she did.' Turning round from the window he said with much more animation: 'Where does your mother live?'

'Oh, she's dead,' said Henrietta, embarrassed.

'Oh, is she?' said Leopold, taken aback. His manner became a little touchy and wary, as though she had been laying a trap for him. Picking Henrietta's monkey up by the ears he examined it distantly: its limp limbs and stitched felt paws hung down.

'Don't!' exclaimed Henrietta. 'His ears may come off!'

'They seem quite firm,' said Leopold, testing them. 'Why do you say "don't"? Do you think it feels?'

'Well, I like to think he notices. Otherwise there'd be no point in taking him everywhere ... Have you been in Paris often, Leopold?'

'Does it squeak?' he went on, absorbed, digging at Charles's belly.

'No. Please put him down. Have you been in Paris often?'

'No. I live near Spezia. Italy's better than France.'

'Why?' said she, nettled.

'It's hotter,' he said, raising his eyebrows, 'and not nearly so shabby. Besides, it has got a king still. Mentone used to be Italy till France took it away. Nobody goes to France when they can go to Italy.'

'Then why doesn't your mother go and see you in Italy?'

'Because it's too far,' said Leopold loftily. Silhouetted against the unsunny muslin blind he began rocking backwards and forwards, from his toes to his heels. Creak – creak went his shoes on the parquet. Intent on balance, he sometimes bowed right forward or jerked hastily back: his hands stayed in his pockets the whole time. He became his own rocking toy whose equilibrium flattered him; meanwhile showing Henrietta that he had no thoughts. She, however, refused to watch. Gazing up at the cornice picked out in grey and yellow, she thought: All he wants is somebody who will notice.

Leopold said, off-hand: 'What did Miss *Fisher* say about my mother and me?'

Henrietta, still with her feet up on the sofa, looked down from the cornice only to stare at the toe-caps of her brown shoes. Then, peering forward earnestly, she read two or three French words on the sheet of *Le Matin* under her feet. Too well she recollected Miss Fisher's taboo. But this was the subject he seemed determined to pitch on, and she found herself burning to know how he felt. 'Oh,' she said, 'she just said your mother lived somewhere else.'

'Somewhere else from where?'

'From you.'

Leopold stopped rocking, bumped down on his heels and stood disconcertingly still, his big-pupilled eyes, set close in, transfixing her so intently that she thought for a moment he had a cast in them. He said: 'So you thought that was funny?'

'Yes, I did,' she said boldly. 'I did think that was funny.'

'If you told that to other people, would they think it was funny?'

'Well, they wouldn't *laugh*, if that's what you mean by funny. I suppose they might think it was rather sort of *peculiar*. But then I promised not to.'

'Tell other people?'

'Mmm.'

'It's not a secret,' said Leopold haughtily.

'Oh, Miss Fisher said it was.'

'Did she tell you not to ask me things?'

'How do you mean?' she said, flustered.

Leopold smiled to himself. 'She told me not to answer, what*ever* you said. She hopes I won't say anything.'

'Then ought you to?' said Henrietta, reproving.

'I don't have to be obedient to Miss Fisher. It's not my fault if you are here while I talk. Look – now your mother's dead so you can't possibly see her, do you still mean to love her, or is that no good now? When you want to love her, what do you do, remember her? But if you couldn't remember her, but heard you could see her, would you enjoy loving her more, or less?'

'I don't see what you mean,' said Henrietta, distracted – in fact in quite a new kind of pain. She saw only too well that this inquisition had no bearing on Henrietta at all, that Leopold was not even interested in hurting, and was only tweaking her petals off or her wings off with the intention of exploring himself. His dispassionateness was more dire, to Henrietta, than cruelty. With no banal reassuring grown-ups present, with grown-up intervention taken away, there is no limit to the terror strange children feel of each other, a terror life obscures but never ceases to justify. There is no end to the violations committed by children on children, quietly talking alone. Henrietta dreaded what he might say next. Helpless tears began making her eyelids twitch.

'Why, are you still unhappy about your mother?' he said.

Henrietta sharply turned her face to the wallpaper.

'I'm not thinking about her. I simply don't like Paris; I wish I was in the train.'

'Well, you will be, soon,' said Leopold, much more gently. For a moment, a smile, his first smile, comprehending and vivid, lit up his face. 'You'll be in the train tonight, and I don't know where I shall be!'

'P'raps in another train,' she replied unfriendlily.

'You see, you and I are just opposites. I *don't* remember my mother, but *shall* see her again.' He watched Henrietta closely, to see, as though on himself, the effect of this.

The effect was odd. Henrietta turned down her eyes, smoothed her dress on her knees and remarked with the utmost primness: 'You must be very glad: no wonder you are excited. I am excited, going to Mentone.' Then, swinging her feet to the ground, she left the sofa and walked to the radiator, above which she spread her hands. Glancing aloofly to see if her nails were clean, she seemed to become unconscious of Leopold. Then she strolled across to examine a vase of crêpe paper roses on the consol table behind Charles's chair. Peering behind the roses, she found they were tied on with wire to sprigs of box. She glanced across at the clock, smothered a yawn politely and said aloud to herself: 'Only twenty-five past ten.' Her sex provided these gestures, showing how bored she got with someone else's insistence on his own personality. Her dread of Leopold gave way to annoyance. Already she never met anyone without immediately wanting to rivet their thought on herself, and with this end in view looked forward to being grown up.

Her married sister, Caroline, commanded all she wanted by sailing along effortlessly, like a swan down-stream. No one overlooked Caroline nowadays. Their grandmother Mrs Arbuthnot's *distrait* expression made her look, as Miss Fisher said, quite above the world, but people did as she liked. From among the many people anxious to know her, she had sorted out two or three friends so distinguished that it was a privilege for Henrietta even to look at them. One of these friends, unbending to Henrietta, had said to her that her grandmother was unique. As no doubt she was, but who is not? And she had minor friends, sub-friends, such as Miss Fisher, whom she remembered when they could be of use. Caroline was as effective as her grandmother; everything was grist that came to Caroline's mill. At one time she had been thwarted and moody, but whatever she touched prospered now she had grown up. Having spent hours unwillingly silent with Mrs Arbuthnot and Caroline and their friends, Henrietta had noted their charm, their astuteness, their command of emotion in others, and could no longer doubt she lived in a world where it was fatal never to make one's mark. Neither Mrs Arbuthnot nor Caroline stopped at anything: possibly only Henrietta knew how far they would both go. They flourished like bay trees without being even wicked: Mrs Arbuthnot looked so vague and untidy that you saw at once that she must be good. Caroline's young husband found her perfect; and though Mrs Arbuthnot had not, this winter, been lent the villino at Beaulieu, she had been lent a flat at Mentone overlooking the sea.

Henrietta inherited from her father, Colonel Mountjoy, fair hair and self-mistrust; her ambitiousness came from the other side. Her father could not do with Mrs Arbuthnot and was always uneasy alone with her. During his mother-in-law's visits, he had the air of wearing his coat-collar up. His wife's death left him helpless: it had seemed highly natural that Mrs Arbuthnot should take Henrietta on. Henrietta trusted her grandmother breathlessly, as one must trust the driver on the Cornici road.

'Twenty-five past ten,' Henrietta repeated. 'How I should like to go out!'

'Well, why don't you go?'

She said firmly: 'I couldn't go by myself.'

Leopold, whom the ever possible fate of little girls in Paris did not concern, looked at her curiously. Now he had said so much his excitement eased a little: he felt a cloudy liking for Henrietta and began to be glad she was in the room. Her matter-of-fact manner made him feel less extraordinary. At the Villa Fioretta, outside Spezia, the solicitude of his re-

lations by adoption, his aunts Sally and Marian and his uncle
Dee, who was at the same time his tutor, drove him into a
frenzy about himself. He was over understood. The repercussions of all that he said and did echoed through the
hollow rooms of the villa, and he knew too well these people
found him remarkable. The chosen childish children with
whom he played made a crook of him, and all the time he
impressed them he despised them for being impressed; he
wanted to crack the world by saying some final and frightful
thing. Only the men on the beach and the clattering servants
did not make him feel he knew more than anyone else. Aunt
Marian and Aunt Sally were faded aesthetic expatriate American women; Uncle Dee, incredibly, was the husband of
Aunt Marian. Before they had bought the Villa Fioretta the
family had lived in Rome, and Leopold still regretted the
bands, the clamour, the pomp. The city became the image of
his ambition, communicating its pride to him so violently
and immediately that antiquity went for nothing: the hills
and columns seemed to be made for himself. To have been
born became to be on the scale of emperors and popes, to be
conspicuous everywhere, like the startling white Vittorio
Emmanuele monument. He was, in fact, full of the bastard's
pride ... But Rome had not been good for Aunt Marian's
asthma, so the family moved. Spezia offered Leopold almost
nothing: his precocity devoured itself there, rejecting the
steep sunny coast and nibbling blue edge of the sea that
drowned Shelley. His spirit became crustacean under
douches of culture and mild philosophic chat from his Uncle
Dee, who was cultured rather than erudite.

The displeased cool manner in which Henrietta had
peered behind the roses, and her glance at the clock, made
Leopold value her: she showed he was nothing to her. All he
had said, having left her cold, was still his. Where he came
from, kindness thickened the air and sentiment fattened on
the mystery of his birth. Years before sex had power to touch
his feeling it had forced itself into view as an awkward tangle
of motives. There was no one he could ask frankly: 'Just how
odd *is* all this?' The disengaged Henrietta had been his first

looking-glass. The idea of her travelling away tonight to Mentone, with the monkey she had always had and her recollection of Leopold, the idea of her gone, made Leopold glance her way with an interest that was half sad. His eyes, at once sharp and shy, rested on the symbol of her departure: the paper-leather dispatch case near the door.

'Is that yours, too?'

'Yes,' she said, with a certain amount of pride. 'It was bought for me yesterday. They're useful travelling, you see.'

'Bought in London?'

'Yes. Have you been there?'

'No. Is it heavy?'

'Depends what you call heavy,' she said.

Leopold, going across to pick up the dispatch case, weighed it and swung it boastfully. '*That's* not heavy,' he said. 'What are all those things rattling about inside?'

'Apples,' said Henrietta, ' – it's not meant to be swung.'

It was not. Its two clasps indignantly sprang open: two apples, a cake of soap and an ebony-backed hairbrush came bouncing and crashing out; the sponge-bag made a damp thud, *The Strand Magazine* and the pink *Malheurs de Sophie* fluttered face down on the floor. The pack of playing cards, happily, stayed in their box. 'There now!' said Henrietta. This confirmed her opinion that all little boys were rough.

Leopold stood grasping the gaping dispatch case, watching one apple roll off under a chair. A smell of shut-up apples and soap filled the room. There was nothing he could say: he stood there unmeaningly. Someone moved upstairs; they heard a step on the ceiling.

'You'll wake Mme Fisher, too.'

'I'm sorry,' Leopold said, with unwilling lips. She could not have believed he could go so small. The catastrophe seemed to seem to him final, for he made no effort to pick anything up but stood frozenly mortified. His face was a mask for Henrietta to laugh at: she did not know what it feels like to look a fool. Leopold looked to her like one of those perplexed comedians who trip over their flat feet or sit on their hats. For the first time this morning a smile twitched up her cheeks, then she laughed outright: she sat on the sofa excitedly laughing, pushing her hair back like a girl at a pantomime.

'Stop that,' said Leopold, trembling.

'You ought to be glad I'm not angry. I did say – '

Leopold raised his eyes in a burning dark look that would have killed if it could. 'I don't care how angry you are.'

'Oh, don't be such a baby!' said Henrietta, unnerved but with her most Alice-ish air. She flopped on to her knees to pick up the cake of soap, and stayed looking round. 'I think you might help,' she said.

'You *are* pleased with yourself,' said Leopold, without moving.

Henrietta, kneeling, looked angrily at his knees. She noticed a scar on one, where he must have tripped up running and come down violently: the idea pleased her. 'Well, what else are *you*?' she said. This produced such a silence that she got still more frightened and crawled off after the apple: 'You're *spoilt*,' she then added recklessly, reaching for it under the armchair.

'What is *The Strand Magazine*?' demanded Leopold suddenly, picking it up as though nothing were going on.

Henrietta was glad of the anticlimax. 'Oh, just a magazine.'

'English,' said Leopold. He pressed his nose into the pages and said: 'It smells English too. What's the Strand?'

'*Hush!*' exclaimed Henrietta, sitting back suddenly. 'Somebody's coming. Miss Fisher's coming downstairs.'

3

Miss Fisher glanced apprehensively round the salon. 'Why, look!' she said, darting to pick up the second apple. When she stooped, a frill of maroon petticoat dipped under her skirt. 'Whose is it?' she said.

'Mine,' said Henrietta. 'It just fell out of my case.'

'It has bruised, I'm afraid: what a pity! Never mind, Henrietta, I will give you an orange. Imagine, tomorrow you may see oranges growing on trees. What a spring you will have – the sun at this time of year. How I would wish to be you!' She brought out her handkerchief and dusted the apple sadly.

'What a pity you can't!' said Henrietta, polite. Leopold looked at Miss Fisher as though she were mad, but her madness was nothing to him, and walked away to the window with *The Strand Magazine*. His presence must have had an unnerving effect on Miss Fisher, who was sillier than she had been before. Now she said with an anxious glance towards him: 'You two have made friends, I see.'

'Yes, thank you,' said Henrietta.

Miss Fisher's uncertain smile faded uncertainly. 'That is very nice,' she said. 'You are company for each other. That will help to pass the day.'

'I shan't be here long,' said Leopold.

'Naturally, naturally not,' agreed Miss Fisher, sending Henrietta a speaking glance. 'Leopold is expecting his mother this afternoon,' she said in a stage voice.

'I know,' said Henrietta basely, 'you told me.'

To hide how sharply she felt Henrietta's betrayal, Miss Fisher made a business of putting down her handbag near the edge of the table beside the apple. She said: 'This afternoon, if my mother can sleep and does not need me with her, you and I will go out, Henrietta, to see a little of Paris.'

'Oh, thank you. The Trocadéro is what I want to see.'

'Don't you mean the Arc de Triomphe?'

'No, thank you, the Trocadéro.'

'But that is not historic, not in very good taste. I had thought we might visit the Luxembourg, so near here. And perhaps Napoleon's tomb.'

'I don't care for Napoleon,' said Henrietta.

'But I think your grandmother might – '

'I don't suppose she'd mind.'

'Notre Dame – '

'I'd sooner see the Trocadéro, thank you. I've got a picture of it in my glove-box at home.'

Miss Fisher, sighing, turned to the window again. 'So Henrietta gave you her magazine,' she said. 'Are you still tired, Leopold? Would you like a glass of milk?'

'No, not milk, thank you.'

'And after the Trocadéro,' pursued Henrietta, 'might we –'

But someone was tapping decisively overhead.

'My mother is waiting all this time,' cried Miss Fisher. 'She did not sleep much last night but slept on into this morning; she awoke most anxious to see you, Henrietta, at any cost. She has so often heard me speak of your grandmother, since the year I returned from Chambéry. So if you are rested now, I think we will go up.'

Henrietta was appalled. 'Isn't she much too ill?'

'Not for a little visit. You will be a great interest. She lies there alone so much.'

'Doesn't she want to see Leopold?'

Miss Fisher turned her eyes down, and if she had not had such a sallow skin might have flushed. 'Leopold ought to rest more,' she said quickly. 'He has to be so fresh when his mother comes.'

Henrietta tugged her red belt round till the buckle came to the front again, and ran a finger inside her starched Peter Pan collar. She felt victimized. 'I don't speak French very well.'

But Miss Fisher, taking no notice, waited with what seemed to Henrietta a smile of the sheerest fanaticism, holding the door open. Henrietta, having glanced once at Leopold, walked out ahead of her. The door shut behind them with a triumphant click.

The Strand Magazine had looked a gold mine to Leopold, but its trafficky cover and glazed smell turned out to be richer than its contents. Frowning with scornful mystification, but still reading, he walked, when the women had gone, across to the sofa, where he lay over the magazine on one elbow, turning over the pages with quick brown

38

hands as though he had England here. He pored over the photographs of statesmen and battleships, the drawings of frank girls, butlers, sports cars and oak-beamed rooms. The funny stories and pictures brought him to a full stop. His passionate lack of humour was native and untutored; no one had taught him that curates, chars, duchesses, spinsters are enough, in England, to make anyone smile. The magazine perplexed Leopold with its rigid symbolism, Martian ideology. A veil of foreign sentiment hung over every image, making it unclear. Once, at the figure of an admiral saluting, something went up in him like a firework. But he did not know what the magazine was *about*. Hoping for something concrete, he went through the advertisements. He sighed, shifted on his elbow and looked away.

Miss Fisher had forgotten her handbag. Set on driving Henrietta upstairs, she had forgotten the rubbed black morocco bag sitting there by the apple. Leopold's eye lit on it with the immediate thought that inside there might be letters about him. Focusing on the handbag, he listened sharply. There was no movement upstairs. Leopold left the sofa, fingered the steel clasp, then opened the bag collectedly. The thing, with its sad grey lining, gave out a musky smell. From between two handkerchiefs and a note-case, Leopold, with the nimbleness of a squirrel, pulled out three envelopes. The other papers – lists in French and a telegram confirming the hour of Henrietta's arrival – were not interesting. Leopold went through everything else twice, to delay for some nervous reason a second glance at the letters. To eavesdrop is an ordeal. Then he shut the bag and put it back by the apple. You could have sworn by its look it had not been touched.

The first envelope bore the Mentone postmark and would be of interest only to Henrietta. He put it aside. The second – light grey Villa Fioretta note-paper – showed the well-known writing of his Aunt Marian. The third, dead white and square, with a Berlin postmark, was addressed in that hand at once dynamic and pausing that he had learnt last week to recognize as his mother's, although she had never written to him. This envelope was thin, it was *very* thin: it was empty. His mother's letter was gone: Miss Fisher had done him down.

Leopold, with his loot, knelt on the end of the sofa, unconsciously holding his head high. He thought: It was Berlin then – she's in Paris now, though. I shall *see* her; I don't need to know what she *said*. That very door will open before it's dark, before it's three o'clock, before Henrietta has got to the Trocadéro. From that door opening, I shall remember on. If I opened that door *now* there would be the hall wallpaper. *Then* when it opens there will be her face. I shall see what I cannot imagine now. Now she's in Paris somewhere because of me . . .

Then he unfolded Aunt Marian's copious letter. She wrote:

My dear Miss Fisher: I have had your second letter, which is most clear, and have to thank you for writing so fully. We shall now put Leopold into the train at Genoa with every confidence. As for the next two days, we must all hope for the best. We, of course, feel bound to defer to your wish and his mother's. I know you will share *our* wish that Leopold should be spared any *trying* scene, which we naturally dread for him, at his age and with his highly nervous, susceptible temperament. Leopold will arrive at the Gare de Lyon at 20.33 on Wednesday night, unless you get any telegram cancelling this. He will travel in charge of a Genoese friend of ours, Signora Bonnini, who has relations in Paris and whom we find sympathetic in every sense. You must expect, we fear, to receive a tired young traveller, for Leopold is highly excitable; I may say we dread the effect of this long trip under *these agitating conditions.* Please do not feed him last thing, as his digestion is delicate and mental tension always affects his stomach. A glass of milk and perrier (equal parts) should be sufficient (or perhaps a *weak bouillon*), whatever he may say. We will tell him to walk right down the train and wait for you by the barrier. He will be wearing a fawn top-coat and blue sailor cap; Signora Bonnini, who says she will wear sealskin and has a slight growth of hair on the upper lip, has promised to wait by him. We are giving Signora Bonnini the photograph of yourself you thoughtfully sent, and are warning Leopold not to consult any stranger or reply to any advance. Though he speaks Italian fluently his knowledge of French is slight; we cannot interest him in it.

We all feel from your heartfelt and *most* understanding letter that you will extend to Leopold thoughtful sympathy. How he has changed from the dark-eyed baby you knew. It is sad that so many years should have gone by without your promised visit, and that your dear mother's health should have been the cause of this. We hope her health is not worse, and that Leopold's mother's visit will not agitate her. We know of your tender feeling for Leopold, which your tie in the past with his unfortunate father will always renew. How undying friendship is! We feel that, apart from the circumstance of his birth, Leopold's heredity (instability on the father's side, lack of control on the mother's) may make conduct difficult for him, and are attempting to both guard and guide him accordingly. He shows extreme sensibility and his mind is most interesting. We believe him to be creative, so are encouraging handicrafts and, so far as possible, relaxing outdoor games. We do not consider him ripe for direct sex-instruction yet, though my husband is working towards this through botany and mythology. When the revelation regarding himself must come, what better prototypes could he find than the Greek and other heroes, we feel. His religious sense seems to be still dormant. We are educating him on broad undenominational lines such as God is Love.

We have of course no idea *what* revelations Leopold's mother may see fit to make, but we do trust you will beg her to be discreet and have regard for his temperament and the fact that he has not yet received direct sex-instruction. Almost any fact she might mention seems to us still unsuitable. We have written her advocating extreme caution, but as she has not replied we do not know in what spirit our letter was received. You will no doubt have a few words with her first, and we should be deeply grateful if you would stress our point. Our position is often trying; you will understand that *we* exercise the very greatest discretion. We dread having Leopold prematurely upset. We have explained to Leopold (though strangely, he never asked) that his father is dead and his mother married in England (for the second time, we allowed him to understand). Why he is *not* with her he has, happily, not asked either. He appears to suspect nothing and exhibits no sign of brooding. We attempt to keep his childhood sunny and beautiful, and do entreat that our work may not be *undone*.

We shall send packed with Leopold two changes of warm underwear, and shall be grateful if you or your maid will kindly see that he puts everything on. Will you also inquire if he has bowel trouble, as the effects of a journey are so binding and his digestion easily gets upset? At midday he eats anything but should be encouraged to masticate. Will you also notify us by telegram as to which train on Saturday we are to expect him home on? Also kindly mention that this letter has reached you. Please also keep a note of any expenses incurred by you during Leopold's time in Paris. Though it is of course possible that his mother may prefer to meet these herself.

Believing we may rely on you to see that the misgivings we cannot but feel are not justified, and with warm good wishes from my husband, my sister and myself. I remain, dear Miss Fisher, Yours most sincerely,

MARIAN GRANT MOODY

The repercussions on Leopold of this letter were such that for some time he seemed to stay quite blank. He sat pulling at his upper lip with his thumb and finger, in the way his Aunt Sally once said would spoil the mouth God had designed, staring at what he now saw from the outside. The revulsion threatening him became so frightening that he quickly picked up Mrs Arbuthnot's letter and read it, as though to clap something on to the gash in his mind.

She wrote:

My dear Kingfisher: *Why* do you never write to me? I had your card at Christmas and hoped for a letter later, but not another word came. I shall begin to think you very much less constant than you declared you were on our drive round the lake. Your pressed wild pansy fell out of de Sévigné only the other day, and I smiled again at that passage we marked together. Am I always to see you standing on top of the rock in your long blue coat, looking down so intently as though you wanted to dive? Never to see you again, I mean? Here (you will see by the top I am at Mentone) I crawl about in the sun, like the many other old women, remembering friends who forgot. Old people, I know, must not make too many demands. And I expect your life is absorbingly full these days.

It comes suddenly into my mind – Do you like prim little girls? I hardly think that you do, but I throw this out. Henrietta, the younger of those two problem grand-daughters (Caroline married last year, she was the one you met) is being sent out to me, to finish the winter here. Her invaluable governess is away, ill, and her father does not know what else to do with her. One is not, as I said before, a grandmother for nothing.

42

Arrangements for the child's journey seem to devolve on me. Caroline has been unusually effective and found her as escorts two travelling women, one to Paris, one as far as Nice. (Nobody for the through train, unfortunately.) But the first woman insists on travelling overnight from London, the second on leaving Paris *late* the following day. Which leaves the child in mid-air for the day in Paris between (it is next Thursday she will be arriving in Paris, by that, I fear, very early train at the Gare du Nord). She could, of course, spend the day at a G.F.S., or some such, but as a first view of Paris that sounds a *little* sad! Though prim, we have our own ideas of things. Whereas a day *chez toi* would be a red letter for her. Dear Kingfisher, could you, I wonder, allow this to be possible? You must not feel bound in any way to amuse her; she reads anything anywhere. Though of course, if you *should* be free, a flying glimpse of Paris would be a delight; she has been nowhere yet and one is only eleven once. She is a responsive, susceptible little person and would, I don't doubt, adore you: in fact, I shall expect to hear for many days of the Kingfisher who forgot me and did not write.

But how I jump to conclusions! There is *no* reason at all why you should meet Henrietta: no time for this, I expect, in a life that I imagine now absorbing and full. Someone (should I like her?) I don't doubt now claims Kingfisher's heart and time. If, however, you should think of meeting Henrietta, will you wire Caroline (now Mrs Wade-Trefusis, 195 Pelham Crescent, S.W.) for times of trains (arrivals, departures, etc.) full instructions and names of the two travelling women, which I fear I forget? I have worked out a dear little system of cherry-pink cockades: one for Henrietta, in order that you may know her at the Gare du Nord, one for yourself for *her* to know you by (in case you should meet her, always in case!) and one for the second woman to wear at the Gare de Lyon, for Henrietta and you to know *her* by. Please also see Henrietta pins on her cockade again before going to G. de L. The second woman (who is, now I remember, called either Watts or Wilson) may not know who she is. I have posted all these cockades to Caroline: see that she *writes* to you, confirming all this and sending you the cockades. She is lazy and given to telegrams. If it is not possible for you to meet Henrietta (as I hardly expect it will be) Caroline must post your cockade to the G.F.S. So perhaps you'd be sweet enough to wire her, either way? I am sorry I cannot give you the times of the trains or the names of the two women, but I find they are in my other handbag at home, and I am writing this

43

on a seat under a palm. However, Caroline knows all that.

No, I must not make claims on you, my dear Kingfisher: my remembering you more often than you remember me is not any reason to do that. If you really did take in Henrietta for Thursday I confess it would be a weight off my mind. Keep accounts of telegrams, taxis and any other expenses and remind Henrietta, who will have money with her, to pay you these back before saying Goodbye. She cannot learn too young to be punctilious.

I often wish very much you could join me here. (Perhaps, however, you do not want to leave Paris?) My little flat has big balconies but such wretchedly small and so few rooms that I hardly know yet how to fit Henrietta in. She is to go to a little school here, so will be out all day: otherwise she and I would not have room to turn round. But there are several moderate and I hear delightful pensions, quite near my little flat. So perhaps I may see my Kingfisher darting and glinting about here in her coloured coat again? This month and March would not, alas, be good for me, as parties of friends here in two of the villas make far too many claims: I had hoped for peace. So I should see not enough of you. If you thought you might come in April, I might attempt to keep on my little flat. If I cannot do this, I must move on to Florence, I fear. But do all you can to come, and we must both hope for the best.

If you should see Henrietta, you will have news of me, for what that may be worth. This letter goes to post now, and I on down to the sea. Always the same old beetle-green parasol! I think I must send you my de Sévigné, with that passage we marked. But I shall keep the pansy! Your affectionate,

                                        PATIENCE ARBUTHNOT
Always hoping to hear from you.

This struck Leopold as a competent letter. He saw at once that Mrs Arbuthnot was wicked, and would succeed. Miss Fisher was not what he had imagined a kingfisher, but he let that pass. Precisely folding up the two letters, he saw he must not return to Spezia. He saw the row of red plasticine figures he had kept out for days on his windowsill because they kidded him plasticine sunbaked hard, and the one vague shape he had modelled that had dismayed Uncle Dee and disappeared in the night. Miasmas crept over all he had done and touched there. He saw himself tricked into living.

Then I will not, he thought. If he could have been re-embodied, at that moment a black wind would have rushed through the Villa Fioretta, wrenching the shutters off and tearing the pictures down, or an earthquake cracked the floors, or the olivey hill above the villa erupted, showering hot choking ash. Let them develop themselves. I will not go back there ... Leopold looked once more at his mother's envelope, at the address dashed off in a Berlin hotel room.

Getting up and pushing back the chairs, he began to pace the salon, with his eyes shut, pressing her empty envelope to his forehead as he had once seen a thought-reader do. Then he began to read slowly aloud, as though the words one by one passed under his eyelids: 'Dear Miss Fisher,' he said.

'It is kind of you to have Leopold at your house for us to meet. I shall be coming at half-past two on Thursday, so please have lunch over and be out of the way. Leopold and I shall go out, *then* you can come back as much as you want. We shall be very busy arranging things, as I am taking Leopold home to England with me. He cannot go back to Spezia as I mean to keep him, the people there must get hold of some other child. I never did mean him to go back, but did not say so for fear they would make a fuss. So they can put that in their pipes and smoke it. When I come, I shall go straight into the room where he is, so please do not be in it. I have come to the conclusion I cannot do without Leopold, because he is the only person I want. We have a great deal to say, so — '

But at that moment the door opened and Henrietta, red in the face, came in.

'Leopold!' she exclaimed, 'Whatever *are* you doing? There are enough mad people in this house!'

4

Mme Fisher's bedroom, though it was over the salon, had two windows, not one. Jalousies were pulled to over the far window, so that no light fell across the head of the bed. A

45

cone of sick-room incense on the bureau sent spirals up the daylight near the door; daylight fell cold white on the honeycomb quilt rolled back. Round the curtained bedhead, Pompeian red walls drank objects into their shadow: picture-frames, armies of bottles, boxes, an ornate clock showed without glinting, as though not quite painted out by some dark transparent wash. Henrietta had never been in a room so full and still. She stood by the door Miss Fisher had shut behind her, with her heart in her mouth. Her eyes turned despairingly to a bracket on which stood white spiked shells with cameos on their lips. The airlessness had a strange dry pure physical smell.

'Here is Henrietta,' Miss Fisher said.

'Good morning, Henrietta,' said Mme Fisher.

'Good morning, Madame Fisher,' Henrietta replied. The hand she saw in the shadows did not stir on the sheet, so she stayed where she was on the parquet beside the door.

'Look, Henrietta, come round this side of the bed.'

'No, let her stay where she is. I see her best in the light.' The voice was less weak than minimized, like a voice far off. 'Go nearer the window, please; I have so very few visitors.' Henrietta heard Mme Fisher breathe more heavily, moving up on her pillows. Miss Fisher stood by, anxious. 'You speak French?' Mme Fisher said with a smile in her voice.

'Not very much.'

'You need not,' said Mme Fisher. 'I have been many years in England. I was a governess.'

'A "Mademoiselle",' said Miss Fisher, also smiling, anxiously.

'Yes,' went on Mme Fisher, 'I rapped very many knuckles, before my marriage.'

Henrietta's own knuckles stung. 'I hope,' she said, 'you are feeling better today?'

'No,' said Mme Fisher, without expression.

'Oh, you do feel better, Mother!'

'You must please let me decide.'

Miss Fisher sat down on the wall side of the bed and took up her knitting passionately, as though to obliterate herself.

46

Transfixed half-way between the door and the window, Henrietta felt that pillow was all eyes. Mme Fisher's unmoved regard was a battery: with an unconscious quiver Henrietta drew in her chin. If she was really dying her head would be flat, she thought. She felt every hair she had, and every freckle, every red bone button down her stomach stand out with frightening meaning: if pictures suffer, she did. 'So,' said Mme Fisher, 'you are the prim little girl?'

'*Mother!*' said Miss Fisher, ducking over her knitting.

'That was a joke of your grandmother's,' said Mme Fisher. Henrietta, for the first time, stared straight between the bed-curtains, meeting lambent dark eyes in a white stained face. Then Mme Fisher relaxed back on the pillow, drawing the bedclothes closer up to her chin. 'Please come by the bed now: we must resign ourselves to talk in the dark. I am too ill for light, you know.'

This had such a mocking ring that Henrietta, edging between the bed and the shuttered window, only brought out, 'I'm sorry,' in an uncertain tone.

'At my age,' said Mme Fisher, 'one must expect to die soon.'

'You have no intention of dying,' said Miss Fisher with energy.

'Naomi will not let me. These days I may do nothing, not even die, I am so much under control.' Lying flat and straight, Mme Fisher turned her head slowly to smile at her visitor. Her dark eyes with their sick brown rims were communicative and mocking. Henrietta found in her smile a perplexingness she had once been told was beauty and learnt to recognize by some pause in herself. The smile was pungent, extraordinary, as deep as darkness and as dazzling as light.

Mme Fisher was not in herself a pretty old lady. Waxy skin strained over her temples, jaws and cheek-bones; grey hair fell in wisps round an unwomanly forehead; her nostrils were wide and looked in the dusk skullish; her mouth was graven round with ironic lines. Neither patience nor discontent but a passionate un-resignation was written across her features, tense with the expectation of more pain. She seemed to lie as she lay less in weakness than in unwilling credulity, as though the successive disasters that make an illness had convinced her slowly, by repetition. She lay, still only a little beyond surprise at this end to her, webbed down, frustrated, or, still more, like someone cast, still alive, as an effigy for their own tomb. Her illness seemed to be one prolonged mistake. Her self looked, wildly smiling, out of her body: what was happening in here was too terrible to acknowledge; she had to travesty it and laugh it off. Unserene, she desperately kept her head.

Miss Fisher pointed across the bed with her knitting-needle, and Henrietta saw a chair and sat down. Mme Fisher's stick to tap with leaned by the bed. The chair was low, the bed high; so that her face was now on a level with Mme Fisher's: she gazed gravely but with alarm into those wells of sockets, those martyred amused eyes. Mme Fisher's foreign accent was marked but in no way quaint: no touch of comedy enlivened their talk.

'So you enjoy travel?'

'So far,' said Henrietta. 'So much happens.'

'Much does not happen here. It is quiet here, I am afraid.'

'Well, there's Leopold.'

'Yes. You travel, I hear, with a monkey?'

'Yes, called Charles. I left him down in the salon.'

'Will he wreck the salon?'

'Oh no, he's not *alive*.'

'That was only my joke.'

Henrietta blushed.

'French ideas of funny are different,' said Mme Fisher. 'That was a joke in English, which you did not expect, perhaps. You are pleased to be going to visit your grandmother?'

'Well, I see her quite often, but it is always nice.'

'You will go to school at Mentone?'

'Yes.'

'That is good, I am sure. Mrs Arbuthnot is busy,' said Mme Fisher in her most hollow tone. 'She has many friends,

48

writes many excellent letters and walks every day by the sea with a green parasol, reading Mme de Sévigné's letters. She goes for carriage drives, and taught Naomi to believe that she, Naomi, resembles a kingfisher.'

'Mother!' said Miss Fisher, 'you are talking too much. I shall have to send Henrietta downstairs again.'

'You see?' said Mme Fisher. 'I am under control.'

Henrietta could not help smiling. But she was taken aback by this view of her grandmother. Miss Fisher was, clearly, mistaken; Mme Fisher had *not* enjoyed hearing about Mrs Arbuthnot. To imagine the two ladies ever together made Henrietta uncomfortable: Mrs Arbuthnot's above-the-world expression bumping against the ceiling while Mme Fisher smiled on in unmoved pain; Mrs Arbuthnot's whimsicality shattered by Mme Fisher's making one of her English jokes. It would certainly never do.

'My daughter is half English,' said Mme Fisher. 'She had a very great faculty for devotion. She was most fortunate, meeting your grandmother at Chambéry.'

'Mother . . .!'

'And I have been fortunate,' pursued Mme Fisher, 'in having heard so much of her English friend. I begin to feel that I know her. Mrs Arbuthnot's friendship has meant much to my daughter, who has much to support.'

There was a pause: Mme Fisher rolled round her head to watch her daughter knitting, unmovedly. One of Miss Fisher's needles clattered on to the parquet and she dived after it: something had been too much. Henrietta wondered if she should go now. She tried hard to catch Miss Fisher's eye, but could not. So she stared at the daylit shell at the other end of the room, till she felt Mme Fisher once more turning full upon her the battery of her look.

'This is your first visit to Paris?'

'Well, yes.'

'You have seen this house only?'

Henrietta hoped that the question of going out might come up now. Oh to exchange those unseen streets, the Trocadéro, even Napoleon's tomb, for this air darkening her lungs with every breath she took, the built-in tree in the court, the varying abnormalities of Mme Fisher and Leopold. The proper French, she thought, cannot be like this. Here she had dropped down a well into something worse than the past in not being yet over. She said: 'But this house is so uncommon.'

'This house? It does very well. It is uncommon chiefly in being a house at all. It was always in my family, and was left to me by my grandfather, who was a notary; it is such a house as you find only now in the provinces. When I am dead, it will be sold at once. One cannot afford to live in a house, in Paris. But I prefer to die here.'

Miss Fisher's interruptions had alternate objects, to save her mother's breath or to turn the talk. Now she said: 'My mother's family come from Touraine: they were always notaries. But my father was a captain in the English artillery. The Fishers were always soldierly.'

'Yes,' said Mme Fisher, 'my marriage was most r-r-r-romantic.'

Mocking herself, she smiled at the memory of her marriage, as at any fanciful object, cameo or painted fan, that might have caught her notice, having its place here and valued once. Whatever she might think of, lying on this high bed, her smile was for the present and Henrietta: an unreminiscent smile. Mrs Arbuthnot spoke so much of living among memories that it shocked Henrietta to feel Captain Fisher gone. His military rattling ardour was silent for good, for where should it be remembered if not here? A man of strange courage, who had begotten Miss Fisher, then, by dying, let flow back an undisturbed solitude. Henrietta, being not ripe for grown-up reflections, did not wonder how he had treated his wife, or speculate as to the lastingness of his passion for the ironical French governess, never pretty, not from the first young. He had married Mme Fisher. Love is the unchallenged motive for some kinds of behaviour: Mrs Arbuthnot said: 'You will understand some day,' and Henrietta was still willing to wait. Therefore she simply wondered what had brought him to Paris (or had they met in

50

England?), what he had done all day here, whether he liked the house. There was comfort in the idea of the plain Englishman's presence: she looked round the crowded walls for his photograph. Mme Fisher had made her mark, she had struck his heart. See what marriage had done for Mrs Arbuthnot and Caroline! But Mme Fisher lay back disclaimingly on her pillows, seeming to say: 'We take nothing out of this world.'

'Yes, look *there* is my father's photograph.' Miss Fisher twisted round to point to it, over her head. Inside its oval frame the photograph had faded. Captain Fisher's moustache chiefly appeared; Englishness or any kind of expression had dulled out after years on the red wall. 'Just before leaving the regiment,' said his daughter. 'Before he married my mother he sent his papers in.'

His widow's hand, in the cuff of a grey bed-jacket, came out over the sheet a moment to pull the bedclothes closer still to her chin. Did she marry because she was tired of rapping knuckles and Frenchmen will not marry you with no *dot*?

Henrietta began: 'My father was in the army; he – '

' – So, Henrietta,' said Mme Fisher suddenly, 'you have not only your monkey but Leopold down there?'

'Yes.'

'And, tell me, do you like Leopold?'

'Oh, I like him. Of course, today he's excited. He – he's not very tall for his age, is he?'

'I have not seen him. I may.'

'Mother ... You slept this morning. Also, I am most anxious to keep Leopold quiet until – '

'He is not quiet down there. What has he been breaking? I heard something fall just now.'

Henrietta said: 'Oh, that was my dispatch case. He, Leopold, swung it and everything fell out.'

'Ah! He likes to touch things?'

'I suppose so,' said Henrietta, perplexed.

'Excited ...' said Mme Fisher, making the first restless movement Henrietta had seen.

'They have been playing,' Miss Fisher said quickly, 'talking and eating apples. It is nice for them both.'

'Oh yes, we've been talking,' said Henrietta. Encouraged by Mme Fisher's attention, she went on brightly, 'He told me about his mother.'

' – Look, Henrietta, my mother gets so soon tired. Perhaps you should go back to Leopold now.'

'No,' exclaimed her mother, point-blank, going under the bedclothes rigid with opposition. How frantically but coldly she loved the present! Henrietta, who had got up, sat down again. The fatal topic of Leopold was magnetic: she was not nearly so anxious to go now. Mme Fisher looked at her avidly. 'Oh, so you made friends, did you, down in the salon? You must resemble your grandmother, it seems to me. Is Leopold not suspicious the whole time?'

'Mother, no; you are quite wrong!'

'I see him suspicious, but still full of himself.'

Henrietta said: 'Well, yes, he is, rather.'

'He likes to talk?'

'*Very* much.'

'I have already heard him up and down on the stairs.'

'He shall come up later, Mother. After – '

'Yes, always "after" no doubt – he has a step like his father's.'

'Oh,' Henrietta said, 'did you know his father too?'

'Quite well,' said Mme Fisher. 'He broke Naomi's heart.'

She mentioned this impatiently, as though it had been some annoying domestic mishap. Henrietta, glancing across the bed, saw Miss Fisher's eyelids glued down with pain. Then, with the air of having known all along this would come, the helpless daughter rolled up her knitting quickly, as though to terminate something, perhaps the pretence of safety, jabbing her needles through it with violent calm. Set for flight by moving up in her chair, she seemed uncertain whether to fly or not, whether or not to show this was unbearable. Her face took a watchful look, as though somebody else might come in at any moment. Her prominent mouth, not unlike Charles the monkey's, formed an unwilling smile; her eyes fixed with an unmeaning expression the white quilt rolled back at her mother's feet. Sudden tragic importance made her look doubtful, as though a great dark plumed hat had been clapped aslant on her head.

Mme Fisher's detachment, Henrietta could see, had its iron side: she no longer felt, so why should anyone else? Grown-up enough to shy away from emotion, Henrietta felt she had seen Miss Fisher undressed. Half of her blindly wished to be somewhere else, while the other half of her stood eagerly by. She knew one should not hear these things when one was only eleven. All the same, she felt important in this atmosphere of importance: she liked being in on whatever was going on. Mrs Arbuthnot did not deal in broken hearts; she said only housemaids had them – but the Fishers were French. Henrietta knew of the heart as an organ; she privately saw it covered in red plush and believed that it could not break, though it might tear. But, Miss Fisher's heart had been brittle, it *had* broken. No wonder she'd looked so odd at the Gare du Nord.

'However, we cannot judge him,' said Mme Fisher, turning to look arrestingly at her daughter as though she had not seen this so plainly before. 'You were determined to suffer, you gave him no alternative. Max was fatal first of all to himself.'

'Leopold's father is dead now,' said Miss Fisher, looking at Henrietta across the bed.

'Happily,' said her mother.

Henrietta began in confusion: 'Leopold didn't say –'

'Naturally,' said Mme Fisher. 'He has never heard of him.'

Having said this with some impatience, she shut her eyes. Henrietta, getting up cautiously, smoothed out the pleats of her dress. The incense cone had burnt out, its fumes were gone: the red wall opposite the window brightened; the winter sun was trying to come through. Henrietta's mind worked round to the Trocadéro: she wondered if she could ask for tea in a shop. She really dreaded another *séance*

53

with Leopold. Shifting from foot to foot she stared at the bracket. 'It must be quite late,' she said.

'Yes. Look, Henrietta: my mother must really sleep now.'

'I must not, but I will.'

Henrietta did not know whether to hold her hand out. 'Well, good-bye, Madame Fisher, thank you so very much.'

'Come again to see me before you go to your train.' Her voice took for the last time its parody note. 'Who knows where I may be when you pass through Paris next time?'

Henrietta laughed politely, half-way to the door.

'Yes, that was one more of my jokes – Oh, Henrietta!'

'Yes?'

'Your grandmother sent you to us. You must never distress your grandmother.'

Going with Henrietta as far as the door, Miss Fisher shut it behind her gently. She must have stayed silent by it for some time, for no sound came from inside Mme Fisher's room.

5

Henrietta's relief at finding herself alone was overcast by the prospect of returning to Leopold. Feeling like a kaleidoscope often and quickly shaken, she badly wanted some place in which not to think. So she sat down on the stairs, with her eyes shut tight, pressing her ear-lobes over her ears with her thumbs: she had found this the surest way to repress thought. But something had got at her: the idea of Miss Fisher's heart.

Why could it not mend, like Caroline's?

Caroline was eleven years older than Henrietta. Summers ago, when Henrietta was six, they had shared a seaside bed-room, a room with blowy white curtains and china knobs on the furniture: here, early one morning, she had woken to find Caroline in tears. Nothing had had time to happen, the morning was still innocent, but here in the stretcher-bed beside Henrietta her big sister lay twisting with sobs, eyes blubbered and scarlet in a tear-sunken face. Sunshine made the room foreign to any kind of despair. Henrietta, who had a regard for Caroline, had said after a moment: 'Shall I come into bed with you?' Her sister's body looked lonely.

'No, thank you. Go to sleep.'

'But it's today now.'

'I know. I hate it,' said Caroline. She sat up and looked with horror round at the furniture, as though she had hoped against hope to find something gone: her hair hung round her shoulders matted, dull. Her poise and her calm regard for herself had vanished. Something she saw on the wash-stand or some new pain made her roll round in bed again, biting her wrist. This paroxysm abated to hopeless hiccups. 'Mr Jeffcocks is married,' she said at last.

'Who to?'

'He told me last night.'

'Has he got any children?'

Caroline writhed at this like a hooked fish. 'I wish I had died,' she said, 'when I was your age.'

Henrietta, frightened, had got out of bed and looked out of the window as though for help. The sea, heartlessly blue and glittering with sunshine, carried two sailing ships: below the tamarisk hedge the shingle shelved to the sea in smooth orange steps. Mr Jeffcocks had already cast a blight on the holiday, for Caroline had devoted the fortnight to running after him, she could not be got to come on picnics or any-thing. She had bought a red glacé belt and spent hours up at her window re-whitening her shoes and looking out for him; she would stand against the bright sea staring down the prom-enade towards the glass porch of his hotel. Nobody knew for certain how she had picked him up. Their mother, who was alive then, took no notice, but Mrs Arbuthnot, who did not in those days see eye to eye with Caroline, was with them also, and the affair had made her anxious and cross, which had fallen heavy on Henrietta ... When Caroline saw Henrietta get out of bed she had said, 'No; don't go.'

'I was going to see my starfish.'

Starfish seemed to have fatal associations, for Caroline wept again. Then she got up, sobbing, to stare at herself in the glass. 'I've gone all different,' she said. 'Say something.'

Henrietta thought, then said: 'Today we're going to Dymchurch.'

'Tell mother I'll stay in bed. And *don't* let them come in here.'

'And *miss* Dymchurch?'

Caroline picked up a comb and blindly tugged at her hair.

'Why do you comb your hair?'

'Something has gone inside me. My heart, I think.'

But Caroline had had to get up, of course. She behaved for several days as though she were ill. Meanwhile, Mr Jeffcocks took Henrietta out in a boat and showed her photographs of his two little girls. Caroline began to show she was uncertain whether he had betrayed her or were just simply common. She no longer slipped out directly after supper, but sat in the sitting-room helping Henrietta sort shells. That autumn they sent her away to a finishing school, from which she came back next year with an unchippable glaze. She said she saw now how morbid one was when one was young. Growing up very fast, she learnt to be so amusing about her early humiliations that soon no one believed they had ever been. She seemed to have been born lucky. At twenty she married, and only Henrietta, fidgeting in the aisle in her Second Empire little girl's bridesmaid's frock while Caroline, white and distant, knelt at the altar, spared a puzzled thought for Mr Jeffcocks that day. On no other occasion did Caroline speak of her heart. The vulgar affair of Mr Jeffcocks blew over, as Mrs Arbuthnot had always foreseen it would.

Mme Fisher's scornful exaggerations on the subject of dying levelled that and everything else flat. Caring for nothing, she seemed to keep every happening, like rows of sea-blunted pebbles with no character, in her lit-up mind. Her eyes still looked through the door to disconcert Henrietta. For growing little girls are tempted up like plants by the idea that something is happening that they will some day know about. Mme Fisher's eyes, her indifferent way of talking, made Henrietta feel that nothing was going on – never had, never would: you knew that when you knew. Henrietta could not understand why that picture of Mrs Arbuthnot walking by the seashore with her green parasol had made her so nearly blush: she only knew she felt guilty, involved in a wrong smile. The fact was, Mrs Arbuthnot did not like anybody to debunk life: though always she said she regretted nothing, she liked to feel there was much to regret if one chose.

A smell of cooking began to come upstairs: lunch would be soon – after that, Leopold's mother. Henrietta, eyeing the barlike stripes of the paper, felt a house like this was too small for so much to happen in. All these things that were still to happen waited: for all she knew this might always be so in Paris ... On the landing above the sick-room door opened; Miss Fisher began to come down. Henrietta contracted her shoulder-blades.

'Why, *Henrietta,* what are you doing here?'

'Just sitting down.'

'But it is so lonely for you.'

'In England I often sit on the stairs.'

Miss Fisher came three steps lower to say: 'Do not, please, repeat what my mother has said to Leopold.'

'Oh, goodness, no,' said Henrietta, impatient.

'I was for a short time engaged to marry his father, then we found it unsuitable.'

'Oh. Am I to see Leopold's mother at all?'

'Oh, no; I am afraid that is impossible. But I will take you to see the Trocadéro, certainly.'

'Do you think we could have tea at a shop?'

'Anything, Henrietta.'

'Thank you. Perhaps I may think of more things.' She went on in a lower voice: 'What is his mother *like*?'

'English in type, beautiful. My mother took in *pensionnaires* here until her illness, and Karen – she – was one of them. Naturally, she has changed a little since then.'

57

'Mrs *what* is she?'

'Oh, I think it is useless to tell you. I should think of her as Mrs Brown.'

'Why?'

'That would be better.'

'What's Leopold's other name, then?'

'He is called Grant Moody.'

'Oh, goodness! That doesn't suit him!'

'He has taken the name of the family that he lives with. They are very kind, good: he should be happy with them.'

'But why is he not with her?'

Miss Fisher, tired of bending over to answer in a discreet voice, sat down also, one step below Henrietta, with an uneasy sigh. 'Please Henrietta,' she said, 'you must be content not to ask me so many things. You make the day more difficult. I did not see, I think, how difficult it might be. No doubt your grandmother will tell you more about life when she considers you old enough. I have a great regard for her understanding. I think now you should go down and play with Leopold.'

'We don't really *play* very much.'

'He is a little shy, perhaps.'

'*I* should call him superior.'

Miss Fisher, after a nonplussed silence, said: 'Have you let him play with your monkey yet?'

'– Mayn't I stay on the stairs?'

'It is a little sad for you,' said her hostess decisively.

If Miss Fisher had had the idea of going downstairs when she left the sick-room, she clearly gave this up, for she went back again, shutting the door behind her firmly: Henrietta, lagging downstairs, heard her going off behind it in French. Her head, Henrietta thought with justifiable crossness, seemed to have been affected more than her heart.

So that coming into the salon to find Leopold in exalted abstraction, an envelope to his forehead, his eyes shut, made Henrietta feel that fumes of insanity must have twisted down here. Or had he always been 'queer'? She said what she said sharply.

58

'I am thought-reading, naturally,' Leopold said. But she saw that he did not like her having come in.

'*Can* you, Leopold?'

'Naturally, or why should I? If you hadn't come in – '

'Well, I have got to be *somewhere*. I can't just melt.'

Irritably contracting his forehead, as though the shock of her entrance had struck him there, Leopold went to the table and put the envelope back in Miss Fisher's bag.

'Oh, you oughtn't to thought-read letters to someone else!'

Leopold, stuffing a handkerchief carefully over the envelope, took no notice.

'It's dishonourable to *touch* other people's letters,' Henrietta went on.

'I've no idea what you mean,' he said scornfully. 'Anything from my mother is mine, of course. But this letter had been taken.'

'Your mother would hate you to!'

'You don't know her.'

'Neither do you, either.'

'She's the same as me; she would see why I do things!'

'*Is* her name Brown?'

This, for some reason, sent him into a passion. Colour rose under his eyes; he looked at the handbag as though he meant to fling it across the room. Then his eyes met Henrietta's. Control made his unchildish passion alarming and Henrietta retreated behind a chair. He said at last: 'Her name's Forrestier.'

'Do you really know?'

'I found out.'

'Then why are you Grant Moody?'

'Because no one knows I'm born.' He said this with such an air of enjoying the distinction that Henrietta exclaimed: 'I should hate that!'

'I expect you would. You couldn't possibly be me.' He went back to lean on the mantelpiece with his hands in his pockets, as she had seen him after she first woke up. 'Everyone else is the same as everyone else. That is what *I* should hate.'

Henrietta said: 'My comb is still on the floor.' Tears of chagrin, angrier than her first tears, started into her eyes as she knelt down to pick the comb up, letting her hair fall over her flaming cheeks. The lines of the parquet swam. 'You go on like God,' she said.

'I haven't hurt your comb. Whatever is the matter? You've got your grandmother. And when you got out of the train you didn't know there was me.'

'I wish I didn't know now.'

'I don't see why you're crying.'

'Well, I think when you upset my things you might pick them up. Miss Fisher talks as if we get on so well.'

'I think she's mad, don't you?' he said, far more engagingly. The weeping-willow fall of her hair as she stooped and the sturdy way she got up, tugging her belt round to bring the buckle over her navel again, pleased Leopold. Whenever he looked direct at Henrietta she was not an enemy. Her grey eyes, stretched wide open to keep the tears back, met his when he said Miss Fisher was mad: he saw in her eyes the elm-grey autumn park where the little girl in the lithograph bowled her hoop. Instantly, she became part of his mother's English life.

'She almost married your father.'

'Who almost did?'

'Miss Fisher. She said so on the stairs.'

'Then he must have been mad too. I don't believe it. What did Mme Fisher say?'

'I think she made some joke.'

'If Miss Fisher is not mad, then she is a liar. When we were coming here last night from the station she told me it was my mother she liked. Anyhow, it doesn't matter: he's dead.' He looked at the clock and added: 'She's coming at half-past two.'

'That's when I am going out,' said Henrietta, sighing.

'Perhaps you may see her some day. We're going to live in England.'

'Miss Fisher doesn't say so.'

'She doesn't know.'

'But you live in Italy.'

'No, I don't now.'

Leopold's calmness dumbfounded Henrietta. He looked again at the clock with masterful confidence, as though its hands moved faster the more he looked. A great many 'buts' shot up in Henrietta's mind, the first being: But we're children, people's belongings: we can't – Incredulity made her go scarlet. 'Do you mean you're going *back* with her? When?'

'Oh, today or tomorrow.'

'But the people in Italy – '

'They can't do anything.'

'But where can you go if nobody knows you're born?'

'They will; she'll soon tell them about me,' he said. 'She wants me more than anything. She did not say this to Uncle Dee and Aunt Sally because of the fuss they make when it's anything about me. Nobody speaks the truth when there's something they must have.'

'But don't you like them?'

'I had to when I was there – '

'But how do you *know* you're going to England?'

'I know.'

Fascinated by what was going on inside him, Henrietta was drawn across the salon to where he stood. Still looking doubtfully at him, she came to stand by his side with her back to the mantelpiece, bracing her shoulders, also, against the marble, to feel as nearly as possible how he felt, and, as though in order to learn something, copying his attitude. She thought: I am taller, but . . . He noted her nearness without noticing her. She studied the stiff blue folds of his sailor-blouse sleeve, and looked attentively at the lines round his collar. A scar from some operation showed on his neck; at her side, under the jaw. She looked at his ear and, unconvinced, touched her own, to assure herself he and she were even so much alike. She found herself for the first time no more asking for notice than if she had stood beside an unconscious strong little tree: moving her elbow his way she felt his arm as unknowing as wood. Perplexity and sudden unchildish sadness made her remove her touch. 'But what are you going to do in England?' she said.

'We shall be together.'

Henrietta thought: Which is ordinary, after all. But his manner had made it sound supernatural. She tried to see him going to school on a bicycle, or being asked by his mother to clean his nails. But each picture had a heroic light: she could not see them lower or less happy. She thought dauntedly: They may really live like that. Henrietta's abstract of another child's mother was a lady with tight pearls and a worried smile. But Leopold's mother swept brilliantly through one's fancy; he commandeered, to make her, every desire, not only his own. He was a person whose passion makes its object exist. She will be in his image, she will not hesitate or mind what they say. There seemed no doubt he and she would go to England together to live a demi-god life there, leaving Henrietta forgotten, luckless, cold.

(But they haven't met yet: they may disappoint each other. She may be wrinkly now, with timid fussy ways, a face just like a mouse, the tight pearls and the smile.)

'But look here,' she said, 'who do you really belong to? I mean, who buys your clothes?'

'Well, they can keep those, can't they?'

'But haven't they been kind to you?'

'I can write and thank them.'

'I really do think you're selfish!' Henrietta exclaimed.

A parade of uncaring expressions crossed Leopold's face. Stepping away from her, still without seeming to notice she had been standing there, he picked up her box of playing-cards with the pink and gold ship and rattled the packed box with a sardonic, but, she noticed, faintly placating smile. He said suddenly: 'Can you tell fortunes by cards?'

'A governess I had did.'

But as she spoke, the kitchen door at the end of the hall, opening, let out a blast of finished cooking. A tray rattled past the salon; the purposeful stump of the maid's returning footsteps, then a heavier rattle, told Henrietta lunch must be coming in.

After lunch, Miss Fisher left them to go back to Mme Fisher; they saw her go upstairs with a special tray. It was still only half-past one. Leopold had not eaten much; he jabbed blindly at his food with his fork, leaving his knife propped at the edge of his plate – but Henrietta's stomach felt as tight as a drum and she had far fewer thoughts. The salon felt chilly after the dining-room. Leopold, as though lunch had never happened, went straight back to the cards. 'Did you say you *could* tell fortunes?'

'I said my governess did.'

'Can you remember how?'

'Twenty-six cards in a ring ... The knaves used to be lovers.'

'Then throw them out. It's the future I want to know.'

'But I don't think – '

'Try. Make up anything. If it's really the future it will come out somehow.'

'Then why don't you try?'

'No. I want to watch.'

'Very well,' she said quickly, tossing her hair back. 'Shuffle and cut to me.'

Having done this with alarming concentration, Leopold pushed the round table to one side and turned back the edge of the rug. He pressed the reshuffled pack between his palms. Henrietta, between misgiving and self-importance took the pack and, kneeling down on the parquet, dealt out in a circle round her twenty-six cards, face down. Leopold squatted outside the circle and they both breathed intently. She said:

'You mustn't think.'

A tide of pale sun reflected from outside swept over the parquet and caught the tips of her hair. Looking up to think, she saw the limbs of the plane glisten and wet yellow light sweep over the wall behind. Upstairs, Miss Fisher shut the other shutter: her mother would now be entirely in the dark. Inside courtyards and twisted alleys, the sound of Paris took on a clearer ring. The sun coming out made Henrietta more nervous, as though heaven opened a window to watch. Leopold's soles creaked as he squatted behind her.

'Turn up any card,' she said.

He did. 'Ten of spades.'

'Oh, that's misfortune. A death.'

'Why?'

'Spades are used to dig graves.'

'Perhaps that is Madame Fisher. What do you do with those other twenty-six cards?'

'Oh, they come in later. Draw again. Show me. Oh, a woman is going to cross your path. Is your mother fair or dark?'

'I don't know. What are diamonds?'

'Money.'

'Look here, are you sure you're getting this right?'

'I don't see why I shouldn't be. Go on drawing. Oh dear, Leopold; really you *are* unlucky. Spades again. Ace, too: that's the worst.'

Leopold, who had crawled around outside the circle and now knelt in front of her, threw down the card angrily: 'I don't think your governess knew,' he said. 'What are hearts – love?'

'Yes – ' A bell tringed through the house; Henrietta looked up, surprised – this was the first indoor bell she'd heard today. One forgets that such things go on in Paris too. Mariette shot out of the kitchen, went to the hall door, murmured to someone, shut it. Leopold, oblivious, stared at the face-down cards, but Henrietta still listened: a woman cannot ignore what goes on in any house. She heard Mariette wait, then start heavily upstairs.

'Look here, the king of hearts.'

'Oh, you'll be lucky in love – What *was* that, do you think?'

'Oh, something. Go on.'

'What do you want to happen?'

'Crossing the sea.'

They heard Miss Fisher come to the top of the stairs, where Mariette and she interrupted each other's French. Henrietta could contain herself no longer; she sat back on her heels. 'Something must be happening,' she said. 'I think someone's brought a note.'

'Well, we can't help that.'

'I wish we hadn't done cards; I think it's made things happen – It's all very well to shrug, but suppose it's about you.'

'Perhaps your grandmother's dead,' retorted Leopold sharply.

'That would be a telegram.'

'Well, perhaps it is a telegram. Oh, damn all these cards! You don't know how, you don't make anything come!' Leopold impatiently broke the circle, sweeping the cards into a porridge with both hands. The gilt ships slipped over each other, here and there a card bent, its edge caught on the parquet. 'Muddle – muddle – muddle,' he muttered, stirring them rudely. 'I thought you said you could do this. What *can* you do, then?'

'Oh, shut up, Leopold: those are my cards!'

'I don't – Here she comes!'

The cautious steps of women when something has happened came downstairs, sending vibrations up the spine of the house. The women came down with a kind of congested rush, like lava flowing as fast as it can. The soughing of Miss Fisher's petticoats made the house sound tiny. Nothing was said: Henrietta could almost hear them make warning eyes at each other. Then the flat step of Mariette went away down the passage; Miss Fisher was left waiting outside the salon door, so acutely silent you only knew she was there. Henrietta and Leopold both dreaded, as she was palpably dreading, her coming in. Their eyes met; they stared at each other; she saw his pupils had prune-coloured settings, yet seemed at once to be seeing her own eyes. Miss Fisher's entrance sent a beforehand echo, a quiver through both of them.

'I knew that would be us.'

Miss Fisher's entrance, like anything much dreaded, happened at no one moment; she seeped in round the door. She seemed, *now*, to have been standing between them always, with the telegram shaking in one hand. Her eyelids, red, were turned down in humble stupefaction, as though she had done some terrible thing. Her manner seemed to have frozen.

'Henrietta,' she said, 'run away for one minute, dear.'

This let Henrietta out. 'Why?' said Leopold sharply.

'Run and play in the dining-room.'

'I want Henrietta here,' said Leopold, going white.

Henrietta edged away round the table; it agonized her to be present but nothing would make her go. Acting abstraction, she bent over the table to see her face in a pool of shiny walnut, stamped her two hands palm down on the polish, then watched the misty prints they left disappear. She felt an intense morbid solicitude, as though Leopold were about to be executed in front of her. His cut-off air, white face and trembling defensive anger heightened the thought, as Miss Fisher, farouchely, lost to all but the crisis, held her arms out to him, dropped on her knees and advanced on her knees, arms out. Her eyes streamed as she rode at him like the figurehead of a ship. Leopold backed, his arms close to his sides. 'What is it?' he said. 'What's happened?'

'You must be very good. Your mother – '

' – Oh. Dead?' he said quickly.

'No, oh no. Only, only a change.'

Leopold, having backed as far as he could, suddenly put up nonchalance at Miss Fisher. Haughtily, he touched the tie of his blouse. His small dark figure, one arm up in the act, flattened against the mantelpiece like a specimen. She, dumb again, knelt there frustrated in the patch of weak sun – was her only object, then, to spill tears on him? Henrietta, waiting, breathed on the table and absorbedly wrote an H in the mist.

'What change?' said Leopold.

'Your mother is not coming; she cannot come.'

Part 2

The Past

I

MEETINGS that do not come off keep a character of their own. They stay as they were projected. So the mother who did not come to meet Leopold that afternoon remained his creature, able to speak the truth.

She did not come. When it was half-past two by the salon clock the door did not open, her face did not appear, he had nothing to remember on from then. But by her not coming the slate was wiped clear of every impossibility; he was not (at least that day) to have to find her unable to speak in his own, which were the true, terms. He did not have to hear out with grave discriminating intelligence that grown-up falsified view of what had been once that she, coming in actually, might have given him. She, in the flesh, could have offered him only that in reply to the questions he had kept waiting so long for her: 'Why am I? What made me be?'

He expected from her a past as plain as the present, simply a present elsewhere. She was his contemporary. When he said: 'We shall understand each other,' he had not boasted. He and she had shared experience once: to his pre-adolescent mind his having been born of her did not shut a gate between them. And there had been his father. He expected her account of what is really: apples and trains, anger, the wish to know: what else is there?

Actually, the meeting he had projected could take place only in Heaven – call it Heaven; on the plane of potential not merely likely behaviour. Or call it art, with truth and imagination informing every word. Only there – in heaven or art, in that nowhere, on that plane – could Karen have told Leopold what had really been. Possibly when she was in love she could speak like that, but she had not been in love for more than nine years, now. Actually with him – in Mme Fisher's salon this afternoon, with her fur hanging over the scrolled end of the sofa, her gloves on the table beside Henrietta's apple – to speak would have been impossible. The moment, with its apparent reality, dwarfs and confuses us. But as she did not come he was never to know this. They might meet later, but nothing then could impair what had not been.

So everything remained possible. Suppose it had all *been* possible, suppose her not only here today in the salon but being as he foresaw, speaking without deception as he had thought she would. There is no time for the deception of her being grown-up. Having both looked at the world they know that, as you compose any landscape out of hills, houses, trees, the same few passionate motives go to whatever happens. Experience at any age has the same ingredients; the complexity of the rainbow is deceiving but its first colours are few. He has travelled less, so his imagination is wider; she has less before her but a more varied memory: referring backwards and forwards between imagination and memory she relives scenes, he sees them alive. The mystery about sex comes from confusion and terror: to a mind on which these have not yet settled there is nothing you cannot tell. Grown-up people form a secret society, they must have something to hold by; they dare not say to a child: 'There is nothing you do not know here.'

Talking to a very young clever person, you do not stick at hard words; on the other hand, you do not seek mystery. In the course of that meeting that never happened, that meeting whose scene remained inside Leopold, she would have told what she had done without looking for motives. These he could supply, for he would understand. You suppose the spools of negatives that are memory (from moments when the whole being was, unknown, exposed), developed without being cut for a false reason: entire letters, dialogues which, once spoken, remain spoken for ever being unwound from the dark, word by word.

This is, in effect, what she would have had to say.

Morning comes late at sea when you lie in your berth under the porthole, hearing the sea sough past. Karen Michaelis lay watching a round of daylight whiten on the wall opposite; the ship's vibration went steadily through her body; her head was full of cloudy, half-awake thoughts. It had been calm all night. When she sat up, she saw green hills beginning to slip by; each time she looked these had come in closer, so presently she dressed and went on deck. This was an April morning ten years ago and they were steaming up the tidal river to Cork.

She felt calm enough to have steadied a ship in a rough sea. A month ago, she had promised to marry Ray Forrestier: they had been friendly and watching each other for four years, ever since Karen was nineteen. Just when she was beginning to wonder why he did not want to marry her, he had asked her to marry him; taking her more by surprise and pleasing her more deeply than she had ever imagined would be the case. Her mother had never asked questions about Ray, but when Karen told her of the engagement her exclamations, like so many fireworks, lit up what must have always been in her mind. Karen then saw that in Mrs Michaelis's view a woman's real life only began with marriage, that girlhood amounts to no more than a privileged looking on. Her own last four years showed up as rather aimless; it was true that her painting lately had been half-hearted; she seemed to have lost sight of her ambition. There is more art in simply living, Mrs Michaelis said. Karen was glad to fall back on her mother's view of things.

She was not married yet: at the same time, she had no right to be still looking about; she had to stop herself asking: 'What next? What next?' She had firm ground under her feet, but the world shrank; perhaps she was missing the margin of uncertainty. The day after the engagement appeared in *The Times*, Ray had had to sail for the East as secretary to a very important person, on a mission so delicate that it must not appear to be a mission at all: Karen was left to deal with everyone's pleased excitement and to find out how uninfectious this was. 'You must be so very happy,' they kept saying: she felt the expected smile so pasted across her face that she even sometimes woke with it. Having to speak of Ray so publicly and constantly began to atrophy private tender thoughts; she began to dislike London where everybody knew everything. Wanting to rescue something at any price, she had written to the most unconscious of her relations, Aunt Violet Bent, inviting herself on a fortnight's visit to Rushbrook, County Cork. Aunt Violet had written back with warm vague pleasure. So Karen was crossing to Ireland, not long after Easter, which fell early that year. Having since last night left London behind, she already felt calm enough to steady a ship.

It was natural that she should feel everybody knew everything: she had been born and was making her marriage inside the class that in England changes least of all. The Michaelis lived like a family in a pre-war novel in one of the tall, cream houses in Chester Terrace, Regent's Park. Their relatives and old friends, as nice as they were themselves, were rooted in the same soil. Her parents saw little reason to renew their ideas, which had lately been ahead of their time and were still not out of date. Karen had grown up in a world of grace and intelligence, in which the Boer War, the War and other fatigues and disasters had been so many opportunities to behave well. The Michaelis's goodness of heart had a wide field: they were not only good to the poor but kind to the common, tolerant of the intolerant. Karen, seeing this, had been surprised to discover that her family roused in those friends she had made for herself, at the school of art and elsewhere, a writhing antagonism. Had the Michaelis been bigoted, snobbish, touchy, over-rich, overdevout, militant in feeling or given to blood sports – in fact, absurd in any way – Karen's new friends might have found them easier to stomach. But they offered nothing to satire; they were even, in an easy endearing way, funny about themselves. That unconscious sereneness behind their living and letting live was what Karen's hungry or angry friends could not tolerate. Nowadays, such people seldom appear in books; their way of life, though pleasant to share, makes

70

tame reading. They are not rococo, as the aristocracy are supposed to be, or, like the middle classes, tangles of mean motives: up against no one, they are hard to be up against. The Michaelis were, in the least unkind sense, a charming family. Karen had had no reason to quarrel with anything, no dull times to be impatient in. She went where she wished and met whom she liked where she liked; but those easy guests at her mother's table made her less easy friends look one-sided and uncouth. She saw this inherited world enough from the outside to see that it might not last, but, perhaps for this reason, obstinately stood by it. Her marriage to Ray would have that touch of inbreeding that makes a marriage so promising; he was a cousin's cousin; they had met first at her home. Her only brother, Robin, had come safely through the war to marry a very nice woman with property in the North; he managed his wife's property, hunted two days a week, sometimes published clever satirical verse and experimented in artificial manures. This was the world she sometimes wished to escape from but, through her marriage, meant to inhabit still.

While Karen sat at breakfast in the saloon, trees began to pass the portholes; soon she went back on deck. The sun brightened the vapoury white sky but never quite shone: both shores reflected its melting light. The ship, checking, balanced uncertainly up the narrowing river, trees on each side, as though navigating an avenue, leaving a salt wake. Houses asleep with their eyes open watched the vibrating ship pass: against the woody background those red and white funnels must look like a dream. Seagulls, circling, settled on mown lawns. The wake made a dark streak in the glassy river; its ripples broke against garden walls. Every hill running down, each turn of the river, seemed to trap the ship more and cut off the open sea.

On the left shore, a steeple pricked up out of a knoll of trees, above a snuggle of gothic villas; then there was the sad stare of what looked like an orphanage. A holy bell rang and a girl at a corner mounted her bicycle and rode out of sight. The river kept washing salt off the ship's prow. Then, to the right, the tree-dark hill of Tivoli began to go up, steep, with pallid stucco houses appearing to balance on the tops of trees. Palladian columns, gazeboes, glass-houses, terraces showed on the background misted with spring green, at the tops of shafts or on toppling brackets of rock, all stuck to the hill, all slipping past the ship. Yes, this looked like a hill in Italy faded; it stood in that flat clear light in which you think of the past and did not look like a country subject to racking change.

Smells of wood-smoke from cottages on the waterfront overhung the spongy smell of the tide; the smoke went melting up white against the woods.

The river still narrowing, townish terraces of tall pink houses under a cliff drew in. In one fanlight stood a white plaster horse; clothes were spread out to dry on a briar bush. Someone watching the ship twitched back a curtain; a woman leaned out signalling with a mirror: several travellers must be expected home. A car with handkerchiefs fluttering drove alongside the ship. On the city side, a tree-planted promenade gave place to boxy warehouses; a smoky built-over hill appeared beyond Tivoli. But Cork consumes its own sound: the haze remained quite silent.

Karen, her elbows folded on the deck-rail, wanted to share with someone her pleasure in being alone: this is the paradox of any happy solitude. She had never landed at Cork, so this hill and that hill beyond were as unexpected as pictures at which you say 'Oh look!' Nobody was beside her to share the moment, which would have been imperfect with anyone else there.

Passengers were beginning to crowd on deck with their baggage; the docks, where Uncle Bill Bent would not fail to be, were in sight. Karen's heart sank at the thought of being met. She was startled to find how unwilling she was to arrive: she had thought of the journey as, simply, going away. But you never get quite away. Rushbrook had sounded airy because she did not know it, but that would be spoilt soon. There would be a good deal of talking and explanation; she was afraid they might press her to have breakfast again. She wished Uncle Bill were not certain to be punctual. He and her Aunt Violet had not been long married; the most that was known of him was that he was never late. In this and other ways he was unlike one's idea of an Irish landowner; he looked despondent and peaky, and lacked gusto. Karen had met him once at a family party, where he had lifted unhappy eyes from his teacup only to glance mistrustfully at the clock. Would he know her again? Or suppose she walked straight through him, as though she had lost her memory in the night?

Going to meet a stranger or semi-stranger, can you help asking yourself what *they* are coming to meet? The sun, melting through the white film, struck the water, and Karen felt reflections playing over her face make bright liquid curves, a smile not her own. Her own smile was not complex. But leaning over the rail, giving her face to the trickery of sunny water, she felt this mysterious smile cast on her cheeks. What pleased her was not mysterious, and she could smile only when she was pleased. Her character was in her look (she had learnt before she was twelve). She looked at people at once vaguely and boldly; for years she had learnt from other eyes what hers did. This makes any lover or friend a narcissus pool; you do not want anyone else once you have learnt what you are; there is no more to learn.

But she had a more outside knowledge of what Uncle Bill would see. When she had no other model, she propped up her board by a looking-glass to work at a self-portrait, intently dispassionate. As a model's, the face was not bad. The eyebrows were lightly marked but their structure was definite; the eyelids straight, lifting warily, as she worked, from the board to the looking-glass. The nose was her mother's nose. The mouth was the clear-cut mouth in her own portrait at twelve; the same arbitrary calmness, but the lips fuller now. The chin, cleft a little – and so on. Effect of the whole face: breadth and delicate planes. But her pencil had always lacked something, not quickness or energy, simply power, perhaps. Her impatience with it always stamped itself on the portrait, which kept, like so many self-portraits, a fixed, challenging look. She was fair, not blonde.

The boat was late this morning. When Karen came to know Uncle Bill's habits better she could guess how distractedly he must have paced the quay. She would know he would have been there an hour early, having driven in breakneck from Rushbrook along the estuary, casting frantic backward glances at the water for fear the boat should be overtaking him. He had never been late, ever. But dreams of unpunctuality woke him, sweating, quite often, Aunt Violet said: your poor Uncle Bill. Tearing up to find the quay deserted, what should he think but that the boat had slipped in, then out, unseen? Common sense did nothing for him. His mind raised whole crops of irrational fears, his anxious love for his wife at the root of all. When signs of life on the quay brought no signs of the boat, he thought of unexplained tragedies at sea. They had all gone down. Or worse still, Karen was overboard and the captain had not the nerve to come in without her. It would be like fate to single out Violet's niece. Anything not only might happen but almost certainly would: was not *The Times* simply a catalogue of calamities? How should he break this to Violet? . . . Only towards the end of her stay at Rushbrook did Karen begin to realize all Uncle Bill went through.

When the boat did come in and she did step down the gangway, Colonel Bent's beaky nose under the flat check cap bobbed anxiously among the crowd at the barrier; he was not tall. He looked through her; she waved resignedly, whereupon he eyed her with some alarm. Snatching her suitcase suspiciously from the porter, he spoke in a muted voice, as though her nerves could not bear much, and when she failed to hear him went unhappily pink. Ladies of his generation did not expect to travel well, they crushed like chrysanthemums and took days to revive. So that Uncle Bill seemed uncertain whether he ought to talk, but to be silent with her made him still more shy. He tucked her into his car as though she were made of glass, then started the car with a jolt that would have shattered anything. They drove cautiously towards Rushbrook along the Tivoli bank, Uncle Bill sounding the horn with a note of entreaty when anything seemed likely to come their way. Karen saw it would be friendlier to be tired: she looked up at the gardens, which smelt gummy and sweet. Her uncle did not expect her to show character: if I had burnt my head off and put on a black pot instead like the child in the story, it would not matter, she thought. Her family were amusing, though not unkind, about Uncle Bill: it was not easy to see why Aunt Violet, who had got on so happily as a widow living outside Florence, becoming each year more like an ageless primitive angel, should have married this hysterical little person who had not even a place: his house, Montebello, had been burnt in the troubles.

But the Bents went on sounding happy; this was the most they could do, for the family had only met them together once. With the compensation money for Montebello they had bought a small house at Rushbrook, overlooking the harbour of Queenstown, now called Cobh. Its avenue ran uphill and its garden was too steep, but Aunt Violet liked seeing some of the sea, not all of it, and he liked watching the shipping through a telescope mounted at the edge of the tennis court. Ghastly black staring photographs of the ruins of Montebello hung at Mount Iris outside the bathroom door; downstairs was a photograph of the house as it used to be, in winter, a grey façade of light-reflecting windows, flanked each side by groves of skeleton trees. It could never have been gay or homely. But Rushbrook is full of Protestant gentry, living down misfortunes they once had. None of them, as a matter of fact, had done too badly, or they would not be here, for most of the big villas are miniature 'places' that need some keeping up. The nineteenth-century calm hanging over the colony makes the rest of Ireland a frantic or lonely dream. The bay is sheltered, the gardens full of exotic shrubs that grow nowhere else. Quiet roads run uphill, with lamps clamped to the corners of garden walls. From the harbour, Rushbrook looks like a steep show of doll's-houses; some gothic, some with glass porches, some widely bow-windowed and all bland. Yet this unstrange place was never to

75

lose for Karen a troubling strangeness, a disturbing repose. Marshes threaded with water, pale tufts of pampas, grey bridges, a broken tower lie for some flat miles between here and Cork.

It was hard for Aunt Violet's family to see why the Bents could not have chosen to settle – for instance – in Devonshire. Perhaps Uncle Bill clung to the edges of his own soil; and it was like Aunt Violet to set, so unconsciously, a premium on her company by living across the sea. Florence had seemed less distant; the Michaelis connection all knew Florence well. 'Abroad' was inside their compass. But the idea of Aunt Violet in Ireland made them uncomfortable; it seemed insecure and pointless, as though she had chosen to settle on a raft. It would have distressed her to know they felt this. But she had always done as she wished, mildly: she was a tranquil woman, obtuse and sweet.

2

When Uncle Bill drove Karen up the avenue, Aunt Violet's bedroom curtains were still drawn. However, hearing the car, she came down to meet them in her blue dressing-gown, her hair hanging over her shoulders in two fair faded plaits: she kissed Karen on the stairs. Rightly concluding that it was too late for breakfast (it was now half-past ten) she said nothing about it; she did not speak of Karen's engagement, either – she may have felt it was too early for that – but, having kissed her niece, looked at her happily. Karen could not have found a more grateful incuriosity on the subject of love than these two elderly lovers'.

An American liner was due at the mouth of the harbour that morning; the tender would about now be starting to meet it, so Uncle Bill went out to adjust the telescope. Aunt Violet went back to her room to dress. The house, like all houses whose mistresses come down late, was silent downstairs and still inanimate. Now and then, the hum of a motor came up from the Cobh road as Karen walked through the

76

rooms. She did not so much ask herself why she was here as why she was ever anywhere. She supposed that is partly why women marry – to keep up the fiction of being the hub of things.

It is a wary business, walking about a strange house you know you are to know well. Only cats and dogs with their more expressive bodies enact the tension we share with them at such times. The you inside you gathers up defensively; something is stealing upon you every moment; you will never be quite the same again. These new unsmiling lights, reflections and objects are to become your memories, riveted to you closer than friends or lovers, going with you, even, into the grave: worse, they may become dear and fasten like so many leeches on your heart. By having come, you already begin to store up the pains of going away. From what you see, there is to be no escape. Untrodden rocky canyons or virgin forests cannot be more entrapping than the inside of a house, which shows you what life is. To come in is as alarming as to be born conscious would be, knowing you are to feel; to look round is like being, still conscious, dead: you see a world without yourself ... Through looped white muslin curtains the unsunny sea daylight fell on French blue or sage-green wallpapers with paler scrolls on them, and watercolours of places that never were. The rooms smelt of Indian rugs, spirit-lamps, hyacinths. In the drawing-room, Aunt Violet's music was stacked on the rosewood piano; a fringed shawl embroidered with Indian flowers was folded across the foot of the couch; the writing-table was crowded with brass things. In a pan-shaped basket by the sofa were balls of white knitting wool. Aunt Violet seemed to have lived here always. The fire was laid but not lit. Each room vibrated with a metallic titter, for Uncle Bill kept going a number of small clocks. Out of these high-up windows you saw nothing but sky. The rooms looked not so much empty as at a sacred standstill; Karen could almost hear Uncle Bill saying: 'I have touched nothing since my dear wife's death.'

That evening, Aunt Violet remembered to ask about Ray; she had somehow got the idea he was in the army and supposed this must be because he had gone away. They went to bed early, as on all other evenings. After that, the days here began to slip by faster and faster, not touching anything as they passed. Some afternoons, Karen walked inland behind Rushbrook, into bare open country near the mountains – which are dark and rocky, though no higher than hills. But the dry whistling upland grass and lines of windbent beeches along the ridges, the dipping spaces of pale distance and air, said no more to her than Aunt Violet's bric-à-brac. She either felt nothing or felt, wherever she was, the same something approaching, like steps in the distance making you stand still. Her passivity made the hills, like the indoors of Mount Iris or the view of the harbour, seem to be behind glass. This was more than having no human fears. She felt hungry all day and slept deeply at nights.

Then one day had character. Ray's first letter to Rushbrook came, on the ship's notepaper, asking Karen to say if she truly *wanted* to marry him, or had only been rushed into saying she would. He said he had somehow got an impression, which worried him, that she had not given the question her whole mind. Perhaps he was wrong, perhaps being idle at sea made him think too much, perhaps being apart from her simply did not agree with him; or this might be a touch of liver brought on by the sea air. But loving her made him want her to have a fair break. He only wished to be clear how they *did* stand.

Karen had thought this was all perfectly clear. His letter came as a shock and was, naturally, upsetting. It would have been more of a shock if she had not already detected in Ray what she liked least: a liking for going over things carefully twice. He liked to tot everything up, and this seemed to her a wretched way to treat feeling. She was angry with him and wrote back with a good deal of impatience that she could not say more than that she *did* want to marry him. What more did he want? What did he mean by her whole mind? No, she did not wish him to answer. Only one thing, she said, seemed more futile than these months of waiting about: his question, any one of the things he had just asked. Had he forgotten that evening before he sailed? Had she been half-hearted then? Well ...? She wrote all this very fast, in uneasy anger. Then she stopped. Could he be attracted by somebody on the ship? Could this be an uncertainty inside himself? She saw the unkind white height of the ship she had seen him off on, and saw it forging ahead, directly away from her. She saw Ray's wish for her attenuated by distance, like those hot glass ropes you see spun at Murano, that, stretching, thin, then cool, go brittle and snap. That made her miss him so much that it seemed startling she had not missed him more. Going out to pace the garden she found herself in a fever; the calm of Rushbrook became a blanket she wanted desperately to throw off. She went back to stamp her letter, then hurried down to the pillar-box: dropping in the letter she thought: What more can I do? ... I cannot stay here, she thought, letting this go on going wrong. Uncle Bill and Aunt Violet filled her with impatience as she stared into the grin of the pillar-box. She wanted to be with some gaunt, contemptuous person who twisted life his own way ...

An hour later she went to the post again, this time with a letter to Mme Fisher in Paris.

On her way up from the pillar-box through the garden, she came upon Uncle Bill, rooting daisies up with a spud round the edge of the tennis court. The net to keep balls from flying into the view had been put up, the court had been marked once, but they had not played yet. It seemed to her that he looked more alarmed than ever, but she supposed that was only her own mood. But, suddenly looking up, with his creased face red all over from stooping, he said: 'Do you think your aunt is looking well?'.

'Why, yes,' said Karen, surprised. ' – Can I find another spud? I should like to do daisies too.'

'There isn't another,' said Uncle Bill distractedly. His face twitched; he looked quickly away from Karen. 'She's going to have an operation, you know.'

'Aunt *Violet*?'

'No, you couldn't know; we're not telling the family; she won't hear of upsetting them.'

'Oh – Is it – is it as bad as that?'

Up there in the drawing-room Aunt Violet began playing Schubert: notes came stepping lightly on to the moment in which Karen realized she was going to die. Phrases of music formed and hung in the garden, where violently green young branches flamed in the spring dusk. A hurt earthy smell rose from the piteous roots of the daisies and those small wounds in the turf that her uncle, not speaking, kept pressing at with his toe. Down there below the terrace, the harbour locked in green headlands lay glassy under the close sky. No one familiar in Karen's life had died yet: the scene round her looked at once momentous and ghostly, as in that light that sometimes comes before storms.

'But she's just like she's been always.'

His desperate little blue eyes inside their network of creases crept round to meet Karen's, then guiltily crept away. 'I shouldn't have told you,' he said.

'No, I'm glad you did.'

'It's on my mind,' he said helplessly.

'Then it was better to tell someone.'

'Maybe you're right.'

'But operations are to make people get well.'

Uncle Bill's unflinchingly wretched silence sent Karen down on her knees to heap up the daisy roots. Feeling mown grass brush the sides of her hands, which shook, she swept the daisies round her into a heap. She said, thinking aloud: 'But everything here goes on as if it would never stop.'

'That's what she wants, you know; she likes things to go on.'

They did go on. Every fine morning, Aunt Violet was to be seen trailing about the upper terraces of the garden, followed by Uncle Bill until twelve struck, when she sent him down to the town. There was always some little thing to be done in town. She did not go too, because everything was down hill, which meant walking back up the steep avenue. She said there was always something in the garden to go on doing, but what she did there never showed much. On cold mornings or when it rained, she wrote letters slowly at the table in the bow-window, among the crowd of brass objects, candlesticks, scales, paper-weights, racks and trays. Now and then she would pause and look at the skyline, looking for the right word or something to say next. At one they sat down to lunch at the table decked with daffodils, and Uncle Bill told Aunt Violet whom he had met in town; he never failed to meet somebody. After lunch she went up to rest, Uncle Bill darting constantly in and out to make sure she was still resting. Karen went for her walks then. At a quarter to five tea was carried into the drawing-room, a brass kettle on a tripod over a thin blue flame. No gong rang for this; Aunt Violet appeared by instinct, her back hair a little matted from lying down. Her hair, fine and limp as silk, was built up elaborately in an Edwardian manner and only re-done once a day, before dinner. Almost at once, as though waiting for one another, Aunt Violet would lift off the tea-cosy by its frill and Uncle Bill raise the lid of the muffin-dish to see what kind of hot cakes there were today. The hot cakes were always running with butter: she would look to see if he were pleased, he always was pleased, then they exchanged a smile. Neighbours sometimes came in to tea, but nothing held up the smile between Uncle Bill and Aunt Violet; they only talked rather more about old times and how one had to make the best of things now. After tea she played the piano or did not play the piano, while Uncle Bill kept within earshot to hear what she was at. Aunt Violet came down to dinner wrapped up in old lace, with a submerged diamond brooch glittering through; Uncle Bill put on a velveteen smoking jacket. Later, she sat with her feet up on the sofa, knitting the balls of white wool away, near a lamp, while he rustled through the day before's *Times* forebodingly, and Karen, looking up from some book she had found here, found her thoughts circling objects and light in the room as aimlessly and returning as a moth . . . All the ticking clocks did little to time here. Here they hung on their hill over the inland sea, and seemed as safe as young swallows under an eave. But fate is not an eagle, it creeps like a rat.

'I ought not to have come,' said Karen.

'No, no; she was specially glad.'

'You can't want me here, when . . .'

'Your aunt feels you are company for me,' he said.

'Is this . . . on her mind at all?'

You could see they never spoke of it. The music indoors stopped, which made Uncle Bill look anxiously at the house. Aunt Violet appeared in the French window, touching her back hair vaguely with one hand. With eyes in this light grey evening startlingly light and blue she looked down at them, and Karen saw she already did not live where she lived, but was elsewhere, like the music that had stopped. She saw, too, why the peace of Mount Iris was so fatalistic, as though those two were a couple expecting their first child. Aunt Violet came down the steps from the top terrace to look at the heap of daisies. 'Poor little things,' she said, 'it seems waste.'

'I must get them done before dinner,' exclaimed her husband, and hurried off to the end of the court with his spud.

'We ought to get the court marked again and have tennis soon,' said Aunt Violet. 'I know Uncle Bill would enjoy playing with you.' Was she perhaps conscious something was in the air, like a very light rain of ashes? She glanced up at the sky. Then, taking Karen's arm as though to say: 'Come away from this,' she walked with her to the parapet at the edge of the lawn. They stood looking out through the mended net at the view. 'You were well-educated,' she said suddenly.

'Why?' said Karen, feeling with horrified tenderness her aunt's hand on her arm.

'You always seem to know what you want to do next. I mean, going off for walks by yourself and knowing where to go to. I never did much until people suggested things.'

'Yes, I know what I want at the moment, but not always after that.'

Her aunt did not take this in but gazed at her own hand lying on Karen's arm intently – surprised, perhaps, that so much had got itself said, for she never spoke much, or as though the hand were a mystery to herself. She was simple enough not to be alarmed by personal talk. She went on: 'As a child, even, you used to have so much character. I remember I always felt you would have an interesting life. You do, I expect, don't you?'

'I suppose so,' said Karen.

'I never had very much character. But people have always been good to me. Perhaps that was the reason.'

'Which was the reason for which, do you mean, Aunt Violet?'

Her aunt, after a moment, said resignedly: 'I'm afraid I don't know.' Karen, looking across the harbour one saw from here, felt her Aunt Violet studying her profile, no more intrusively than if they had been standing yards apart. It was disarming, this disembodied closeness. But then the middle-aged woman withdrew a little, glancing down at her own breast as though Karen's clear-cut outline had made her suddenly shy. 'One sometimes wishes one had done more,' she said.

'But you being you is enough for anybody.'

Aunt Violet took this with such unmoved stillness and sadness that Karen realized how often it must have been said, and what a stone for bread the remark was. There had been her two happy husbands – apart from everyone else. Letting go of Karen's arm, she sat down on the parapet with her back to the view and began to pull rather helplessly at an ivy stem. 'I meant, selfishly,' she said. 'I was thinking more of myself.'

This was like hearing a picture you had always loved to look at, dearer than a 'great' picture, sigh inside its frame. That it should be less sustaining to be than to see Aunt Violet struck you with remorse. To something proud and restless – the spirit, perhaps – that looked out from inside her, nothing must make death more humbling than the idea of its ease: death should have a harder victory. *This* was stepping through still one more door held courteously open for her. Better to be rooted out hurt, bleeding, alive, like the daisies from the turf, than blow faintly away across the lawn like a straw. All these years she had stood by, uncritically smiling, had she been wanting really, like other women, to be the heart of things, to *be* what was going on? No wonder she gave such tender attention to small everyday things, living as people wish they could live over again, slighting nothing. The writing-table overlooking the sea, where she rested her elbows among the brass ornaments, her bedroom curtains drawn across the daylight must be heavy with her regretful wonder, not about death, about life. Every afternoon when they had finished tea, she blew out the wavering blue flame under the kettle, then glanced round the drawing-room where she still was. Closing her piano, she heard the silence. Wherever she had lived, her life had been full of people dropping in for a minute from somewhere else, or making her their somewhere else. No one asked her to understand, or wanted what happened to them to happen to her. Could she have wished to be trodden down in a riot, be a mark for anger or go down on a helpless abandoned ship? Her life here was very much confined, for she must on no account walk uphill. Did she ever think, Well, what if I walk uphill?

'Oh, Karen,' she said presently, as though she had to be clear about some plan for tomorrow, '*are* you going to marry Ray?'

'That's what he asked this morning,' said Karen, startled.

'Then it's not quite settled?'

'I thought it was. We seemed to be as much engaged as we could be. I can't see why he has brought it all up.'

'People like to be certain,' said Aunt Violet.

'I don't think it's so much that. He can't be content with just me; he keeps wanting to know my feelings, or whatever it is. What I do is not enough, he always wants to know why. Surely our being happy should be enough for him? Outside, he is so different; you could never guess that. If he wants me, he shouldn't keep asking the whole time. If one begins to think, why should one ever do anything? Marry most of all. Yes, I want to marry him. But I don't want to do anything

84

that a reason's been found for; I want to do something I must do. My painting used to be that.'

Aunt Violet said humbly: 'Couldn't love be a reason?'

'If you look close, there may be a reason for love.'

'Oh! I had never thought of that.'

'I shouldn't want to marry anyone else. He really is a plain man; simply, it doesn't suit him to keep on asking questions. If he must have reasons why we should marry, there are really only too many: we are the same kind of people, we think the same things are funny, we do not embarrass each other, we should have enough money and everybody we meet out at dinner will say what a charming couple we are – Aunt Violet, I know you know I should not go on like this if there were not really something much more. I know the third thing there when we are together is good. And I want him, in every way. No, I know I couldn't bear him to marry anyone else.'

'I don't suppose he'd do that,' said Aunt Violet placidly.

'I don't know. Something funny might happen.'

Her aunt turned on the parapet to look at the view, and the whole question of marriage went out of focus. Karen, stepping up on to the matted ivy beside her, looked across the harbour too. Standing like that, she towered over Aunt Violet as she had been made to feel she towered in character. She felt she was expected to carry anything off: our elders deceive themselves by their hero-worship of youth. Aunt Violet had spoken of Karen's marriage as, simply, a pleasant plan for tomorrow: having been so much a woman all through her own life, had she hoped her niece might be something more? Her open-minded questions touched a spring in Karen that young people dread: all your youth, you want to have your greatness taken for granted; when you find it taken for granted, you are unnerved.

'You will keep up your drawing?' said Aunt Violet. 'I am sure it would be a pity to give that up.'

'No, I may stop; I'm afraid of finding I can't draw – You're cold, Aunt Violet, you shivered: ought we to go in?'

'No, I'm not cold. I just want to watch that ship.'

They both watched the trawler with red funnels clear the Lee estuary and steam down Cobh harbour towards the open sea. Round an edge of cloud, the last of an unseen sunset shed light that made the veined leaves under the terrace sharp and still as a photograph.

'The harbour is good company,' said her aunt.

Karen, with her eyes on the ship, said: 'And yet in a way I would rather fail point-blank. Things one can do have no value. I don't mind feeling small myself, but I dread finding the world is. With Ray I shall be so safe. I wish the Revolution would come soon; I should like to start fresh while I am still young, with everything that I had to depend on gone. I sometimes think it is people like us, Aunt Violet, people of consequence, who are unfortunate: we have nothing ahead. I feel it's time something happened.'

'Surely so much has happened,' said Aunt Violet. 'And mightn't a revolution be rather unfair?'

'I shall always work against it,' said Karen grandly. 'But I should like it to happen in spite of me.'

'But what would become of your Uncle Bill? He has always been so good, and no one would think of him.'

Karen saw this was too true. Stepping down from the parapet, she stood frowning at a green stain on the toe of her white shoe. Aunt Violet, still watching the trawler, said: 'Was there anyone else you liked?'

'Yes, there was. But he made me miserable.'

3

Uncle Bill's guilty eyes, following Karen round, implored her to forget what had been said. But you cannot forget: now she saw the shadows over this house like clouds coming up faster; what was going to happen stood at the door. Only Aunt Violet went on being herself. She said she felt Karen should see more of the country, so Uncle Bill took their niece for drives inland and Aunt Violet thought this delightful for them both. Perhaps it was good for him to get right away from the house; all the same, it seemed unfair when there was so little time left.

County Cork is netted with white by-roads running up hill and down. Karen saw the gorse pouring burning like lava into the green valleys, down the sides of the hills; the car hummed through empty country full of this gold glare. Country people transfixed them with sombre unseeing blue eyes and goats lurched off through the uncurling fronds. Lonely white farms, rocks and valley poplars washed over her mind on a tide of light. All pleasure in looking seemed to have left her; she wanted the unkind edge of feeling again. Uncle Bill used to talk about Montebello: how it had been built, what improvements he had made, how even the stables were cut stone and what each room had contained.

At Mount Iris, the pits left in the lawn by the daisies healed; the court was re-marked and friends came in to tennis. Aunt Violet looked on while Karen and her uncle sprang about actively: balls pinged on the net at the sea side of the court. Warm weather set in and several more Rush-brook neighbours unburied themselves like tortoises. The more lifelike life became, the more Karen felt she must get away from Rushbrook while everything lasted. But she could not think how to make her visit end before the date she had said without making her going away the beginning of the disaster. At nights she began to lie awake, hearing the land-ing clock march ticking on through the dark; even at lunch she thought: This is no good. The drawing-room lamps began to shed less light and, sitting between her uncle and aunt after dinner, she no longer liked to raise her eyes from her book. Aunt Violet's probably dying was not only Aunt Violet's probably dying, it was like ice beginning to move south. Useless to wish she had never come to Mount Iris; the cold zone crept forward everywhere.

Getting away turned out to be quite simple: one day at lunch Karen said she must be back in London by Saturday of this week. Aunt Violet was sorry but not distressed. She did not say she was afraid it had been dull here, or ask Karen her plans. 'Uncle Bill will miss you,' she said. 'He's enjoyed your visit so much. We shall feel quite a small party.'

The Cork boat to Fishguard sails at about six. That last Friday afternoon, several people came in to tea. Someone soon to start on a journey is always a little holy, so Karen was allowed to stay outside the talk. Looking round the room she had looked round that first morning, she found it new now in an unforeseen way, for she was not likely ever to see it again. The milk-glass Victorian lamps with violets painted on them, the harp with one string adrift standing behind the sofa and the worked Indian shawl for Aunt Violet's feet would no longer be themselves, once put apart from each other and gone to other houses: objects that cannot protest but seem likely to suffer fill one with useless pity. Shrubs outside the window had come into leaf during her visit, and now cast blurred shapes on the wall. Beside Uncle Bill, a visitor's dog sat up to beg politely; he, frowning carefully, dropped tea-cake into its mouth.

He was determined she must not miss the boat, so they left before tea was over. Karen got blindly into the car, leaving Aunt Violet, in the porch, looking as though she had still something to say. From Mount Iris gate to the Tivoli end of the Cork tram, Uncle Bill drove in silence. Between Tivoli and the quay, he said: 'Well, don't tell your mother. *She* doesn't want that. She may write herself; I don't know; I've no idea . . . You mustn't worry.' He said: 'Don't worry,' three times. He came on board to take her things down to her cabin. She kissed him goodbye: tears started into his eyes and he walked quickly away.

Ray's next letter had not reached Karen at Rushbrook. Two or three days before she left she had written:

Ray: I am leaving here on Friday, so your next letter here may miss me; they'll send it on, I suppose. I know I had said I would be staying longer, but Aunt Violet is going to have an operation next month, so I cannot take up more of their time. If anything happens to Aunt Violet I shall inherit Uncle Bill, as there seems to be no one else, so I hope you will like him. He is like an unfledged bird that has already been blown out of its tree once.

I wish you were not away.

I didn't like the last letter I wrote you, but something in Ireland bends one back on oneself. One doesn't think exactly, but it upsets one – How is Sir H.? Has he begun to be difficult? You said something about liver, I hope that did not last. Aunt Violet loved the sapphire in my ring.

You said before you went away, do you remember, why didn't I go to Paris for part of the time? Well, I did get so far as writing to Mme Fisher, but have just heard she cannot have me, as her house is full up with two American girls. Oh, and here is some news (at least, it is news to me). Naomi Fisher is going to marry that man Max Ebhart, that French-English-Jewish man in a bank that they always see so much. I forget if I ever spoke of him. She adored him when I was there, but he made her too frightened to speak and me too angry to speak. He was really entirely Mme Fisher's friend, which makes me wonder if *she* can have made the match. I don't think Max E. could have thought of it on his own account; he has been used for years to seeing Naomi there but not seeing her (if you know what I mean). It was Mme Fisher he came to talk to: they had a kind of salon all to themselves, just they two. I think the Fishers are mad: he is not a person to trust. The way he and Mme Fisher ignored Naomi, and at the same time lorded it over her, always made me furious. He is not the sort of person you would care for at all. I cannot think what he wants Naomi for. Mme Fisher did also mention that they have come in for some money, a sister of Captain Fisher's has died in London. I do not think Max E. exactly mercenary, and even if he were, any Fisher money could not be enough to interest him. But this means the Fishers can stop taking in girls; these two Americans are to be the last. I expect they must be glad.

I'm sorry to write so much about people you've hardly heard of. But Mme Fisher's letter only came yesterday, so it is in my mind. And you know how fond I have always been of Naomi; now this news about her brings her so close. If he does not make her happy, I shall be miserable. I shall be seeing her: Mme Fisher also writes, which is good news, that Naomi is in London *now*, for a few days, on business about the legacy; seeing her makes one more reason to go back. Max E. is over too, helping about the business, I may have to see him too but rather hope not.

No special news from home. Christina and Robin are back from Spain, and glad to hear about us (they're up North again). I suppose they'll write. I have had sixteen more letters while I've been over here. We are certainly doing the right thing. Father sounds much the same. Tell Sir H., mother met a cousin of his at dinner at the T.'s, but unfortunately I cannot remember his name.

Forgive my impatient love. I suppose it's because I miss you.

KAREN

Are the people on board nice on the whole?

The boat did not sail up to time. Going down river on the tide in the bright green April dusk, Karen watched hills, houses, trees slip behind to become the past. The plaster horse still stood in the fanlight; the chestnuts would flower soon. But that first morning's mysterious clearness was gone. In less than a fortnight, how much had happened? Everything or nothing? You look at places you are leaving, thinking: What did I hope to find? She had had Ray's checking-up letter, learnt that Aunt Violet expected to die next month, and that Naomi was going to marry Max. When she got home they would ask: 'Well . . .? So . . .? What was it like?' Could she say: 'Like a long afternoon with three telegrams'?

Karen felt hungry, empty instead of sad. Everywhere, widening water and darkening shores, with unlit mansions standing in knolls of trees. She went below to dinner before they cleared the estuary, so as not to have to look up and see Rushbrook. The saloon was already more than half full.

After a minute in there, a girl with high pink complexion, in a lemon-yellow hat, pulled out the other chair at Karen's table and bumped down on to it. Several other tables were still empty and Karen glanced at them pointedly: she did not want company. But Yellow Hat's face swooped across at her confidentially: 'D'you mind if I come?' she said. 'There's a fellow after me.' Her round slate-blue eyes rolled in a woman-to-woman way.

'Do,' said Karen with a polite smile.

Yellow Hat, who was large, billowed out pleated jabots between the lapels of her opulent fur coat. She had a highly respectable kind of flashiness, and was not what Mrs Michaelis would have called quite-quite. Karen had seen her being seen off noisily by a number of friends. Whoever the fellow was, he must be exceedingly bold. Yellow Hat heaved herself out of her coat and reached for the menu.

'Not much choice,' she said, 'but it's always good. I always go for the chops; they give nice loin chops. Of course, it depends how much the crossing upsets you. Me sister can't take a thing but tea and plain steamed fish. But they'll get you that if you ask, or I'll ask, if you like. I'm in with all the stewards; I cross this way so often. D'you often cross this way?'

'May I look?'

'Oh, so sorry!' She passed across the menu. 'Wasn't that Colonel Bent from Rushbrook with you just now?'

'Yes,' said Karen vaguely. 'Why?'

'I know him by sight at the Yacht Club; he's quite a dandy ... I'd like to bet *you*'re not Irish?' said Yellow Hat archly.

'You would be right.'

'Over here for a bit of fun?'

'My aunt married Colonel Bent.'

'It's not been at all the same since the Army left.' Yellow Hat, sighing away regretfully, spread over half that table her elbows and bust. 'I guess you think we're all mad?' she went on invitingly.

'No, not specially. Why?'

Yellow Hat looked rather annoyed. 'Well, we are,' she said. 'Mad as hares. Reckless and mad and bad – that's what they say, you know: there's no harm in us. There's no holding us once we're off, though ... You ought to see the way all of us go on at home.'

'If I were mad, I don't expect I should know.'

Yellow Hat leaned across. 'Listen now,' she said recklessly. 'Will we split half a bottle of white wine?' When Karen nodded she grabbed at a steward's coat-tails and ordered Graves. 'That's a nice sweet wine,' she said. She seemed to be one of those decent pink pious racy girls who screech a good deal, speak of their fathers as Pappy and are really rather severely kept down at home. She could not help acting Irish even at Karen: once in England what a time she would have! The relation between the two races remains a mixture of showing off and suspicion, nearly as bad as sex. Where would the Irish be without someone to be Irish at? 'Now tell me,' said Yellow Hat, 'was this your first time over?'

'Not quite; I have been in Dublin.'

Yellow Hat had stopped listening; boldly, she was eyeing the sapphire on Karen's left hand. She said, '*You're* lucky, I see.'

'Yes.'

'Well, I suppose we all come to it,' said Yellow Hat piously. – 'Tell me, did you ever meet any Irish boys?'

'I don't think I did: no.'

'They're terrors,' said Yellow Hat, closing her eyes impressively.

'Are they?'

'Yes. Did you see that fellow with the red choker scarf saying goodbye to me on the deck just now? It was he spotted Colonel Bent saying goodbye to you. And it wasn't the colonel he spotted first, I may say! Now there's a terror for you: Jimmy Whelan, his name is. I wouldn't trust that one far! Is that tongue you have there? I didn't see tongue on the menu.' She sipped away at her Graves like a chicken drinking; generous colour spread over her face. 'Come on,' she said, nodding at Karen's glass. 'Your health.'

Karen said: 'Any terrors I've ever met have always been rather dull.'

'Ah, but,' said her friend astutely, 'perhaps *your* poison's not mine!'

Karen looked round reflectively, turning this idea over. The lit-up saloon was by now noisy with eating passengers. On the tables, glasses of porter had yellow slime round their rims; sauce-bottle stoppers were buttons of bright red; the cruets plied up and down. Business men shot their cuffs clear of the gravy and got down to it in a business-like way. People forked potatoes across each other and yelled at each other kindly above the zoom of the boat. Under this flashing chatter you heard the rush of strong dark unwilling water being cut through. Milky-faced Irishwomen looked round like

92

vacant madonnas, their unspeaking eyes passing slowly from face to face; women like this accept that all men are the same, simply one fact: man. Of the short-headed, roaring and tusky Irish there were a great many, but here and there a long bluish-white Celt face hung on the smoky air like an unkind mask. The brass-rimmed portholes darkened: Rush-brook must be behind now ... This bright snug scene sealed up everyone in itself and made them seem bound for no-where.

The saloon vibrated once; the engines checked and ground on. The ship had turned out to sea.

'I don't know what my poison is,' said Karen, smiling.

'Then beware, as the gypsy said!' exclaimed Yellow Hat. Her big silly face took on that immortal look people's faces have when they say more than they mean. The look passed; she twisted her string of pearls; her eyes rolled into Karen's with roguish morbidity. 'A girl never knows what may happen,' she said. 'Every time I get on this boat and the boys come to see me off I think: Well, who knows? A month is a long time!'

'Are you afraid of the sea?' Karen said disjointedly.

'Oh dear no, dear: are you? This is *my* eleventh crossing.'

'You just mean, it makes you wonder?'

'It's all in the stars, they say – However, of course, *you*'re settled,' said Yellow Hat, with as plain a stoppage of interest as was polite. The pot of tea she had ordered came; she poured it out hot and strong, then brooded over her cup with such an inward air that Karen repeated 'Settled?' rather un-easily.

'Surely to dear goodness,' said Yellow Hat, nodding glumly at Karen's ring, 'you wouldn't look beyond *that*? You know what's coming, all right.'

Karen poured out her coffee. 'For all we know, we may not get to Fishguard, but – '

' – Oh well, you see, dear, I've crossed eleven times – You ought to drink up your wine. D'you not like wine?'

'I was forgetting.' Melancholy filled Karen as she looked at her fingers through the yellow Graves that Yellow Hat would have liked. Catching sight of herself in a strip of mirror, she eyed her image with an unfriendly frown. How pettishly she took pleasures that came along! She disliked her pearl ear-rings, even, for looking bloodless. She returned to eye humbly and with no inner smile Yellow Hat's heavy frills and honest, heated face. 'I meant, apart from ship-wrecks and outside things,' she said, 'surely what happens to one is what one makes happen oneself?'

Lighting a cigarette with momentous boldness, Yellow Hat let this pass. 'I have a sister married in Liverpool,' she said. 'Were you ever there?'

'Once. Is that where you're going?'

'I'm not, no; I'm going to Cardiff. I've cousins there, too. That's a fine town.'

'I live in London,' volunteered Karen, still looking at Yellow Hat with respect.

'Think of that! You're quieter-looking, if you'll excuse my saying, than most London girls. I never care for their style.' Her eye, running over Karen, made it plain that she thought well, if not very much, of her. She did not wonder about her, they were much too unlike. Karen saw she must look to Yellow Hat like something on a Zoo terrace, cantering round its run not knowing it is not free and spotted not in a way you would care to be yourself. She thought: She and I belong to the same sex, even, because there are only two: there should certainly be more. Meeting people unlike one-self does not enlarge one's outlook; it only confirms one's idea that one is unique. All the same, in the confusion of such encounters, things with a meaning ring, that grow in memory later, get said somehow – one never knows by whom ... 'D'you dance much?' said Yellow Hat.

'Yes, quite often. Do you?'

'I'm crazy about it,' said the great strapping girl. 'D'you know the Empress Rooms? Aren't they grand?'

'Grand.'

'Well, who knows we may run into each other there! I wear emerald green and I've got a mole on me back. If you see me passing, give me a good slap.'

The steward brought their two bills. The fellow who must have been after Yellow Hat pottered twice past their table, then gave up and went away. Yellow Hat, having watched him go round her yellow hat-brim, dived for her bag and hitched on her fur coat. 'We're pitching a bit,' she said. She added a shade doubtfully: 'Will we go up now and have a look round the lounge?'

'Do you know, I think I'll go straight to bed.'

'I daresay you'd be right: me mother's the same,' said Yellow Hat with an air of distinct relief. Smiling kindly at one another they got up and zigzagged out; the ship was pitching a bit. They paused at the foot of the stairs; the rubber-floored passage to Karen's cabin went on ahead. Yellow Hat seemed to feel: One can't just let people *go* . . . She became embarrassed all over. 'Well . . .' she said.

'Well . . .'

'I'll watch out for you at Fishguard,' said Yellow Hat, gathering speed. 'Try cotton wool in your ears. Well, so long till then.'

Forgetting to smile, they looked at each other askance, nodded, and parted – for ever. The ship ploughed ahead steadily through the dark.

4

Nobody could have offered more of contrast to Yellow Hat than Naomi Fisher, found waiting downstairs at Chester Terrace next morning when Karen got home. The morning-room where they had put her was a bleak restless place where nobody ever settled. It was behind the dining-room and had two doors: the service-lift groaning up a shaft in one corner alarmed you if you did not know what it was. The main telephone was in here, with a plugboard for extensions, a bureau, with a dry ink-well and rack of telegraph forms, and an unsmiling row of directories and old *Who's Whos*. From the top of a case of exiled books, a bust of the Duke of Wellington frowned down at you blindly; the walls were

95

hung with engravings of the Virtues in action which Mrs Michaelis had never liked. The gas-fire had a stiff tap and was seldom on. To be put in here by a servant showed the servant's distinction between being shown in and being asked to wait. Naomi's anxious brown eyes and humble manner must have led Braithwaite to think there must be something she wanted; and that therefore she was no lady. What she did want, and wanted badly, was to see Karen: a need so pressing as to be without grace. So here, when Karen came in quickly, she was sitting, at the edge of a cold leather armchair. All 'endy' black furs and French-virginal primness, she sat with strained dark eyes fixed on the opening door. She had heard the taxi out there, then Karen's voice. Emotion, odd at so early an hour, kept her speechless till after they had kissed.

'Your face is cold,' said Karen. 'It's terribly cold in here. I'll kill Braithwaite one of these days!'

'I have come too early.'

'No, why?' said Karen, pulling off her gloves.

'You must be tired,' Naomi said, anxious.

Karen was – or was it dazed? 'I did sleep in the train, though. How much of you have I missed? How long have you been in London?'

'Just four days, Karen. Next Tuesday we must go back.'

Naomi spoke with an unreproachful sadness that made Karen exclaim: 'Why didn't you let me know? I needn't have been away. But I only heard by chance.'

'I should have thought. I came round here at once, they told me you were away,' said Naomi, gazing at her with fatalistic love.

'I was in Ireland; I don't really know why.'

'Oh, but that seems sad, when you went so far! You see, I had to come over here when I could, and that was quite suddenly; between two American girls and two more American girls.'

'Bother those girls!' said Karen. 'Are these really the last?'

'Yes, these are the last. We had not been intending even to

take them, but they were friends of old friends and we did not like to refuse. It is for two months only.'

Impatience on Naomi's behalf had made Karen angry ever since, as a young girl, she had been at the Fishers' herself: at this moment, kneeling to light the fire, impatience made her bruise her thumb on the tap. She had decided not, after all, to bring Naomi upstairs, in case they should run into Mrs Michaelis. Though bound to be specially nice to Naomi Fisher because she wished she were not there, Mrs Michaelis would be wanting, naturally, to hear all about Rushbrook from her daughter. So, when the gas had popped alight, Karen and Naomi stood to talk in the window, each leaning a shoulder into a curtain and looking across the small garden at the dark brick mews behind. Naomi was in black from top to toe, for the English aunt who had died leaving her the money. She explained to Karen she was staying at Twickenham in dead Miss Fisher's house, with a cousin called Helen Bond, a co-legatee and executor, going through clothes, papers, books and those sad meaningless things that are called 'effects', getting the house ready for the auctioneer. (Helen Bond and she had agreed to sell.) Though she had only known her aunt so slightly (Miss Fisher had disapproved of her brother's French marriage) all this was sad work, Naomi said. Dust from her aunt's life seemed to have settled on Naomi, making her voice husky, her skin unalive. But, though she did not look it, she had a turn for affairs; Karen had no doubt she would get through everything well. It was nice to think of Naomi's having money.

'Max has helped me,' said Naomi.

Then, as though she had drawn undue attention to something, she stared nervously at the window-sill, seeming to shrink all over. Karen's heart smote her; she saw *she* ought to have spoken of Max first, and how unkind on her part the omission was. She should have cried: 'I'm so glad!' before she was into the room. But ungladness made her perverse and shy. And Naomi looked so much more like someone who'd lost an aunt than someone who'd gained a lover. Max should have given her something to smile about, or, at least, violets to pin on her black fur. Karen's thoughts at once leaped to attack him, as though they had been waiting. Naomi remained with her eyes down, as though imploring Karen not to feel she must speak. She had outgrown years ago any girlish naturalness, without having learnt how even to imitate any other. You could see that her tremendous inside life, its solitary fears and fires, was out of accord with her humble view of herself; to hide or excuse what she felt was her first wish.

'Oh, my *dear* Naomi . . .'

'Yes, Karen?'

'You know how glad I must be that you're so happy!'

'But you are happy yourself.' Naomi looked up almost accusingly, as though her friend spoke too much from the outside. She fixed her eyes on Karen as though daring her to stay calm. Her timid husk dropped off, or she lit up inside it; she stood with face and eyes exposed, turned burning to Karen, as much as to say: 'Look . . . Surely you are the same?'

Karen said: 'Yes. But we are not at all the same.' Naomi, now again no more than herself, agreed: 'Yes, Life is so different for you and me, naturally.'

Karen felt she had reason to be tired. Even without a journey, she could not discuss her heart at eleven o'clock. She felt in her overcoat pocket for her cigarette-case and sat down, noncommittally smiling, in the leather armchair. Sun, then shadows of clouds on the brick mews made the room lighten then darken uneasily. The time in Ireland, like one long day spent waiting, hung on her mind. She was in that flagging mood when to go on living seems only to be to load more unmeaning moments on to your memory. Pulling off her hat, she tilted her head back and impatiently rolled it, as though to shake off something, on the leather chair-back – like, Mme Fisher once said, a young English boy.

She knew Naomi loved her with that touch of devotion that can be on one side only; a thing you cannot return. All Karen herself felt was: here was this bond between them, or

band round them, forged in that year in Paris (yes, forged –
it was metal, inelastic, more than chafing sometimes) when
she was so young, so much frightened of Max, so unable to
ignore him, that Naomi there was what you had to have. But
since then, there had been everyone else, and her conscience
began to send in bills about Naomi. She ought to want to
thank Max for making all that all right ... Holding her
cigarette at arm's length she watched it fuming away. 'And
so Max is over here with you?' she said.

'At a hotel in the Adelphi.'

'Oh. On a holiday?'

'He has some business here, but also helps me with mine.'

'I'm sorry I may not see him; there's so little time left.'

'Oh, but three days more! Oh, I beg you to!' exclaimed
Naomi. Turning round from the window to face Karen she
interlocked tightly her black-gloved fingers, then drew them
apart slowly, as though with pain. 'To go back to Paris without that would disappoint me, Karen.'

'But it isn't as though he and I hadn't met, Naomi. I once
saw him so often.'

'You did not like him in those days.'

'In those days I was stupid.'

'But I beg you now to meet him again.'

Karen said easily: 'Can't we wait till we're married? Till
we're all married, I mean? You still have Ray to meet.
There's so little time now, and I want to talk to you. After
all, I have met Max, but you can have no idea what Ray is
like.'

'Perhaps I have,' said Naomi disconcertingly.

Mrs Michaelis said, whenever she met the Fishers, that
she did wish Naomi had a less emotional manner. 'She does
not do herself justice; her eyes start out of her head. Do you
never find it a little trying, Karen?' 'I know what you mean,
but she's perfectly calm really; I think I should miss her
manner,' Karen often replied. The conclusion used to be,
always: 'The fuss she makes flatters you.' This morning, she
did find Naomi trying; she could feel her mouth setting in a
smile like her mother's – a too kind, controlled smile.

'Naomi,' she said, 'you know I want to like Max: I *must*, now. But if I still didn't, you wouldn't blame him, you'd blame me. How could you not, as things are?' She added, glancing up at the bust of Wellington: 'Did he ask to?'

'Ask to see you? No,' said Naomi, still more disconcertingly. 'Not so far, at least.'

'I don't think I take that well.'

'You were never friendly to him.'

'Oh, that is absurd! You know how frightened I was of him. I used to think *he* knew, too. You mustn't encourage him to be touchy, Naomi; you make him sound like a man who cannot pass a looking-glass. Surely people *should* be indifferent, even if they are not?'

'Oh, Karen, there are no giants.'

'Surely there should be.'

If Karen's passion for indifference took Naomi aback she did not show it, but, as though to counter the Mrs Michaelis Karen had so suddenly put on, put on Mme Fisher herself and said, with her mother's smoothness: 'Perhaps in your world, Karen. You live, you see, in a more fortunate world.'

'Do I?' said Karen moodily, dropping her mother's manner.

Naomi's gloved hands made a level movement, as though to say, 'But of course.' She looked through her friend with unenvious dark eyes.

'I wish you would take your gloves off,' exclaimed Karen. 'It is dreadful in here at the best of times, and when you stay with everything on, Naomi, you make me feel we are in a waiting-room – I am not as unfair as I sound; you know I admire Max; all I meant was, he was sarcastic when I was eighteen. But if there *is* time to meet, why on earth shouldn't we?'

'That will make me very happy,' said Naomi.

Evidently, her heart had been set on this. When Karen was eighteen, the immense store Naomi – so often disappointed – set by small things had seemed natural to her. But since those Paris days they had seldom met without Karen's beginning to wonder which of them could be mad. The strength of Naomi's feeling about marriage could be foreseen; also, she had loved unrewardedly for so long. But at any time she had a way of making straight lines bend and shapes of things fluctuate as though a strong current were flowing over them. With her there, there seemed to be no more facts. Under her unassumingness, Naomi had a will that, like a powerful engine started up suddenly, made everything swerve.

In Paris she had been subject to Mme Fisher and her own tongue-tied silence. Karen and Max, two people, were her objects; even with them she did not pursue anything; she was pure in heart. No wonder she frightened you ... The hall clock struck: it was now half-past eleven. Karen thought how much she should like a bath. Would Braithwaite have told her mother she had come home?

'Your poison's not mine,' she quoted.

Naomi, meekly pulling off her gloves, said: 'Please?'

'A woman on the boat was saying that last night.' Both Naomi's hands emerged with an odd nude air. Karen suddenly said: 'And Max loves you very much?'

'Yes,' answered Naomi. 'Naturally, I have asked myself many times, am I stealing him? I am in no way his type; I am utterly unlike anyone he frequents. I am not *femme du monde*. You know how it is, how nobody looks at me. My mother has all the wit: I inherit nothing from her. How often have I said: "But what can I *do* for you?" There seems to be nothing that I can do. But he says yes, that there is, and wishes me to believe him. I, necessarily, believe him.' She straightened out, then folded her gloves gently, as though they knew better than she did what Max meant.

Karen felt she should say something at once. 'Mme Fisher is very pleased, I expect?'

'No. Oh no. My mother opposed the match.'

'But he and she are such friends.'

Naomi's face went pinched and monkey-like, lines appeared round her mouth. She stared at the gas-fire. 'That alters nothing,' she said. 'She is not pleased with us.'

Karen, startled, said, 'Does she interfere?'

'Not any more now. She simply smiles and says nothing. She washes her hands of me.'

This brought up a lively picture of Mme Fisher. Karen herself had more than once been the victim of that unspeaking smile. Mme Fisher always withdrew opposition in such a way as to make your motive snap. If you went against her, she said: 'But naturally, you know best,' which at once drove dismay in. If you knew best too often she packed you back to your mother, writing: 'Your daughter is growing too wise for me.' The waiting list for a place in her house was so long that she could afford to be high-handed. The girls in her house (of whom Karen had been one) were her guests (at a price) not her charges: she always made this clear. She undertook to exercise no direct authority. If that was what mothers wanted, there were the finishing schools. She did not undertake, she said, to impart any kind of 'finish', or, in fact, to receive young girls still lacking that quality. She would receive only young girls of good understanding and manners, who would not abuse a freedom she had no means to restrict. In short, she would keep no girl who did not know how to behave. They were there to attend the Sorbonne or to study music or painting. She offered, simply, she said, a roof, a modest table, the French of Touraine and a nominal chaperonage. She was, herself, a blue stocking, an unworldly woman. Not for nothing had Mme Fisher lived years with the English and discovered their liberalness and liking for the half-way. All this went down with some English and more American mothers. Her unofficial prospectus (always the same letter in answer to an inquiry) pleased mothers to whom the trimming and stuffing of daughters, in Paris or elsewhere, for an immediate market did not commend itself, or who wanted for their dependable daughters freedom inside the bounds of propriety. A mark between student wildness and the suspicious primness of an 'establishment' was thus brilliantly struck. Mme Fisher met a felt need. Mothers were enthusiastic and daughters did not complain. Mme Fisher appeared to put herself to no trouble; once you were there you were there, and she hoped your studies went well. She put up with your presence amiably. She asked no questions, but knew: she knew where you went, why, with whom and whether it happened twice. Though Paris was large, you were never out of her ken. The girls, discussing this, hovered between an idea of the supernatural and Naomi's having been told off to shadow them. Nobody knew how Naomi spent her days – but how could Naomi shadow two girls at once? There must be more to Mme Fisher than that: her marked unobservingness and withheld comment gave her terrific power over the girls' ideas. They might do as they wished, but did not, for she made it too clear that nothing they did could be what they really wished to do. If she did not apply polish, of which she said she knew nothing, she applied to young wood that emery-friction of satire without which first, no polish will 'take'. Her non-presence in the salon, on those afternoons when she handed over the room to the girls for their friends' visits, was as constant, uncommenting as the tick of her clock. She was *some*where all the time. For ten years now, ever since Captain Fisher's death, well-bred, well-fed, well-read English-speaking girls had been passing, two at a time, through her small house in the Rue Sylvestre Bonnard. Of all these, only Karen had left a mark, known Naomi, had more than a word with Max or crossed Mme Fisher without being packed home. Perhaps only Max knew how far all this had gone. Now the English aunt's death, the small legacy, Naomi's coming marriage – no more girls.

'Where shall you live, Naomi?'

'Oh – with my mother.'

Karen opened her eyes. Naomi added: 'I could not leave her, you know, and Max would not wish me to. And there is the house; we cannot – '

'No. I see. So you'll all go on just the same?'

Naomi looked at Karen askance, as though hearing something unfriendly in her friend's tone. A little stiffly she said: 'With no more girls.'

Mrs Michaelis – who, it turned out later, had been told Naomi had called and been put in the morning-room, and heard later that Karen was back and in the morning-room too – came downstairs firmly, at this point, and looked in. She had been waiting some time, full of patience and humour, for Naomi to finish her heart-to-heart, but felt it really ought to be done now. She very naturally wished to talk to her daughter herself. She greeted Naomi with absolute friendliness, but Naomi, going governessy and frightened, looked about for her gloves, preparing to go away.

5

Naomi's dead aunt had a flowering pink cherry at the foot of her garden at Twickenham. Karen spread a sheet of newspaper on an upturned packing-case under the tree: dark pink lights and splashes of sunshine where wind parted the branches came spilling through. This last day of April was warm and idle, like summer. Inside the French window with its white frame in sunshine, the aunt's house was hollow, completely dead. But someone else would move in almost at once, and be here next spring, no doubt, to enjoy the cherry.

This was Monday, the afternoon before they went back to Paris. While Karen spread the newspaper tablecloth, putting a stone at each corner to keep it on – and, even so, the slight wind came creeping under – Max and Naomi were indoors, boiling the kettle and looking about the kitchen for left-over china for tea. They made a great point of tea when they were in England. In an hour or two they were going to lock up the house, and drop the key at the agent's on their way into London. Karen kept half turning to watch the windows; she wondered which would come out first, Naomi or Max.

It was Max's step she heard on the basement stairs, then crossing the bare drawing-room. He stepped carefully through the window, carrying the laden black iron tray. The sun struck on his forehead, wrinkled with carefulness, and on the white china. He put the tray precisely down on the packing-case, so that a rim of newspaper stuck out all round. Then, straightening himself, he looked up through the cherry, which was so pleasant there was nothing to say.

However: 'Where shall we sit?' he asked. 'There are still those three chairs, but they are too high.'

'Why not the grass?'

Max felt the grass. 'Yes, it's dry enough,' he said. 'But whoever pours out must kneel.'

'That will be Naomi – what is she doing now?'

'Still waiting for the kettle to boil.' There was no teapot on the tray yet.

With nothing more to arrange, they became silent. Karen stood pressing her back against the tree-trunk, touching the bark behind her with one hand.

Their meeting, yesterday, had been pointless and pleasant. Karen and Naomi had lunched with Max at his hotel in the Adelphi. In five years Max had not changed; he was still very much himself in unmoved disregard of how you might feel. What Karen remembered best about him in Paris was what she had kept expecting and he was not. What he was on Sunday in the Adelphi he must have been always: whatever more she had seen she had made herself. This year, he must be thirty-two, but still looked, as in Paris, some special age of his own. That nervous, rather forbidding stillness still swung back on him, now and again, like something that he would rather you had not touched. What few gestures he made, from the wrists only, moulded sharp surprising shapes on the air. The turn of his head was polite, attentive, slow. Slowness of movement in a quick-thinking person makes you feel some complication of thought or feeling behind anything that is done. His smile, which was gentle, narrowed his eyes slightly; Karen saw why she had thought him sarcastic then ... All the same, her memory had exaggerated him. The meeting she tried to avoid amounted to almost nothing. All through lunch, she was conscious of something missing its mark in her, and did not know whether she were sorry or glad.

Max's forehead was high and narrow, his dark hair with a spring at its roots brushed carefully back. Bony structure showed at his temples and cheek-bones, the bridge of his nose and along the line of his jaw. His dark eyes, softened by childishly long lashes, were set rather close in. An unexpected movement of those long lashes would make his face appear flinching and sensitive: mostly, it was impassive. He looked either French or Jewish, perhaps both; his mother had been French and his father an English Jew. Intellect, feeling, force were written all over him; he did in fact cut ice. Mme Fisher had once remarked that a darting womanish quality, enforced by a manly steadiness of will, made him the figure he was, or promised to be, in his own, the banking, world. In any field (she said) success is possible for the artist. But he must put up with being more admired than trusted. He might not arrive where he should for many years more; he would have, first, to be right an unfair number of times, and must lack scope to be right until he was recognized. No plain man would ever care for his mouth. But he was in no way supersubtle or florid, and no doubt could have been a gentleman had he wished.

But Mme Fisher did not want Max as a son-in-law. Karen wondered how he took his old friend's unfriendliness. What Naomi said was true, he *did* mind everything; a harsh edge you sometimes felt in his manner being chagrin, perhaps, at minding so much.

This Sunday, away from Paris, it was startlingly simple: they were all three good friends. Karen had blushed inwardly to remember the scene she had made with Naomi – though it was quite a small scene – yesterday morning, about not wanting to meet him. Whatever did I think could happen to me? His charm remained – if it ever had been charm. But by now, she had lived several years in a world where it was almost everyone's business to please. She looked back at that broken-off talk with Aunt Violet both watching the trawler: *then* she had thought she had something still to dread. It had been the air of Ireland, perhaps, or the shock of having just heard about Aunt Violet. But now I am back here, where I really belong . . . Sunday London silence filled the half-empty dining-room, with its unbright silver and lifeless wall-mirrors. She watched Max's hand, while he talked, touching objects – the stem of a glass, a salt spoon, a cigarette – she looked at objects he picked up when he had put them down. Becoming Naomi's lover 'placed' him, and far away.

All through lunch, the Paris past stayed unreal. Karen looked back at it boldly, surprised. She remembered, for instance, being so much unnerved by the bare idea of meeting him that she would turn back upstairs again when she heard him cross the hall. But if he did not cross the hall, but stood back himself in the open door of the salon, she would creep on down, casting round for something to say: at the same time feeling her heart thump. She saw now that his frequent presence about a house where young girls were could have been thought irregular, had he not made such a point of ignoring Mme Fisher's young girls. A cold, withdrawing bow was the most most of them got. Those darkish late afternoons he was there so often, waiting for Mme Fisher to come in or be free to talk to him: when he was not really there, some shadow often deceived Karen, or she would be misled by a door ajar: uncertainty, at that special time of day, made her life pump through her furiously, uselessly. When they were in the same room, his weight shifting from foot to foot, as he leaned on the mantelpiece talking to Mme Fisher, filled her with uneasiness. Every movement he made, every word she heard him speak left its mark on her nerves. He was the first man I noticed, she thought now.

She thought, young girls like the excess of any quality. Without knowing, they want to suffer, to suffer they must exaggerate; they like to have loud chords struck on them. Loving art better than life they need men to be actors; only an actor moves them, with his telling smile, undomestic, out of touch with the everyday that they dread. They love to enjoy love as a system of doubts and shocks. They are right: not seeking husbands yet, they have no reason to see love socially. This natural fleshly protest against good taste is broken down soon enough; their natural love of the cad is outwitted by their mothers. Vulgarity, inborn like original sin, unfolds with the woman nature, unfolds ahead of it quickly and has a flamboyant flowering in the young girl. Wise mothers do not nip it immediately; that makes for trouble later, they watch it out.

Mrs Michaelis was wise: whatever she saw, she said nothing. Only, when Karen came back from Paris, her mother saw to it that Ray, for one, was about. The rule of 'niceness' resumed in Karen's life. She grew up, her regard for order overtook her sensations. She took herself up again from where she had been at twelve: a discriminating little girl who spent her tips on antiques. What would not do, did not do. She had come to look back at Max as a person who would not do. But in that she had been unjust, as she discovered on Sunday; as Naomi's husband he would do very well; her Michaelis view of life quickly fitted him in. She was ashamed, looking at Max across the table, of the unfair way her fancy, then her revenge on her fancy, had misused him.

For Max was very nice. As her host at lunch today she met him for the first time.

First love, with its frantic haughty imagination, swings its object clear of the everyday, over the rut of living, making him all looks, silences, gestures, attitudes, a burning phrase with no context. This isolation, young love and hero worship accomplish without remorse: they hardly know tenderness. 'The Queen of Spain has no legs' ... But in the Adelphi dining-room, Max reappeared dependable, solid, shyish, with a touch of Ray about him: domestic man – hanging Karen's fur over a chair-back for her, slipping Naomi's gloves out of reach when she played with them, refusing sauce, looking anxiously down the wine-list, failing once or twice to catch the waiter's eye. His wish to lunch somewhere gayer had been evident, but Naomi had said it would be quieter here. He looked the Frenchman with a good English tailor, and had a slight cut on his chin. Only those small worries of hospitality at an English hotel altered the pleased unsmiling calm of his face. His and Karen's talk was light, unadvancing: proper Michaelis talk. Naomi listened to them with pride and pleasure, not adding much. A weight, some remaining preoccupation, seemed to have lifted off her since they had sat down. She looked ten years younger than she had ever been.

But Karen, looking at Max, against a stuffy draped curtain, thought: This is like an epilogue to a book. You hardly read on, the end is so near: you know.

That had been yesterday.

Besides the pink cherry tree, there was not much in the garden: a stretch of lawn, now unmown, between the tree and the window, two lolling bloomy borders of lupins not yet in bud. The aunt must have lived indoors. But every blade of grass, pricking up, shone; the wind puffing the poplars in other gardens shook white light from the April sappy leaves. Many sensations of pleasure made up the moment and hummed in the silence between Max and Karen like bees in a tree. The yellow-brown brick house with its dark windows glared at them down the lawn. Not speaking, and their pleasure in not speaking, made an island under the boughs of the cherry. But silences have a climax, when you have got to speak.

'What can Naomi be doing?'

Max said: 'Still standing beside the kettle.'

'She must be making it shy.'

'Are you thirsty?' he said with his oddly inflected voice.

'This time tomorrow, you'll both be – where?'

'Still in the Nord train. We do not reach Paris till six.'

At his words, the English Channel rose to cut them off like a blade of steel. The fine-weather blue the sea would have tomorrow, puffed into smiling ripples, could not disguise from her how fatal it was. She even smelt the salt air that would blow on deck. She said with a touch of pretty-woman extravagance: 'I feel you are both going away for ever.'

'Please miss us,' said Max with the same ease. 'But we are a couple of foreigners, after all.'

'Foreigners, though, belong somewhere else, and you and Naomi don't.'

'No; we are not rooted anywhere like you are.'

'Am I? All I meant was, I wish you lived here.'

'No, *that* would be the pity,' he said with surprising force. 'In London, we three should soon not even meet. No, we make better visitors.'

The ironic humbleness of his manner offended Karen, who looked up through the tree wishing she had not spoken.

'I do not want to go back,' he went on briskly, 'or, at least, not to go back yet. But there can be no question of anything else. I must return to work – yes, this has been a holiday – and now Naomi has finished in this house she has no good reason to stay on, either.'

'It is those wretched American girls, waiting. I suppose they feel, as I probably felt at their age, that the Fishers exist for them.'

'You still exist in that house – haunt it, if you prefer. They are not likely to.'

'How I wasted that year!'

'How?'

'In being eighteen.'

'But you were studying art.'

Going on standing up in a rather rigid way, as though lashed to the tree-trunk, she looked at the shadows moving at their feet on the grass. Max's sudden unhumour made her feel silly, as though he and she had been playing catch idly and he had got bored and flatly let the ball drop. This too often happened. He was a foreign man, with no idea of saving anyone's face. Unconscious, and thinking rapidly on beyond this, Max sat down at the foot of the tree, clasping his hands, ridged with fine stretched bones, round his knees and leaning his body back. It had been foolish to stand, as they had, so long. She looked down uncertainly at the top of his head. Then she slid down too and sat with her feet stretched out at the far side of the packing-case. The cracked white cups took pink lights as the sun, already descending, slanted across the cherry; the tree filled the air with its heavy scent-lessness.

Max brought out his cigarette case, opening it thought-fully. 'But how should it waste time to be eighteen? Any year of one's life has got to be lived. Five years hence, you may dislike what you are now.'

'I may. But not so much.'

'You were more serious then – will you smoke?'

'After tea, thank you – to be serious is absurd; it is useless: what can one do?'

'So you gave that up, since eighteen?'

'I had no sense of humour then.'

'Oh, good God!' said Max sharply.

'Why?'

'What you say is deadly. Must everything be funny?'

'One's life is.'

'No wonder you get on nicely.'

Karen, with an uninnocent sigh, bowed over her knees and pressed the back of a hand to her forehead, staying like this. To burlesque despair at herself was the only way she had to make his reproof absurd. The movement was so quiet that it might have been natural; the curled ends of her hair fell over cheeks, which she felt burning unintentionally. Beyond the tray, Max sat smoking, not looking at her.

'When I was eighteen,' she said, 'you were unfair to me because you made me exaggerate. I had to say something when I didn't know where I was. Did you expect me to be like Mme Fisher? To say what one means one has to be her age.'

'To *know* what one means is always something,' he said.

'Well, I know now,' said Karen, hearing a hard note in her own voice. 'If I exaggerated again just now, it was because today is hardly a day, is it? Here we are in a place that's hardly a place at all, in a house belonging to somebody dead. I'd never been to Twickenham till today, and I suppose I may never come again. If I did come, I might never find this house. I don't know the address; I suppose it has one.'

'Yes,' said Max. 'You are certainly off your beat.'

'As a rule, you are quite right: I get on nicely.'

Max looked up and smiled at the French window. He said: 'Here comes Naomi.'

6

Naomi stepped through the window, in one hand a brown teapot, in the other a kettle with a trail of steam. Having been busy up to the last moment, she still wore a white overall over her dress and a white handkerchief round her head like a coif.

'How cool you look there,' she said, coming happily down the lawn.

'Come and sit down, Naomi.'

'I think I have done now – how sweet the tree smells,' she added, looking up.

'Not the flowers,' said Max. 'Simply, the leaves smell gummy.'

Perhaps it was his exactness that had such a calming effect and made her sit back quietly on her heels. He never went rocketing off – so she would check in mid-air and come quietly down again. His precision about any fact was passionate: she would not have loved him for years if he had been cold. Her second look at the tree was meek and tutored, as though she expected to see its gumminess drawn out by the sun. Her hands, reddish from being scrubbed in cold water, lay peacefully on her white overall. Being Martha became her now. She had always been hard-working, mechanical with her fingers, but in Paris she raced through work in a grey abstraction, exiled from half she did. At Twickenham her hands became herself; putting away her aunt's home she began building her own. She touched no object without sympathy; Max's touch had given all others nature. She threw herself into the day's business for him.

For Karen, she was the after-dark Naomi who used to slip into your room after lights were out to put mended stockings back in your drawer. She was not supposed, of course, to mend Karen's things. Thinking you were asleep she would creep softly past the bed; as she pulled the drawer open you heard her hold her breath. Light coming in from the landing fell on her face – unconscious, intent, calm. But a word brought her to sit on your bed and talk – in a whisper, because of the other girl. She was Naomi then, not Miss Fisher.

This afternoon, the shadow under the tree lay on her as soothingly as the dark. Her brown eyes, whose sockets looked less hollow, turned contentedly from Karen to Max. Touching the packing-case to make sure it was steady, she said: 'Have I kept you waiting long?'

'I meant to have helped more in the house,' said Karen. 'I went in, but everything seemed to be packed up.'

'You know what Naomi's like,' said Max. 'There is only one way she can bear to have things done; while you do them some other way she looks on like a wounded bird.' He watched Naomi's stiff-overalled figure, like a white wood-carving, kneel down beside the tray. She touched the handkerchief bound round her forehead, knelt upright and started pouring out tea as if this were home. Perhaps it was their first home. As lovers, Max and she were a couple of refugees, glad to find themselves anywhere. He had been right in saying they were not rooted. Now they had inter-locked, like two twigs on a current that, apart, would have gone on twisting perplexedly. They both had the hybrid's undefendable shyness that no one else can gauge. She had waited years for him to discover her as a refuge; his smile as she came through the window was her reward.

For Karen, the silence of that first minute with Max under the cherry had been spoilt since: they had both spoken and not said what they meant. Still, she could not wish herself back in London, or any place but here. 'All the same, I came here to help,' she said.

'I have only to lock up now – what have you talked about?' Naomi said eagerly.

Max wrinkled his forehead. 'Sense of humour,' said Karen.

'She thinks so oddly,' said Max. 'Naturally, so much

belongs to the English, they can afford to be moderate. But nowadays the world is in bad taste; it is no longer "history in the making", or keeps rules or falls in with nice ideas. Things will soon be much more than embarrassing; I doubt if one will be able to save one's face. Humour ... no longer possible. Karen will have to find herself something else.'

Karen putting down her cup on the grass, said: 'Irony seems less childish, I daresay.'

Max glanced across the tray to see if she were angry. She sat pressing her hand with Ray's ring into the grass, feeling the helpless colour come up her face. He was behaving like those rather cruel young uncles who mock one's youth.

'Possibly, less childish,' he said. 'Humour is being satisfied you are right, irony, being satisfied that they should think you wrong. Humorous people know there is nothing they need dread. English good-natured jokes seem to me terrible; they are full of jokes about mortification – the dentist, social ambition, love.'

Naomi, looking ever so slightly anxious, said: 'Oh, you have nothing to eat yet. You did not unpack the buns!' She tipped the bagful of buns she had bought at a pastrycook's, on their way here, on to a plate. 'I think that humour is English courage,' she said.

'Ostrich courage,' said Max.

'Please,' said Naomi, 'do not be anti-English – Karen, please eat a bun.'

Max ate two mouthfuls of the bun, then said: 'Humour is like a silly vow of virginity.'

'Max was saying,' said Karen, 'how well I get on these days.'

'You should be glad,' said Max, 'I wish I got on as well.'

She saw him glance at the ring on her hand on the grass without comment in his dark eyes – as though her hand were exposed in a museum glass case or the ring itself had been dug up out of a tomb: something that mattered once. 'But chaff is English, Max: you are being jolly,' she said.

'Max thinks too much of ambition,' Naomi said, like a loving young governess.

'So does Karen; she is ambitious to live.'

'What old friends we are,' said Naomi, 'telling each other truths.' She refilled the teapot happily.

Karen smiled across at Naomi briefly, then dropped her eyes, refusing to look at Max. She sat with her knees crossed, digging the heel of one shoe into the grass. With three or more people, there is something bold in the air: direct things get said which would frighten two people alone and conscious of each inch of their nearness to one another. To be three is to be in public, you feel safe; the person so close before becomes a face at the other side of a tray. Are you less yourself than you were? You will never know.

'But take care, Max, or Karen will never visit us.'

'I am sorry,' said Max. 'I am not accustomed to holidays. Satan finds mischief for me, I daresay. Will you have more tea, Karen?' He reached round and took her cup.

Naomi filled his cup too, and put it down by him. Still propped on the grass on one elbow, he irresponsibly tore a handful of grass, and, smiling, tossed the blades on his hand, to show how much he was enjoying his holiday. Then he kept his hand still and stared at the grass; his thoughts had gone somewhere else. They were not thoughts but thought, hardening his eyebrows into a metal line. A man with two women, devotedly watched by one, unwillingly watched by the other, often looks foolish: whatever he does is too weighty. His thought withdraws and there is an attentive hush – but all the same, they are making a child of him. 'Look how hard he can think.' It said much for Max that Naomi's adoration did not make him more foolish. But his silence, cutting across the idle warm afternoon, had the proper ring: forbidding and unemotional. However fondly she spoke, it was true: he was ambitious. Wind fanning across the gardens through the poplars, knocking off pink petals, the absurd tray, the smell of torn grass made the afternoon a pleasure he did not share any more. Had the holiday lasted a day too long?

A doorbell sounded inside the empty house. 'That must be the carrier come for Helen's books.'

'Aren't you selling all the books?'

'No, Helen wants to keep some. They are going across to Highgate.'

Max said quickly: 'Shall I go to the door?'

'No, I must go,' said Naomi. She got up and went in.

Max threw away the handful of torn grass. He gave Karen a cigarette and, pushing the tray away from between them, lit it for her. Shielding the match for himself, he said: 'She thinks you are hurt.'

'She always thinks things will hurt people she likes.'

'What a good thing,' said Max, 'you are not as touchy as I am.'

Karen had nothing to say. She wondered how much of the Saturday morning talk Naomi had repeated: Naomi's own good faith was so entire that it would never occur to her not to repeat anything . . . Outside the edge of shadow, the lawn blazed in sunshine up to the French window: Naomi's voice and the carrier's echoed indoors and Karen sat trying to fix her mind on them, trying to think what books Helen Bond would be likely to choose to keep. Naomi was coming home with Karen this evening, to spend her last night in London at Chester Terrace, but Max had a business dinner tonight, so, when the rattling journey back to London was over, that would be all. Looking down the garden, she saw ink-dark lines round everything, even between the roof and the blue sky: for a moment the garden looked as unbearably vivid as a garden the moment before you faint. Thinking: Gone tomorrow, she felt her own hands clasped round her knees loosely: surely if this were frightful they would be clasped tight? A coin of light from the trees slid off Max's foot. She said: 'All the same, I don't like being attacked, Max.' Watching the coin of light, he said nothing, which had been what she had dreaded.

'I will let Miss Bond know,' said Naomi, now in the hall.

Mrs Michaelis, who had met Max once, yesterday afternoon, thought him an excellent person for Naomi to marry, though that she should be marrying still seemed odd. He belonged to an order of people she felt about most kindly, who, agreeably present when they are present, melt into air when the servant has shown them out. Knowing this is to be, you part excellent friends. Being a very exact and sincere woman, she knew where a thing should stop. She did not make copy of people by drawing them out; no one had cause to regret the success they had had with her, or feel small or betrayed later. She said Max's personality was striking – of course, it might seem more striking to her than it was, as she met so few people like that. However, it had struck her. She liked his intellect; you could feel his ability. Though she found him nice rather than exactly attractive, no doubt many people would find him attractive too. Though it was nice for the Fishers that he was marrying Naomi, he could, she thought, have done better if he had wished. But this unambitious marriage showed a good heart.

'Oh, he knows what he is doing,' said Mrs Michaelis. 'Though he has such good manners, I don't think he is as confident as he seems. He looks sensitive, and might easily be touchy. I don't think he would be happy for long married to a woman who made him feel in any way not right. The question of background: curious, isn't it? For instance: here today at tea he was charming; not suspicious or "sticky", not tiresomely at ease. But then, he was alone with us: if we had had him here with so many other people no nicer than he is, and not nearly so clever, he might have been different, on the defensive at once. Yes, it is curious: social things matter so little, yet somehow one cannot be with people who do not "mix" when they have to. But Naomi is odd – and from one's own point of view sometimes a little trying – in exactly the way that would make him feel most at ease. Yes, a wrong marriage, I think, would be fatal for him; he is a man who would quickly outlaw himself. And there is always that touch – Jewish perhaps – of womanishness about him that a woman would have to ignore and yet deal with the whole time. He would see through a strategic woman at once; only a simple good woman would do for him. And Naomi is so good – perhaps that's what's trying about her. *Her* trouble has always been all that bottled-up feeling: he will give that an outlet, and at the same time quiet her down. At tea today I thought she seemed so much calmer. It will be good for her getting away from Mme Fisher, who I have no doubt is rather a wretch.'

'But they are going to live with her.'

'I don't suppose that will last long,' said Mrs Michaelis tranquilly. 'Either he will put down his foot, or Mme Fisher will die – Well, Karen, about tonight . . .'

So Mrs Michaelis dismissed Max; he melted into thin air while still on his way to the bus. Should he ever come up again – which was unlikely, for no one they knew in Paris had heard of him – she would have him at her fingers' ends, to discuss once more with understanding and tact.

As Karen here sat on the lawn beside Max, looking at her clasped hands, what her mother had said after tea yesterday raced through her mind. What Max had said about touchiness set it going. How right Mother had been, how right she was always. All the same, her well-lit explanations of people were like photographs taken when the camera could not lie; they stunned your imagination by *being* exact. Would those unmysterious views in a railway carriage make you visit a place, even in dreams? You could not fall in love with the subject of an Edwardian camera-portrait, with polished shoulders, coiffure and curved throat. The lake showing every ripple, the wood showing every leaf, or the stately neck with pearls are too deadeningly clear. It is more than colour they lack. Without their indistinctness things do not exist; you cannot desire them.

Blurs and important wrong shapes, ridgy lights, crater darkness making a face unhuman as a map of the moon, Mrs Michaelis, like the camera of her day, denied. She saw what she knew was there. Like the classic camera, she was blind to those accidents that make a face that face, a scene that scene, and float the object, alive, in your desire and ignorance. Nowadays, a photograph is no more than an effort to apprehend. So Mrs Michaelis did not like modern photography, which she found exaggerated and woolly. Some recent studies of Karen by one of her friends had been regretfully put away in a drawer. She, not unfairly, found that an over-great sense of mystery too often leads to artiness. Nothing annoyed her more than to be told that the personality is mysterious; it made her think of Maeterlinck, people in green dresses winding through a blue wood. It is inexcusable not to be clear, she said. She preferred to think of people in terms of character.

Karen enjoyed her mother's anti-romanticism. God forbid indeed, that one should have cloudy ideas, or impart to objects one's own shifting moodiness. But the exercise of any sense, sight most, starts up emotion. You cannot debunk everything. Karen's mother was so far right: no objection is mysterious. The mystery is your eye.

What Mrs Michaelis said about Max and his reasons for wanting to marry Naomi would be, no doubt, true – if you pressed him flat like a flower in a book. But he had a thick-ness you had to recognize, and could not be pressed flat without losing form. Looking up to stare at the French window, Karen felt him nearer, as though he had moved – but he had not, he sat still. She glanced round: he was split-ting a blade of grass with his thumb nails; he drew a breath to speak, and then did not. Why split a blade of grass, and not speak? Everything that she knew of him disappeared at a point, like a road running into a dark tunnel.

He took another breath, and looked at the sky. 'An angel must be flying over,' he said.

Infected by his uneasy lightness she said: 'I didn't know you had been in England so much.'

'Long enough to learn what you say when no one speaks. I suppose the French, from talking so much more, more easily let a silence pass. Yes, I stayed here for three years once, working with one of my uncles. I never lived here, naturally.'

'Why, naturally?'

'Why, if I had lived here I should still be someone who speaks English quite remarkably well. It was my father's language, but never mine: he died when I was so young. What I say is correct, but never spontaneous, is it? It is too tight or too loose; it never fits what I mean.'

'How can I tell? It depends what you do mean.'

'Possibly it is an advantage to me,' he said.

'Shall we bring the tray in?' Karen said suddenly.

Leaning over the tray, Max stacked up the odd cups and saucers, and tipped the buns back into their paper bag. Karen saw his face with a tense look, like the face of someone expecting the first arrow, against the fringe of lupins. She felt worlds away from where they sat. He went on doggedly, determined to finish: 'What I say would often be right if I meant something else.'

'We had better give the buns to some child, hadn't we?'

'Where shall we find some child?'

'Oh, on the way home.'

Indoors, Karen heard Naomi shutting the hall door. The carrier must have taken the case of books. No doubt they were sets of classics, better bound than the classics Helen Bond had already. Naomi would be pushing the handkerchief back from her forehead, looking round to see what to do next. There was nothing left to do but lock up the house; a church clock struck six somewhere behind the gardens; they ought to start back soon. The poplars, the crimson-showering cherry, the lawn, the window belonged to the past already. An indoor chill, like in some room where nothing ever goes on, began to settle on Karen.

'We'll bring the tray in when we go.'

But they both sat back, her hand lying near his. Max put his hand on Karen's, pressing it into the grass. Their unexploring, consenting touch lasted; they did not look at each other or at their hands. When their hands had drawn slowly apart, they both watched the flattened grass beginning to spring up again, blade by blade.

Naomi came out busily through the window, taking off her overall, flapping the white sleeves. 'Alas,' she said, 'this time tomorrow we shall be gone, Karen!'

Next morning they left for Paris.

Naomi liked to be seen off, so Karen drove with her in the taxi to Victoria, where Max in a dark overcoat waited beside the barrier. Raising his hat with no change of expression, he watched them come through the crowd. Rock-still among all the pushing and agitation, he looked like a nervous Frenchman determined to travel well. The tip of a long magnetic wave from the Continent touches Victoria platform whenever a boat train starts: Max already belonged among the returning foreigners, though Naomi, keeping her hand on Karen's arm sadly, seemed for those minutes more to belong where she stood.

On the platform before their journey, to speak of a next meeting would have been out of place: even Naomi did not attempt to comfort herself with this. Goodbyes breed a sort of distaste for whoever you say goodbye to; this hurts, you feel, this must not happen again. Any other meeting will only lead back to this. If today goodbye is not final, some day it will be; doorsteps, docks and platforms make you clairvoyant ... Naomi had set store by Karen's coming so far: would she expect her to stay and see the train out?

Once they had found their places and their luggage was on the rack, Karen turned round quickly to embrace Naomi standing in the compartment door. The kiss stopped any protest; in its womanish closeness Karen breathed eau-de-Cologne and camphory fur, and felt Naomi's gloved hand, her wrist with buttons, pressing between her shoulders in an imploring way.

Max, outside, looked along the dark corridor with the expression men wear while women say goodbye. He turned to shake hands, then Karen turned to go. But her way was blocked: from each end of the narrow corridor late-comers just in time, with porters hauling their baggage, came jostling in on them. Stout men agitating from carriage to carriage bore down on Karen and Max, who, standing with their shoulders against the window, found themselves jammed face to face. There was no escape. She stared at his right shoulder. This undid their touch on the lawn yesterday; they faced each other unwillingly, defiant, dead. Then their eyes met; they looked steadily into each other's pupils. All your youth, you are dreading more than can happen. But this was more than she had dreaded in Paris, when she used to wait trembling outside the salon door.

A porter passed, with baggage pitching on his shoulder; Max put up his hand to shield Karen's head. The people had found places; the corridor was now empty. The train stood as though built on to the platform, but Karen walking away down it, steadied herself against the frames of the windows as though the train was rocking at top speed. The platform under the glass roof was quiet; everybody for Paris was now aboard; with used-up smiles their friends waited to see them go. It was five to eleven; today was the first of May. The weighing hall with its pulled-up trolleys was aimless, as though the train had started, as though the last train of all to Paris had gone. This part of the station is quiet between departures, like a country halt, with nobody about. Outside the entrance, under the smoky glass porch, the taxis had all gone. Karen walked into Wilton Road, looking doubtfully at the buses, which like big particles in shaken water swam past. She felt she had left London. Crossing the street, she stood by a shop window, frowning, pressing her thumb to the clasp of her handbag, like a spoilt pretty girl with some contretemps in her day.

She was at home for lunch. Mrs Michaelis said: 'Well, did they get off all right?' She added, she was sorry that they had gone, but after all they did not live here; it would not do if they did. Glancing through the dining-room window at the trees, she smiled and said: 'May today. How nice, Karen, that everything's beginning.' By 'everything' she meant the London season, which sends ripples up every little channel, even making unworldly people smile. That afternoon she and her daughter went to a young man's private view. A picture of a flower-pot on a balcony made Karen decide to go on painting: next morning she returned to the studio.

That end of April had been in itself a summer: no more came after it for some time. The Twickenham cherry must have moulted its petals before another day came when you could sit on the grass. It grew colder; the season had lost its way. May is seldom quite up to time; this year there was a grey chilly pause before her undisappointing brightness settled down over London. Then, tulips blazed in the parks, geraniums hung on balconies, gay awnings unrolled, warm air blew through your thin dress as you walked. Frowsty streets where little dressmakers live began to be full of light and echoes of barrel-organs playing the new tunes. Pattering spring showers brought the trees right out; the last leaves cast their sheaths; thundery light, toppling ink-purple clouds across the ends of streets made the green burn. The suburbs tossed with lilacs and red may. Between thunder and sun, the Nash terraces round the Regent's Park, the trees in their May haze, took on their most theatrical air – but indoors at Chester Terrace, Michaelis family life continued as ever: intelligent, kind, calm. Mrs Michaelis joined two more un-cranky committees. Mr Michaelis left home for his office at half-past nine every morning, enjoying his walk through the park to the Underground. From ten o'clock on, the telephone rang cheerfully; invitations came rattling into the letter-box. They went to the Opera. The cook cooked even better. Two or three really good new books appeared. Everybody they wanted to see was in town.

No news from Rushbrook: perhaps the thing had been put off. Perhaps such things did not happen. News from Paris was that Naomi was safe home; the American girls were there.

Karen thought: the great thing now is to marry Ray. Every day, like an exercise, she shut her eyes so point-blank that Max was gone till next day, when she shut her eyes again. She could not see Ray: his face was gone as though a spot of acid had dropped on her memory. But she thought of their marriage constantly and with hope. This would be the last May of her undecided girlhood; this time next year she would be Karen Forrestier, living in a house she had not seen yet; even, possibly, going to have a child. She saw herself familiar with their new hall door, staircase and firesides, picturing times of day in the future house, making tomorrow fatten thin today. If what was to be expected came of Ray's time with Sir H., Ray's future would be assured; they would live in London. But it won't be the same she thought, even London will change. I shall be different. She found she had come to hope everything of change.

Her expectation that other Mays would be different gave this May, like a tree in front of a cloud, a fragility, or made it the past now. In her parents' world, change looked like catastrophe, a thing to put a good face on: change meant nothing but loss. To alter was to decline. 'Poor So-and-so is so changed.' You lived to govern the future, bending events your way. If change did break in, you bowed and accepted it. In such a world, except for that year in Paris, her mind had always been very clear, with few dreads, though she saw enough to be thankful to be so safe. The in-tuneness of her marriage with all this had pleased Karen nearly as much as her mother. She had not been born Karen Michaelis for nothing; it had been on the daylit side of marriage that she liked to dwell; she had expected, even, to show her friends that there is nothing in love to get so angry about. But since the day she had walked away from Victoria, her thoughts had bent strongly to whatever in marriage stays unmapped and dark, with a kind of willing alarm. She had now to look for Max in Ray.

There was her home, their new house, to assemble. If you want nice things, you cannot begin to look about too early. Tables and chairs that have their period, four legs and their price; they are more than visionary. And for a bed you generally go to Heal's. Mrs Michaelis and Karen often stopped before an antique shop window with the same pleased thought. But not always – an Empire sofa in Wigmore Street one morning suddenly sent the blood to Karen's head. Its unexaggerated sea-green silk curves made her want to exclaim: 'Stop: we won't want that! I can't take it to Paris, to

Naomi's young man!' Which would be like whipping a pistol out of her kid bag and firing at the sofa through the glass . . . If that half-French couple had any place, it was certainly not here. (She liked them as visitors – what Max had said dug in crookedly, like a bent pin.) But since they had gone, since the afternoon of the cherry tree there had been no Today. She enjoyed the sweet light streets, flattering talks, the Opera, in terms of regret, by thinking: Soon I shall be gone. She must rely on marriage to carry her somewhere else. Till it did, she stayed bound to a gone moment, like a stopped clock with hands silently pointing an hour it cannot be.

Ray's married sister Angela was in London this month, and often at Chester Terrace. 'We are all far too alike,' Angela said. 'But after all, there *is* only one way to be nice. Nothing unlike oneself in people really is not a pity. It's better to inbreed than marry outside one's class. Even in talk, I think. Do let us be particular while we can.'

Karen said coldly: 'I shall grow more like you, then?'

'Nonsense; you're so individual.'

'It costs money,' said Angela. 'But that's fair, I suppose.' She had two little girls; she went on: 'No doubt I shall live to see the poor children nationalized, or married in a laboratory. But while we *have* names, not numbers, I think it's nice to be like what one's like, don't you, even if everyone else is?'

To disagree was to be foolish.

'You're not wobbling about Ray?' Angela added.

'No. Why should I be?'

'I thought you looked rather cosmic – it's wretched that your engagement has to be so long.'

The Wednesday after that, a letter came for Mrs Michaelis from Paris, from Mme Fisher. The envelope with the vigorous violet writing sat all that afternoon on the hall chest, waiting for Mrs Michaelis to come in, and Karen found herself always passing it. This must be news. She could not think Mme Fisher had other reasons to write. Had those two, with no more warning, married? No date for this had been spoken of when they left. When Mrs Michaelis did at last come in she took the letter, and others, up with her to the drawing-room. But here she was kept busy pouring out tea for visitors, with her unopened letters tucked under the tray. When the people had gone she glanced through them again and said: 'Oh, look, here's a letter from Mrs Fisher!'

'What does she say?'

'I haven't opened it yet.'

'No, I know. I mean – won't you?'

But London posts do not let you catch up with letters; at this point Braithwaite brought in the six o'clock post on a salver.

'Dublin . . .' said Mrs Michaelis, looking this new lot over.

'Dublin – who?'

'It looks like Uncle Bill.'

Karen's heart stopped. Indulgently, Mrs Michaelis opened Colonel Bent's letter. She paused, put it down, and stared at the rim of the tray; then said after a moment: 'Karen . . . Aunt Violet's *dead.*' Karen, who had got up, came across to stand dumbly beside her mother. They had not met like this before; no one had ever died; her brother Robin had come safely through the war. Aunt Violet was four years older than Karen's mother; she was her only sister but they had never been intimate because of Aunt Violet's being so shy – she had been perhaps less shy with her husbands because men do not expect to know you so well . . . Mrs Michaelis put out a hand towards Karen – not wanting to touch, to show she was glad she was there. There was nothing whatever to say. Mrs Michaelis had not wept for years, and never in the drawing-room; she could not begin now. In a dream she picked up Uncle Bill's letter and went on reading. 'He says they went up to Dublin at the end of last week, then she had the operation on Monday. She would not let him write first, she said she would write herself. Then, I suppose, couldn't bring herself to. He says he thinks she dreaded what we would say. But of course, he should have written; we ought to have known. Poor Uncle Bill . . . Did she say *nothing* about it when you were over there, Karen?'

'No. She said nothing.'

'Why – why did she always live so far away?'

Mrs Michaelis's hand now closed, trembling, on Karen's. 'This is not the worst that will happen, Karen,' she said. They both saw the crack across the crust of life. Mrs Michaelis went over to the window, as though someone, not herself, needed air and had to be taken there. The sea of trees in the Park did not look too smiling: after all, they had not known her. A death can only touch what the life touched. Karen saw the dug-up daisies on the lawn at Rushbrook, while Uncle Bill spoke: the death had been then. She saw the strong grass at Twickenham springing up after her and Max's hands. Watching her mother facing the outdoor air like a self-commanding figurehead, Karen thought: Aunt Violet was wilder, she would not stay with us. Heaven may be peopled with such wild mild figures ... Mrs Michaelis turned to look round the drawing-room, gold with evening sunshine across trees. 'It is the shock,' she said scrupulously, half smiling. 'I don't feel anything else yet.' She picked up her gloves, which were on the back of the sofa; she was still wearing her hat. 'I'm going up,' she said. 'Don't let them disturb me. When Father comes in, tell him, and tell him I don't think I'll see him just yet.' She looked at the tea-table. 'And better open those other letters, Karen, in case there should be anything – '

'And put off the people for dinner?'

From the door, Mrs Michaelis looked back in a fixed way. 'Yes,' she said absently, 'yes.'

When Karen had telephoned – it was in the study – she went back to the drawing-room, where Braithwaite was clearing tea away with a concerned face – if she did not know, she knew there was *something* to know. Karen, picking up the letters, stood with her back to the parlour-maid, nervously saying nothing. She thought: Servants are terrible: why should they share one's house? ... In the sun, the curtains were flame-pink; prismatic crystal candlesticks shot rays out; the flooded empty white room looked like a stage.

She died before this, thought Karen. She would want me, though, to be very sorry for him. She saw Uncle Bill looking up and down the Dublin streets not knowing where to go now, with no one with him to smile and make his face uncrinkle. Braithwaite had shut the door but Karen opened it, to be able to hear her father come in. Waiting like this to hear his latch-key made her too nervous to touch Mme Fisher's letter; she opened the others and put them under a paperweight. How many people wanted to see her mother – did she make them feel safe? ... Her father was late; what could be keeping him? Mother was right in saying worse could happen: once a board gives, the raft begins breaking up. Were not awaited people killed in the streets every day? He was a careless confident vague man. She thought: If Father were killed I could not marry for some time, then began to weep and walk about, repeating 'Max, Max, Max!' This was a moment to meet: life stood at its height in this room and she wanted him to come in.

She heard the latch-key and, going half-way downstairs to meet her father, told him the news. His shocked empty eyes met hers; it shocked Karen to think her life sprang from an impulse of his. 'But don't you think I ought to go to your mother?'

'She said not, Father.'

'But don't you think I ought to go, all the same?'

'If you want to very much.'

'Poor Violet,' said Mr Michaelis. 'Poor Violet. She was a lovely girl.' Then he saw the tear-marks on Karen's face. 'It's too bad,' he said, touching her cheek gently. 'It's too bad; you were with her. You mustn't cry . . . you mustn't cry, little one.' He went heavily upstairs past her, glanced at the flight above but went into his study, shutting the door, still doubtful.

Karen opened Mme Fisher's letter, which had thin purple lining inside the envelope. She *had* had a reason to write; there had been a misunderstanding. A Lady Belfrey, who had written during the winter, then, by doing no more, left matters in mid air, had just written again, apparently taking for granted that Mme Fisher would have a vacancy for her niece. There was no vacancy for Lady Belfrey's niece. Since last month, when Naomi had decided upon this marriage, there had ceased to be question of vacancies for any more girls. The last two girls, Americans (and these two, even, had been received under protest), would be remaining until the end of June. After that no more. Mme Fisher regretted this misunderstanding with Lady Belfrey infinitely, the more because she understood Lady Belfrey to be Mrs Michaelis's close friend. But having heard no more from Lady Belfrey last winter, she had had the impression the matter was to be dropped. She would gladly have stretched a point and taken Lady Belfrey's niece later in the summer, but this was impossible, Naomi's marriage to Max being fixed (so they told her) for early July.

'After which,' wrote Mme Fisher, 'I must expect Naomi to be too fully occupied with her husband's happiness to give the assistance I need, as I grow older, in the supervision, however slight, of young girls. *La jeune ménage* will, moreover, take up space in my little house, and there is the possibility of children to be considered. At my age, one must learn to recede gracefully.'

Mme Fisher had, naturally, written to Lady Belfrey, but dared hardly hope that any explanation of hers would make the mistake less annoying. She was, therefore, writing to Mrs Michaelis to express her regret and explain the position more fully. Such high value did she set on the happiness of her connection with Mrs Michaelis that to disoblige any friend of the family was odious to her. (In short, Mme Fisher suggested that Mrs Michaelis should smooth down Lady Belfrey.) Lady Belfrey was a strikingly stupid woman; there was no question whose the mistake had been. Why, then, should Mme Fisher care? She had said 'no' to a number of stupid women when to take in girls had been the only living she had: now she needed no more girls. What makes her write? Is she writing to hurt me?

She wrote in a later paragraph:

'Naomi speaks gratefully of the kindness with which in London, you received her and her fiancé. She believes the young man pleased you. He has the ability of his race, though some people do not find him sympathetic. His decision to marry Naomi was a surprise to me, as I believed he had other prospects in view. I suppose it can seldom be with complete confidence that one entrusts one's daughter's happiness to another's hands. You, *chère madame*, are in the matter of Karen's marriage most happily placed. I have, perhaps, the too great suspiciousness of a woman who has stood long alone. Till this legacy, upon which we could never depend, Naomi had no *dot*; in my country, where, as you know, such considerations rank high, marriage was not, till now, to be hoped for for her. My son-in-law to be is not a rich man, and though this increase of my daughter's income would not, of course, have influenced him unduly, it cannot, if they are to marry, be immaterial to him. This momentous change in her prospects has elated my daughter: she has a full heart and I hope that there may be no deception in store for her. July 5th, at the *Mairie*, has been fixed for the marriage; the honeymoon will be spent in the Auvergne.

'Tell Karen that she is in my mind often: I feel she will not disappoint the expectations I formed. I shall be sending her, a little nearer her marriage, a small comb set with pearls which should, I think, be her type. The pearls are at present being re-set. (It is an heirloom on one side of my family, from, I think, a maternal great-grandmother.) Naomi speaks with pleasure of Karen's good health and spirits, Max of her distinguished beauty. For myself, I shall wish for her every happiness.

'Receive, *chère madame*, my most . . . etc. etc.'

Somewhere in all that is what made her write, thought Karen. 'Such considerations' – how the French despise us! Did Max really say that? How I used to wonder what they said in the salon. How *she* used to smile when she found me in the hall! Did *she* send Max to England? What did she hope would happen? How like her, writing to Mother. What is she planning now? . . . July 5th: I shall not be married by then.

Braithwaite slipped in to put down the evening paper, folded like a lily for a coffin. She would have heard by now;

news travels downstairs through the bones of a house. Mr Michaelis opened the study door; he and Karen both heard Mrs Michaelis pacing over their heads. In the course of the next hour it was decided that he was to catch tonight's Irish mail, to support Uncle Bill on his journey with the coffin tomorrow. If Uncle Bill had known how to ask for support he should have telegraphed, but they forgave this. Aunt Violet was to be buried at Montebello. Proper clothes were packed and Mr Michaelis seen off, homesick, dumb; he was to dine on the train.

Two days later Mrs Michaelis, seated at her desk in a black dress with pretty touches of white, turned up Mme Fisher's letter, which had got into the file of letters of sympathy. She read it through with a frown. 'Edith Belfrey has made another muddle,' she said. She went on: 'Mme Fisher seems to suggest that that young man is marrying Naomi for her money. How odd the French are!'

'She is terribly unfair.'

'Oh, I've no doubt he is – or that must come in to it. But it's odd of her to tell *me* so.' Mrs Michaelis, putting the letter aside, dipped her pen in ink. 'I don't think one need answer,' she said. 'I'll speak to Edith Belfrey.' She began to reply to another letter of sympathy. Her eyes had blue circles round them, her note paper had come out in a thin black line. She wrote a little, then looked up and said to Karen: 'How unreal it seems!'

8

Before the end of May it was summer; cool in the house but glaring hot in the streets. Mrs Michaelis went on being puzzled rather than sad; she was as right as ever in all that she said and did, but her eyes did not meet yours with the old confidence. Everyone blamed Uncle Bill for letting Aunt Violet's death come as such a shock; Karen did not even ask herself why *she* had said nothing. Karen went to the studio almost every day, but saw nothing but rings of air round the

131

model; she worked away flaggingly, with a dead brush. What she had thought she saw in the flower-pot on the balcony, that had sent her back to painting, was gone now. Her dull work was done for pity (her own pity) like a pavement artist's on a cold day.

One hot night, when her parents were out together, she went into the study to look for soda-water on the tray Braithwaite left ready for Mr Michaelis. With her thumb on the siphon she stopped and looked at the telephone: the window was open behind the curtains and hot night air came in. The telephone held her eye; she saw it going to speak. The bell rang: Karen put down her glass. Was she Paddington 0500? Then hold on for Paris. Karen went to shut the window to keep out London, the door to keep out home. This sealed her up in silence with the telephone and one lamp cut out from darkness under its green shade. When she picked the receiver up they were on the line.

'... Miss Michaelis, please?'

'Speaking ... Hullo, Max.'

'Hullo, Karen. Where are you?'

'Here.'

'In which room?'

'The study. They are out. Where are you?'

'Rue Sylvestre Bonnard. Naomi is at the theatre with the Americans. Her mother has gone to bed.'

'Ill?'

He said: 'She has gone to bed,' in the same tone.

They waited; the line seemed to go dead. 'Max?'

'I was overwrought, I wanted to hear your voice.'

'It's four weeks since –'

'Yes. Will you come to Boulogne?'

'When?'

'Next Sunday. Or shall I come to Folkestone?'

'No, not Folkestone; I've been there. I mean ... Boulogne.'

'The boats will give you some hours. Sunday, then.'

'Yes. Will you meet the morning boat?'

'Yes.'

The line died again. 'Max?'
'Yes?'
'Is that all?'
'Yes.'
'Good night.'
'Good night.'

Karen had hung up; they had had less than three minutes. She looked for a cigarette in her father's box and lit it unsteadily. The clock said half-past eleven; her father and mother, who had been at a concert, must be walking home. He liked to do this on fine nights, so she would pick up her skirts and walk beside him with gallant even steps. Karen opened the window and looked across at the lights in the mews; this was above the morning-room where she had talked to Naomi. Electric silence filled the gardens and courts. Four weeks, she thought. How did I bear four weeks?

On Saturday night, she told them she would be spending tomorrow in the country, starting early, getting back rather late. Her mother said 'Yes?' with the uninquisitive smile that had kept Karen from ever lying before. Never to lie is to have no lock to your door, you are never wholly alone. Her mother's agreeing smile made the world small; there was nowhere left to go to. Her family's powerful confidence was a searchlight that dipped into every valley, not letting you out of view. Since the night Max rang up, all faculty for tenderness in Karen had stopped – perhaps it had stopped before that; it might even lie in Aunt Violet's grave. All she felt, that Saturday, was: She *ought* to ask; I have an unnatural home . . . On Sunday she crept downstairs in a thin dress, with a coat over her arm, to catch the early boat train. Summer mist lay over the lake in the park; what she did had no more colour than going to school.

She sat in the train in her thin dress; everyone else had luggage. The train swayed on the rails, the summer country swayed past: knolls, trees in their early morning blue bloom. Sooty siding walls, a dead bird on a wire, moon-daisies in a cutting: the known county of Kent. Expectation made her

133

hollow. The sea appeared. On board, the vibration of the ship starting half woke her nerves. Looking back at England, she asked herself: Or, is this courage? and walked the deck still not knowing. On this unclear fine morning France could not be seen.

The hills and dunes of Boulogne were chalked green and white against the paper-blue sky: France looked one long low hill. Sea-clearness struck the houses, from the glittering sea. Dykes, earthworks and idle cranes appeared; two long black-and-white wooden piers ran out to meet the ship. Eager trippers and blasé Sunday travellers crowded up to wait where the gangway would be let down. Karen looked up and saw the cathedral dome, ethereal with distance, at the top of the town: thin chimneys stood along the inland skyline. They steamed in past the Casino, which flew two flags; sunny light rippled over its garden trees, so close and bowery that they looked like a wood. The long line of quay-side hotels and cafés smiled, expectant of the incoming ship. France met her approach coquettish, conscious, gay.

Across the water from the hotels, on the railway quay, a group of people were waiting, shading their eyes as the sun struck the bright white ship: women in cotton frocks with their bare arms up. The ship steadied and drew alongside. Karen, looking down calmly, saw Max. Hat off, sun dazzling his unburnt forehead as his eyes searched the ship as calmly, he looked young. Stuck in his coat, a rose that he must have stopped to buy at some flower-gay street corner. Opposite the rose, the holiday town hung like a painted scene: after all, after all, were they not meeting for pleasure? He hasn't seen me, she thought, and looked away gently at the cranes over his head, the crowded shipping behind. It was twelve noon: sharp and deep Sunday chimes broke from two bel-fries into echoing streets. Max suddenly saw Karen. She smiled, and heard them run the gangway across. They stood looking at each other. When the gangway was clear, she landed, last of all.

They walked down the cobbled quay towards the bridge; lines cross the quay and they waited once to let part of the boat train shunt. Max said: 'We have a fine day.' Karen, stepping on air, did not feel the cobbles. Max had put on his hat with the brim well down because of the sun. Their hands, swinging, touched lightly now and then; their nearness was as natural as the June day. Saying nothing, they crossed the bridge and walked down the quay at the other side, along the line of cafés, then turned into one where he ordered Pernod Fils and she said she would have a vermouth and soda, please. The man brought some dusty ice in a zinc pail, and Max scraped the sawdust off Karen's piece of ice with a spoon out of her saucer. The inside of the café was transparently dark, the marble table cold to Karen's bare elbows. Outside in the glare, she saw from the women walking how rough the cobbles had been. A hot breath from the sea made the orange awning flop.

Max spooned the wedge of clean ice into Karen's drink. 'I suppose we shall say something,' he said seriously.

'Do we want to?'

'No-o,' he said, with his funny rising inflection. They looked at each other's drinks; the Pernod with water added turned solid yellow and sent up an aniseedy smell. Karen looked up first, at Max's turned down eyelids, the cheekbones showing under his unburnt skin. 'Do you live indoors?' she said.

'Yes. I am too busy. And games I never play, which is terrible in France. Do you mean, I shall get fat?'

'No, I should think you were born thin.'

'I did play tennis.'

'Well?'

'Fairly well. But in town it is too expensive. When I was a boy, I played in the south of France.'

'Did you know people there?'

'My mother's relations lived there.'

'Are they Provençals?'

'No; my aunt's husband retired there from Le Mans. He had one of those new villas outside Mentone, and grew carnations for market up in the hills. He is dead now.'

'My mother's sister has just died.'

'Your aunt? So many aunts have lately died. Look at Naomi's.'

'I had been staying with her the month before.'

'Then you must be sorry,' said Max. He looked un-understandingly at her, but his dark startled pupils softened with gentleness. She thought of the Chester Terrace drawing-room, blazing, that deathly evening, with sunshine, into which he had not come. 'I was more frightened,' she said. 'It seemed to crack my home.'

'Did it?' said Max. 'I did not care for my uncle, but I remember very well when he died.'

Karen's empty white gloves lay on the table between them; he turned one over, intently looking at it. Nerves in her finger-tips began burning; she looked away from the glove at the grey feathery veins in the marble table-top. Outside, the idle flopping of the awning filled up the pause.

'I've been painting again,' she said.

'I wondered whether you would.'

'When do you think about me?'

'I never know when I may – Did you paint well?'

'No. I can't see things now.'

'Then is it worth it?'

'No. But the day you left –'

'This is better than what we both do,' he said putting the glass down and looking across at Karen.

'You might not think so the whole time.'

His forehead wrinkled. 'I never know,' he said. ' – Have you been in Boulogne before?'

'Only crossing it, landing here.'

'Shall we walk about?'

'I'm rather hungry,' she said. 'I forgot to ask them for early breakfast, so I only had tea before I started.'

He did not seem to hear; he said: 'Will you take your hat off?'

She took off her hat, and he looked at the way her hair grew round her forehead; his eyes fixed unbelievingly on her forehead as though he had not known she still looked like this.

136

Then he said: 'Then we'll have lunch. I know where we will go.' He paid for the drinks and Karen put her hat on. As they stepped out under the awning he said: 'We can't, I suppose, look at each other the whole time.'

Boulogne is less shallow than it looks from the sea. Inland, streets run criss-cross some way up the bluff behind, under the citadel. At the end of May there are still not many visitors; the townspeople took one in with such possessive alert eyes that Karen thought: They must think we are staying here. But however far into the town you penetrate, beside trams, under arches, you never feel inland or forget that the downhill streets have a line of water ruled across at the end. The silence in *culs-de-sac* is the silence of not hearing the sea. Today, the salt sunshine brought every shape nearer, as though distance had been parched out. Doorways, cobbles, arches and stone steps looked sentient and porous in the glare. Buildings basked like cats in the kind heat, having been gripped by cold mists, having ached in unkind nights, been buffeted in the winter. Hot wind tugged now and then at the flags down on the Casino, stretching the flags, then letting them drop again. Flashing, a window was thrown open uphill. What you saw, you felt. Max's presence, and what he said or did not say, made the flags, the steep streets and the window opening familiar; she saw the same deep reason for everything.

The façade of a theatre blocked the end of the street where the restaurant was. Going into Mony's, they sat down side by side on a brown leather bench, unfolding the pressed napkins. Max said he had liked this place before. Karen knew he meant: So I hope we may like it now. But because inside here was so suddenly dark – and so suddenly chilly, making her cup her bare elbows in her hands – because she missed the table with grey veins and the hot orange of the awning, all she felt was: Before? Before? Who with? He had been a man for years, and Boulogne had been here always. With Naomi, who had sat on her own bed in the dark? She did not picture any exact other woman; it was his whole experience that stood over her, while Max read down his menu

Napoleonically, and she looked at her menu blotty with mauve ink. This is the worst of love, this unmeant mystification – someone smiling and going out without saying where, or a letter arriving, being read in your presence, put away, not explained, or: 'No, alas, I can't tonight,' on the telephone – that, one person having set up without knowing, the other cannot undo without the where? who? why? that brings them both down a peg. Jealousy is no more than feeling alone against smiling enemies ... Then Max saw Karen's fingers comforting her cold elbows. He put his menu down. 'Are you cold, my darling?' he said.

'No,' she said, 'not now.'

So he picked up the menu and said: 'Well, what shall we eat?' She said she was not sure, so he chose the lunch. When the waiter had gone, they both looked at the clock. Already, there was one hour less. She saw her boat going one way, his train the other; looking away she said: 'Is Mme Fisher still ill?'

Max pressed his hair back with the side of one hand. As though a wire had been run through his forehead, his eyebrows twitched together and met. Karen saw she had let in an enemy worse than time. 'She was not ill,' he said. ' – You mean, that night? She was tired and there was nothing to say, so then she went to bed.'

'She used not to go to bed when there was nothing to say.'

'There used not to be nothing to say. But she and I had not been alone for some time, till that night, when she found me bad company.'

'How long have you known her? I never knew.'

'Since I was twenty; I was given a letter to her when I first came to Paris. Twelve years. Till this year, I have not tried to separate what she made me from what I am. From the first, she acted on me like acid on a plate.'

'Corrosive?'

'Yes. No. What her wit ate out is certainly gone. But more happened than that; as she saw me, I became. Her sex is all in her head, but she is not a woman for nothing. In my youth, she made me shoot up like a plant in enclosed air. She was completely agreeable. Our ages were complementary. I had never had the excitement of intimacy. Our brains became like senses, touching and drawing back.'

'Then you acted on her, too?'

'To an extent only. She was ready for me when I was not ready for her. She had waited years for what I had not had time to miss. We met in her house, in all senses. Women I knew were as she made me see them: they were not much. Any loves I enjoyed stayed inside her scope; she knew of them all. She mocked and played upon my sensuality. She always had time to see me; she did not turn upon me however angry she was.'

'Is she still angry?' Karen said suddenly.

Max broke a roll in two and dug the crumbs out with his thumbs. Something inside his head being at white heat, his movements were more than ever deliberating and slow; the irises of his eyes, as he turned to Karen, showed that prune-colour angry dark eyes take on in certain lights. 'She does not say so,' he said.

'I think she is in love with you.'

'I cannot think of her that way,' he said violently.

'She suggests you are marrying Naomi for her money.'

Max, unmoved, said evenly: 'I could not marry Naomi if there were not the money; I have not enough myself to support a wife.'

'What she said made me angry.'

Max smiled. 'You think heroically,' he said. 'You are thinking about my honour. Do you want me to mind?'

'Yes. *I* do.'

'When I cut myself even slightly, I bleed like a pig, profusely. Does that make me nobler?'

'But you do mind. You were overwrought when she left you to go to bed.'

'I have told you why. After twelve years – her silence humiliated me.'

'Was that all?'

'No. When she did speak, she spoke of you.'

'Oh! Why?'

Max's eyes now impassive, rested on Karen's. 'She told me you loved me.'

Karen looked at a vase of roses on a middle table, then round the restaurant, with its embossed brown wallpaper, in which they were shut up with what Mme Fisher said. She watched the waiter bring a half canteloupe packed with ice to their table and slice it precisely, then fill their glasses with Vouvray misting outside. The room was beginning to darken with Sunday people, and Mme Fisher seemed to have come in too.

She said: 'But you knew that.'

'But I had not thought about it. Thoughts I might have had would very likely offend you, and I did not wish to offend you even in thought. In regard to you, I have disliked my own mind. When she spoke I heard what I dared not think.'

'Why? What else did she say?'

'She said: "You should be gratified. What do you mean to do?"'

Karen picked up a spoon and began to eat her canteloupe. After a minute she said: 'What did you say?'

'Nothing,' Max said, carefully fitting together the halves of the hollow roll.

'I see. But you rang up.'

'To hear your voice . . .'

'Yes?'

'And be certain you did exist. My only other proof, since we left London, had been the letter you wrote to Naomi.'

'She showed it you?'

'Yes. She is anxious we should be friends.'

'That is English of her, I suppose,' said Karen, looking back in her mind at those streaked white cliffs. She was silent for some minutes then said: 'What made Mme Fisher say that, do you think?'

'The wish to hear me say what I would hate.'

'What would you have hated?'

'Anything I could say. Her other motive – if you want to hear it – to show I should set my cap higher than Naomi.'

Karen coloured. 'That's hideous,' she said.

'That is why I do not think.'

'Oh. Then what does go on?'

'Only images, and desire.'

They did not look at each other. Karen drank Vouvray, pressing her thumb on the stem of the cold glass.

'Nothing I say sounds pretty to you, Karen. But our position is not pretty, you see. Perhaps you have not thought, either? Perhaps you dread thinking, too . . . I knew you first as someone to leave alone. One of her young girls that I might bow to but not meet. That rule of the house still stands.'

'Yes. But you rang up.'

'Yes.'

'Why?'

'I felt: Why not? . . . Why *not*?'

Karen, moving despairingly, caught an edge of the cloth between her knees and the table, pulling the knives crooked: some wine splashed from his glass. She exclaimed: 'Why must I listen to all this when you never say you love me?'

Max's eyes fell from her eyes to her breast.

He and she sat side by side like two wax people while the waiter stretched across to unwrinkle the tablecloth and straighten the knives. Bowing, he took the canteloupe rinds away and, bringing two grilled trout on a bed of cress, served monsieur and madame, refilled their glasses and spread a napkin over the spilt wine. This worked like a change of scene. How well waiters knew their entrances, Karen thought, squeezing a round of lemon over her trout.

'Not too much lemon,' Max said in a friendly critical way.

Karen wiped it off her fingers. 'No,' she said. 'But you do take this for granted, and how can I?'

'The trouble is, you see, that already we've said too much. How can one discuss an unwilling love?'

'And we didn't meet to talk.'

'Is that true of you, too?'

'Yes,' she said, looking round at him quickly and blindly.

141

'If there had been something to say, anything that we could say, we would have written each other letters, I suppose, or talked more when we telephoned. Because there *was* nothing, we're here. There is nothing to say about wanting to be together.'

'Nothing. Except to wish we were alone.'

'If we were, we might not look at each other.'

'I am horribly ungentle to you, Karen. But I dare not be different. What would become of us?'

Speaking as calmly as possible, bending over her plate and trying to look like the other women at lunch here, Karen said: 'But what is worse than being apart always?'

'Think. Yes you must think once. We should never tolerate one another if we were not in love. Even today here, we are both estranged from half of ourselves. You would find my life mean. A good deal of what you are I should not care to touch. I am calculating and like to see my way to my pleasures; to love you would be a leap in the dark. You were not made to leap in the dark either. We were not laughing, at Twickenham, when I said you got on so nicely – too nicely. You do; in my way I do too. We admire that in each other. Why should we bring each other to a full stop? And to leap is not only to leap, it is to hit the ground, somewhere. You have a romantic idea – '

' – No, I have no ideas left.'

'Would you come back to Paris with me?'

Karen felt like a piece of paper rearing up in the fire the instant before it catches, on the tense draughty flame. She put down her glass carefully.

'*That* was an idea,' he said calmly. 'They have too much power with you.'

'Oh! Then you didn't mean . . .'

'You see why it is impossible.'

'Naomi.'

'One cannot simply act.'

'Yes, I saw that once.'

Max looked across the restaurant – at the solid people lunching, the trays of fruit in the middle, the glazed advertisements on the walls – with abstract interest, as though he were alone. Watching a bottle of wine being opened, he said: 'Why are you so anxious to run away from home?'

She could in no way account for her own strangeness, and did not see why she should – to him above all.

Troubled defiance made her look away from him saying nothing, though all sorts of exclamations darted up in her mind. Max went on eating composedly, till he had finished his trout. 'What a pity, Karen,' he said, 'you are letting your trout get cold.'

'Yes, I am,' she said. 'I'm sorry.'

While the next dish came, he said: 'Can you tell me how many times the English besieged Boulogne?'

She was sorry to find she did not know. They began to talk about French kings. He and she could not be, like lucky lovers, provincial, full of little references and jokes. They had been nowhere together, their childhoods had been different, of what people they had in common they dreaded to speak. Their worlds were so much unlike that no experience had the same value for both of them. They could remember nothing that they could speak of, and memory is to love what the saucer is to the cup. But for lovers or friends with no past in common the historic past unrolls like a park, like a ridgy landscape full of buildings and people. To talk of books is, for oppressed shut-in lovers, no way out of themselves: what was written is either dull or too near the heart. But to walk into history is to be free at once, to be at large among people. Art does its work even here in clarifying their faces, but they are dead, immune, their schemes and passions are legacies. For the first time, he and she went into company together. His view of the past was political, hers dramatic, but now they were free of themselves they were one mind. Outside, the street, empty, reeled in midday sun; the glare was reflected in on the gold-and-brown wall opposite; side by side in the emptying restaurant, they surrounded themselves with wars, treaties, persecutions, strategic marriages, campaigns, reforms, successions and violent deaths. History is unpainful, memory does not cloud it;

you join the emphatic lives of the long dead. May we give the future something to talk about.

At three they left, to walk up to the battlements. The wide uphill Grande Rue of Boulogne is certainly not gay. Trams crawl unwillingly up it to the boulevards. It is without interest, uncertainly modern, abstract; its steepness, so tiring to the body, is calm to the eye. Shut shops, this afternoon, made its blankness absolute; massed trees at the top were summer-dark with heat. Max and Karen walked up silently, in what shade there was. They found themselves in the tranquil leafy dullness of the boulevards, out of which the old citadel rose.

The utter silence of the glaring, shuttered streets inside the citadel oppressed them. Everyone in here must be asleep, if not dead of a plague. Karen's feet began to ache from the cobbles; an afternoon unreality fell on her. The cathedral had the same stricken look: its façade was caked with autumn greyness, as though mists left a sediment. People in love, in whom every sense is open, cannot beat off the influence of a place. Max and Karen looked about them vaguely, not knowing why, they were not sightseeing – lost to each other in fatigue and vacancy. Then they turned back to the archway they had come in by and climbed the steps beside it, up inside the old wall to the ramparts.

Trees growing up here, and deep silent grass, make the walk round the ramparts dark green. Between branches there were rifts of blue; the bright sea-lit day shimmered and broke in. They passed the first angle, where a tower-top bulges, then sat down on the parapet. No one else was in view; the afternoon was too hot. The stone up here gave out heat, even in shadow. On the outside, below the parapet, the wall dropped sheer to the boulevards: there were seats the other side of the path, but they preferred this unsafe parapet. Having looked up and down the perspective of green walk they turned to look at each other, still with afternoon vacancy in their eyes.

'You're tired,' he said.

'It's the time of day. And the stones. Will you give me a cigarette?'

144

The leaves behind their heads and the leaves under them kept sifting in the uncertain air that drew out the flags. An incoming tide of apartness began to creep between Max and Karen, till, moving like someone under the influence of a pursuing dream, he drew the cigarette from between her fingers and threw it over on to the boulevard. Moving up the parapet, he kissed her, and with his fingers began to explore her hand. Their movements, cautious because of the drop below, were underlined by long pauses. They were hypnotized by each other, the height, the leaves ... Later, they began hearing voices on the steps; as the sun went down a little, other people came up to walk on the ramparts. Interruptions, making them draw apart, did not alter their sad and desperate calm. Karen could only tell how the time passed by the changing shadows on the roofs below. They got up once and walked right round the citadel, coming back again to where they had been. The apse of the cathedral, the sad windows of houses had looked at them through the boughs.

Before they left, a bar of glittering light struck across the path exactly where they stood, making their figures blaze. They stood and looked at each other. The town below began humming with early evening life. Karen saw his face, drowned in the light, full of tiredness and agony.

At six o'clock, they were walking on the quay again, past the café where they had sat when they first met. The town had high shadows and was vivid with colour now that the sun was amber and less fierce. They had looked into the empty Casino gardens, they had looked at the shore, but they dreaded solitude now. The tide was out, the glass-green harbour water had sunk, leaving dark slime on the embankment walls; Karen's boat waited across the water, against the railway quay. He and she sat down in another café, shabbily modern, full of steel and red paint. He ordered Pernod Fils, she had a vermouth and soda. This ice had no sawdust, but looked grey. Max spooned a wedge of ice into Karen's drink.

She said: 'I can't marry Ray.'

Max said nothing; they looked at each other's drinks.

She went on: 'They'll say, "Why not?" '

'Surely that's your affair.'

'But my marriage was their affair. They don't like change. They'll say, "What next, then?" What, indeed?'

'Well, what next?'

'I don't know. I've never made any break before. What does anyone do next?'

'Would you marry me?'

'But you don't want to marry me.'

Max said: 'It is more or less impossible.'

'Naomi. What about her?'

'Well, what about her? You have got to think too.'

'What would she do next, for instance?'

'You know her life.'

'You see, Ray's a man. He . . .'

'You know we would be wretched married.'

'You would rather marry Naomi?'

He paused, then said: 'Yes.'

'Why?'

'I am at home with her, she reposes me and I need her. I am not ashamed with her; there is nothing to be explained. Also, I love her: I could not hurt her life.'

Karen's arm was on the table: he touched it thoughtfully.

'No, don't,' she said.

'I'm sorry, I didn't realize – '

'I did.'

'She would be my wife,' he said. 'You and I expect so much the whole time. I cannot live in a love affair, I am busy and grasping. I am not English; you know I am nervous the whole time. I could not endure being always conscious of anyone. Naomi is like furniture or the dark. I should pity myself if I did not marry her.'

'That's what my mother said.'

'You should stay with your own people. Go home, Karen. I beg you to go home. I do not want adventure, you are not capable of it – don't weep, you will kill me – you don't know what you want.'

Turning quickly away from all the other tables Karen knocked her tears away with her hand. 'Yes, I do,' she said. 'Why else am I here?'

'Do you want to stay here tonight?'

'Yes, I do. Do you?'

'Not when you are crying; I dread you. But I do. Tonight is impossible; I must be at work tomorrow by half-past eight.'

'Then that means, never.'

'Why?'

She did not speak or look at him.

'Next Saturday,' he said, 'I will come across to Folkestone. By the early afternoon boat. Will you meet me?'

'Yes,' she said. 'But I don't like Folkestone; I've been there.'

'We can stay somewhere else.'

'Hythe is along the coast. About five miles.'

' – Will you have another drink?'

She shook her head. He paid for the drinks and they walked out of the café, then stood, uncertain, on the quay. She said: 'I think I'll go on board.'

As they crossed the bridge, he began to say: 'You know – '

'Oh, please, Max – I'm so tired.'

They walked slowly over the cobbles between the railway lines to her boat. Looking across the water, she saw Boulogne as she had seen it this morning – its façade of gayness and trivial peace. It hung like a painted scene. The melancholy boulevards, the silent citadel were out of view. The Casino trees stood still in yellow light; the flags had dropped and hung lifeless down their poles.

'Then, Saturday,' he said.

'Yes. Don't write before then.'

'No. There is nothing to say.'

'No,' she said.

9

Rain drifted over the Channel and west over Romney marsh; there was no horizon, the edgeless clouds hung so low. Centuries ago, the sea began to draw away from the cinque port, leaving it high and dry with a stretch of sea-flattened land between town and beach. The grey barracky houses along the sea front are isolated; if the sea went for them they would be cut off. Across fields dry with salt air, the straight shady Ladies' Walk, with lamps strung from the branches, runs down from the town to the sea: on hot days a cool way to walk to bathe. Inland, in summer, a band plays in a pavilion beside the canal, whose water is dark with weeds that catch at the oars of pleasure boats, and overshadowed by trees. On and off, there is rattle of musketry practice from the ranges along the edge of the marsh. West of the town, the canal bends under a bridge then goes straight to Lympne between the hills and the marsh; across the marsh martello towers in different stages of ruin follow the curve of the coast towards Dungeness, where at nights a lighthouse flashes far out. On its inland side, the town climbs a steep hill, so that the houses stand on each other's heads. The beautiful church must have crowned the town; now new houses spread in a fan above it, driving back the thickety hazel woods. Back from the brow of Hythe hill the country – cornfieldy, open and creased with woody valleys, Kentish, mysterious – stretches to the chalk downs. Now and then you hear bells from Cheriton, or distant blowy bugles from Shorncliffe camp: this week-end, they were muffled by low clouds.

Not having been here before and now coming with Max made an island of the town. It stayed like nowhere, near nowhere, cut off from everywhere else. Karen cannot divide the streets from the patter of rain and rush of rain in the gutters. She remembers a town with no wind, where standing on the canal bridge you hear trees sighing with rain and the sea soughing on the far-off beach. All Saturday night, rain rustled the chestnut across the street from their window;

on Sunday morning the lace mats on the dressing-table were wet. The handkerchief she had left lying the night before was wet too; she wiped her pearls but when she clasped them on again they were cold round her neck. Though the window looked on the High Street, nothing was opposite except the chestnut, growing in an old garden.

Rain in summer seems a kind of disaster. The idea of this rain being disaster, though they knew it was not, had hung over Max and Karen meeting on Folkestone pier on Saturday afternoon. They said nothing about the broken weather till, waiting for a taxi outside the harbour station, she brushed rain off his overcoat sleeve with her hand. After that minute or two crossing the gangway, drops hung on the heavy English stuff. Karen said: 'You've come with no mackintosh?' 'I did not think; it only began raining outside the Nord, when there was no time to go back. I can buy one somewhere in Folkestone.'

'But haven't you one already?'

'It would be no harm to have two,' said Max.

So they stopped in Guildhall Street and bought him a light fawn mackintosh with a buttoning-up collar. Karen wanted to go out to Hythe by bus, but he said they might as well keep the taxi. The mackintosh, with its new rubbery smell, slid about during the drive out, showing its check lining and the chain inside the collar to hang it up by. Max leaned back, smoking cigarette after cigarette, knocking the ash off over the window and only glancing at Karen now and again: his deliberateness struck her as never before. There are degrees in being alone with someone. It was not till they had driven down Sandgate hill – not till they were, even, clear of Sandgate itself, on that flat stretch of road above the beach, passing cream-coloured houses with gardens of tamarisks – that she saw what made them completely alone for the first time: there being no sun. Always before, at Twickenham or Boulogne, the sun by happening to shine had been a felt presence, adding itself the whole time. It had been insistent on the flowery pink tree, the salt quay stones. Till today, they had not, when alone, ever been two; always either three or one. Now, what they did was cut off from any other thing, their silence related to them only. Tamarisks flying past the rainy windows were some dream – not your own, a dream you have heard described. Not what they both saw – the sea, the bare hill, the railway arch, trees, villas – but the sense of *not* seeing these stamped their drive for her.

She had taken off the sapphire ring that morning and put a bought wedding ring on the finger, which had so far made her keep her left-hand glove on. Seeing HYTHE on a yellow sign made Max stoop to pick up their scattered things and rout for her other glove in the folds of the mackintosh, as though they arrived somewhere like this every day. The taxi drove down the High Street and pulled up; Karen got out and, waiting outside the Ram's Head, felt rain from this new sky on her face. She looked at the wet green tree across the street and, inside the porch, at the brass-railed door of the inn. Under the cloud-bound sky a clock, uphill, struck. The struck hour sounded final: from then on the day governed itself. Max put a hand under her elbow and they went in.

A real ram's head glared from the hall wall; the manageress looked through her hatch with glass eyes too. 'Number nine,' she said. The head-maid's bumping backview, with crooked apron-string bow like a white scut, went on up. The stairs split, left and right.

'Mind, m'm,' said the maid, ahead in a dark arch. This unlit floor was all steps, two dull square glass panes only in one door. 'Mind, m'm; it's dark here when you don't know.' 'I can see that.' It had to be dark, built in between the hill and the tight street. The maid said: 'Number nine,' ahead, opening a door. Karen saw the chestnut over the white blind. She looked round and put her hat on the bed. The boots brought the bags up; the maid who would not go re-folded a towel over a jug; Number Nine shuffled with servants staring into your back. 'The gentleman said, tea in the lounge.' The maid, the boots had to go; the door shut. Karen looked at her face in the strange glass. She thought: 'I must go down,' but stopped to see the room behind in the glass.

Rain made the day dark for day, but till late the light did

not change. Saturday stayed late, reflected on wet roofs and straight wet paths uphill. The west broke, the grey went white, lightening across the rain that did not stop but still veiled darkening houses and trees. At nine they went out and stood on the canal bridge; the band pavilion was empty, the chairs stacked up. Hearing the sea creep on the far beach, they walked that way, along the Ladies' Walk. Along this tunnel of trees lights hung quenched under arching branches, rain glittering past, no June moths. On a bench back from the walk another couple of lovers were blotted out, faceless, sheltered by the unfrequented night. On the embanked sea-front a house with a tower stood up; next door, in the lodging-house terrace, someone played a piano, but then stopped. Here the sea air was washed unsalt by the rain; you only smelled tamarisks and wet grass. The sea crept on the shingle with a half-living rustle; on its far-out silence Dungeness lighthouse flashed, stopped, flashed. At the sight of this one light Karen remembers her hand, wet with rain and for some minutes forgotten, tightening on Max's wet india-rubber sleeve. He made her face inland, where the High Street lights rose steadily through the rain and windows studded the hill where many people would sleep tonight.

'I am supposing,' he said, 'that you know what you are doing. It will be too late when you ask yourself: What have I done?'

She asked herself: What have I done? at about three o'clock. She only knew she had slept by finding an hour missing on her luminous watch. She thought, how frightening luminous watches are, the eye of time never stops watching you . . . The street lamp still lit up the chestnut tree, cut out its fingered leaves on the dark above and cast the same inescapable barred square on the ceiling over the bed. The mantelpiece and the wardrobe with its mirror stood each side, darker than the dark walls. Having done as she knew she must she did not think there would be a child: all the same, the idea of you, Leopold, began to be present

151

with her. This made her lean over, trying to see Max's face. But there was not enough light and his face was turned away from her in the cleft of the pillow. There was something cast-off about his way of lying, as though whatever it was had finished with him, too. They had both come a long way, without consulting each other, to sleep under a ceiling with this barred light. Between the tamarisks passing the rainy window and this lamp-invaded darkness, nothing remained. She began to count how many hours were left before his ship sailed tomorrow night – no, tonight. Her sleep of an hour had let tomorrow in.

The weight of being herself fell on her like a clock striking. She saw the clothes she would put on to go home in hanging over a chair. While it is still Before, Afterwards has no power, but afterwards it is the kingdom, the power and the glory. You do not ask yourself, what am I doing? You know. What you do ask yourself, what have I done? you will never know.

Had this not been escape? She was washed back ashore again. Further out than you dare go, where she had been is the outgoing current not strong enough not to let you back? Were you not far out, is there no far out, or is there no current there? I am let back, safe, too safe; no one will ever know. Naomi and my mother, who would die if they knew, will never know. What they never know will soon never have been. They will never know. I shall die like Aunt Violet wondering what else there was; from this there is no escape for me after all. Max lies beside me, but Naomi sat on my bed in the dark; she was there first and will never go away. I have done what she does not know, so I have not done what I dread. Max said at Boulogne: 'One cannot simply act.' I thought he meant, must not, what it meant was, cannot. People must hope so much when they tear streets up and fight at barricades. But, whoever wins, the streets are laid again and the trams start running again. One hopes too much of destroying things. If revolutions do not fail, they fail you.

This seemed to have to be, when nothing had ever had to

be, so I thought it would be all. It looked like the end. I did not see it would have an end. These hours are only hours. They cannot be again, but no hours can. Hours in a room with a lamp and a tree outside, with tomorrow eating into them. The grass sprang up when we took our hands away. The maid will make this bed and fold back two corners of eiderdown like they were folded back when I put my hat on it. If I could brush the rain off his sleeve again, and drive past the tamarisks, and walk up behind the maid with the bumpy bow on her back, and put my hat on the bed –

Now nothing more has to be. Whatever may happen this morning, it will be part of afterwards. I wish there were fewer hours before he sails. I shall be glad to be back again in London; they are always delighted to have me home. Is one gentler to older people because their death is nearer? I thought tonight would be the hour of my death but here I still am, left to die like Aunt Violet after mother has died like her. To be with Ray will be like being with mother; that is why my marriage makes her so glad. Max was the enemy. It is true he hurt me, but now nothing more has to be. I cannot see him, only touch him, and that is over. At Boulogne, to touch was to see, to see was to touch. But all that time we were travelling to only this: a barred light on a ceiling, a lamp, a tree outside.

I cannot see him to see what a child would be like. Though there will not be a child, that is why I want to see him. If a child were going to be born, there would still be something that had to be. Tonight would be more then than hours and that lamp. It would have been the hour of my death. I should have to do what I dread, see them know. There would still be something to dread. I should see the hour in the child. I should not have rushed on to nothing. He would be the mark our hands did not leave on the grass, he would be the tamarisks we only half saw. And he would be the I whose bed Naomi sat on, the Max whose sleeve I brushed rain off: tender and guardable. He would be the Max I heard talking when I stood outside the salon, the I Max rang up: that other we were both looking for. I could bear us both lying tired and cast-off if it were for him, if we were his purpose. Paris then Twickenham, the boat train at Victoria, Boulogne, the sea-front last night – if he ran through those like a wire they would not fall apart. The boat going up the estuary, the silent mountains, the harbour the day I knew Aunt Violet would die – those would not have been for nothing. He would have been there then and then and then.

– He would be disaster. They would not know where to turn to save me for themselves. They would have to see me as someone poisoned. Only poisons, they think, act on you. If a thing does act on you, it can only be poison, some foreign thing. 'Your poison's not mine,' she said ... What made Naomi insist on Max and me meeting last time? What made Aunt Violet look at me like that? *She* saw Ray was my mother: did she want this for me? I saw her wondering what disaster could be like. The child would be disaster. But there's no question of him.

Looking at her clothes on the chair near the window Karen must have fallen asleep again, for she seemed to be putting them on to hurry home in and they were ice-cold, heavy and wet with rain. The way they stuck on her skin was terrifying. She woke, and the chestnut leaves cut out on dark were terrifying. Her life had been full of warnings; the first was: 'You will get wet.' They warn you because they love you and because you are theirs. Now, here she lay as it would be death to those loving warners to know she lay. Not her hiddenness now but her unhiddenness made her heart thump chokingly, as it did years ago when, playing hide and seek, she heard the steps of the seekers go by just the other side of the curtain, or heard them come into the dark room where she hid. The curtain would fall, the light would discover her before she could slip out to bolt for 'home', which used to be by the gong, at the foot of the stairs. Once you were 'home' you won, you could not be caught. So sometimes you struck the gong.

Being caught is the word for having a child, sometimes. Then Ray would not marry me; mother would not buy me the sofa I wanted to shoot. The street would stay torn up,

154

the trams could not begin again . . . How silent it is! Surely it must be time for a clock to strike? You would never think there was the street out there. Yes you would; it takes a street to be silent, a stone silence going nowhere. Besides, we walked back down a street last night . . . I wonder whether so much rain tires that tree? When do they put lamps out? This is the time of night when they say you feel most afraid. Only, I have nothing to be afraid of: no one will know.

No one will ever know. When Naomi came out, the print on the grass was gone. He will never be born to be my enemy. The sky *is* paler; I see the top of the tree. Today is showing; I shall be home tonight. My clothes are not really wet; that was the dream. 'Home' was always downstairs; downstairs is always safe. Upstairs is crazy with dreams or love. Once 'home' you are safe; you cannot be caught; no one knows where you were hiding. Is Max hiding from me? He seems to sleep with his will, as though he had chosen sleep. He said: 'Naomi is like furniture or the dark.' Here are furniture and the dark, but he is asleep. Perhaps that is what he meant: you can sleep, you need not know them. For her, this will be the dearest part of the night . . . That is what Mme Fisher can't bear, the thought of their quiet sleep. She killed all wishes by saying: 'Do as you wish,' but she cannot kill their wish. If she had been standing on those stairs today, smiling, when I came up behind the maid, I should have turned back and gone, away from where Max is. But if her smiling would stop me, she would not smile. She is a woman who sells girls; she is a witch. She is here; she is that barred light. She can never have wanted Max to be quiet; when he's quiet he's not hers. He was hers tonight when we saw the lighthouse, hers when we came in. Did I dream the sky was lighter, or is it lighter? If I don't sleep again, today will be so long – She turned her pillow over and rested on the cool side; the rain was falling more loudly and heavily and she tried to imagine she was the tree.

When she woke, Max was standing in daylight by the window: Sunday footsteps had begun in the street. She put her hand to her forehead to shield her eyes.

'I thought your things would get wet; I got up to move them.'

'Are they wet?' she said indifferently.

'No, the rain did not come so far. The things on the table are wet, though.'

'Need we wake up?'

'No.'

He stood looking at her, then presently came back to the bed and took Karen in his arms.

When the bells had stopped, after eleven o'clock, and everyone was in church, they walked uphill by one of the asphalt pathways broken by steps. Near the top, the church-yard with wet crosses lay behind a flint wall; across the path, gardens of sodden flowers. The heaviness of the climb in rain-muffled air, in their dragging mackintoshes, made them feel bent on something that must be done. They stopped and turned to look down at the town roofs making the rain smoky, the smudge of sea. Max leaned on the churchyard wall, his hands in his pockets, locked into himself by the first pause since they had started out.

'Can you imagine living here?'

'No,' he said, as though speaking for the first time today. 'No – '

'I – a port with no sea, a hill you could not drive up without going a mile round – it has too much nonsense about it.'

'Never mind,' she said calmly.

'You're right; it doesn't hurt me.'

'Do you want a funicular?'

'Yes – I like hills better without places, but if there are places there should be funiculars.'

'But what should we do this morning?'

'Go up in it.'

A martial hymn tune came from trees beyond the canal. Karen said: 'The Salvation Army Band.'

'If they are out of doors, their music will get wet. But perhaps they are not?' Looking at her dispassionately, he said: 'The rain gives you pink cheeks; you don't look like yourself, you look like an English girl.'

'Is that all right?'

'Yes,' he said, with that ironic tilt-up in his voice, like a smiling shrug, that she could never account for. Talk between people of different races is serious; that tender silliness lovers employ falls flat. Words are used for their meaning, not for their ring. If she had learnt to dread that kind of talk about art and life, most of all about love, to which literalness is deadly, she would have suffered more ... Above where they stood, a level road behind a row of white posts cut across the path, along the face of the hill. When they went on, they took it and walked more easily. Max seemed indifferent to the rain; though he certainly would not seek it, alone, for pleasure – in fact he might feel a cat's repugnance for it. Possibly this steep walk, this driving damp on his face, seemed part of the desperateness of their meeting, to be taken in his stride like their being here at all. What they had said had always been under pressure, the quick talk of people who act without asking why. She had seen, before this, his dislike of romantic inconvenience, and was not surprised that he liked funiculars.

This road had, on its uphill side, villas with climbing gardens and new white gates; on the other a brick-topped wall overhung the town, and, as the hill bent inland, a wide view of the marsh. Midday smoke blurred the roofs and rain-veiled trees: you could almost hear, below, the clatter of oven doors as Sunday joints were put in. Women in white gloves would be coming home from church, and after lunch the bells for children's service would ring. Sunday comfort, peace hung over all she saw, as though this were a picture saying only one thing. The stretch of forlorn marsh and sad sea-line made the snug town an island, a ship content to go nowhere ... Karen, walking by Max, felt more isolated with him, more cut off from her own country than if they had been in Peru. You feel most foreign when you no longer belong where you did ... A lady, opening one of the white gates, glanced at them curiously, then turned away her polite eyes. About a mile further on, the road ended in a path cut through a hazel wood.

10

After lunch, Max went to a table in the Ram's Head lounge and sat down to write a letter. Someone played the piano and several people were talking round the wet-day fire, but he wrote straight ahead, immovably, stopping once to crumple a sheet and pull another impatiently from the rack. From the window-seat, Karen kept looking across – at first, because she *had* never watched him writing, later, because she began to dread what he wrote. Nothing said at lunch had led to the writing-table, and this unexpected act of his struck cold on her; that unaware face with the lower lip pressed in, that unpent speed starting from the tip of the pen. At all other times he paused before any action – like a car slowing up for a cautious minute where a railway with no gates crosses the road. (The motorist, sitting back, hears the wind in the wires and looks at the skull-and-cross-bones warning nailed to a post.) But writing he did not deliberate. He writes like a man on the stage, she thought, so much not caring who watches, he almost writes to be watched. Not a pause: what he writes must have been here all this morning, mounting up. So we were not alone . . . She knew she paid the penalty for having come too close, but had not looked in him for any one enemy. His cigarette-case was open on the table beside him, and she came over once for a cigarette. He did not look up; she went back to the window-seat.

Several more people, crowding through the swing doors, sat down in the ring of chairs between her and him, where she and he had sat at tea yesterday.

Their looking at Karen made her at once pick up an old copy of *The Sketch*. Her night thoughts in a heavy flock had now settled at the pit of her mind. At last Max stood up and looked about for her sharply, not knowing where she sat; then he came over and said: 'I want a stamp; where can I get one here?'

She looked straight at the letter in his hand: it was to Naomi.

'Max . . .'

'I suppose we can get a stamp at the office?'

'Must it go today?'

'Yes.'

'Why?'

'Why else should it be written?'

She did not know what to say. They went out and bought the stamp at the office, and he stamped the letter. He went to the hall letter-box, but Karen caught at his wrist: the manageress stared. Face to face, as when they got jammed in the train corridor, Max stared Karen out with unnaturally dark eyes. 'Don't post it here,' she said. 'Not this minute, not here. Let's take it out somewhere.'

'Out?' Max said, touching the envelope corners with unkind finger-tips. 'Surely we've walked about enough.'

'I want air very much.'

'Why – is your head aching?'

'No – yes. Wait while I get my things.' She began to go upstairs, but turned at the bend to say: 'Max, you won't post it? Wait!'

'Don't be long,' he said. When she came down the letter was still in his hand.

From the Ram's Head door they turned right, down the High Street in the direction of Romney, the silent ranges, the marsh. Shutters up, blinds down behind shop windows darkened the street: the street reflected the blind windows and a strip of unalive wet sky. Today having been blotted out of its place in summer, everybody had taken to indoor sleep; fumes of sleep seemed to creep round the windows, staling the out-of-doors.

Karen looked at Max once or twice, but her lips stayed gummed together, and he walked fast, not looking at anything.

'What made you write?' she said at last.

He turned an iron face to her. 'What makes you ask?'

'What are you saying to her?'

'That we cannot be married.'

'Give me the letter.'

'Why?'

'Only to carry.'

Max passed her the letter without looking at it. 'Keep it dry,' he said. 'Put it in your pocket.'

'But you cannot – '

Someone opened a window with a creak of the sash: Max started and said: 'We are in the street.'

'They don't care,' she said, but stopped all the same.

At that end, the High Street bends into a square where the Folkestone buses turn to go back. Max guiding Karen's elbow in keyed-up silence, they crossed the empty square to the Romney road canal bridge. On from the bridge the canal and the road straighten out and run parallel, with a strip of grass between them, both overcast by trees. Max and Karen, seeing a trodden path beside the canal, took it: the grass deadened their steps. On to the dark unmoving canal water drips fell from the trees on the far bank. From behind the trees, through a thicket, a row of barracks peered across the canal. Though rain fell no faster the sky steadily darkened, filling the air between trees and water with dusk.

She went on: 'But you cannot do that to Naomi.'

'Did *you* always think so much of her?'

Karen flinching, said: 'I suppose that's fair.'

'You foresaw nothing?'

'Not this, no. Nothing. No change. This was quite apart from her. I did not see it would hurt her in any way. I thought this left you unchanged.'

'You thought I would come so far for a little thing?'

'Little when it had happened.'

'Little to you?'

'No. But I thought you felt as I did, that this finished the past but did not touch the future. Being here does not seem to belong to now, it belongs to the year in Paris when I used to want you so much even to look at me. If I had not felt this was something that should have happened long ago, and that belonged to when it should have been, if I had known you loved her and felt she was the *now*, I should never have come, Max.'

'Then you were – extraordinary.'

'You knew that from the first.'

'Because I said to you that I had no honour, you thought this need have no weight.'

'I am sick of honour. But I thought there was your heart – not for me, for her, I mean. There was no question of your loving anybody but her. Did you not know why I came? Since you were in London in April, then went away, I have been either possessed or else myself for the first time. I found I was in prison – no, locked into a museum full of things I once liked, with nothing to do now but look at them and wonder why I had. *They* keep me away from everything that has power; they would be frightened of art if I painted really well. When it thundered last month I used to wish I could be struck by lightning.'

He said coldly: 'I did not know you had so much reason to come.'

'Reason? You might as well say, what *reason* has one to answer the telephone?'

'You believed in my marriage because it seemed – unpolitic. You agree, then, she is not a woman to marry without love?'

They walked some way in sharp silence. Karen said: 'Not to marry without love for *her* sake, you mean?'

'I half mean that: yes.'

'But she has not altered: oh, *she* has not changed. What you wanted, you want: it is still there.'

'I know.'

'What has happened?' said Karen, stopping beside the canal.

'Not so much,' said Max, impatient. 'It is just her that I have been mad to think I could marry for love, *her* love, her love only. I see now that that is what I cannot accept.'

'What made you think you could, then?'

'I looked back at my humiliations, my ridiculousness and self-deceptions, and dreaded others. You do not know what it is to be suspect and know why. What it is to have no wall to put your back against. For years her mother did much to

161

show me my insecureness; Mme Fisher has taught me to be suspicious less extravagantly, but with more reason, by showing me where I stood. – I asked Naomi to marry me one afternoon in the salon, towards the end of March. Her mother had been with us, then gone out. Or rather, Mme Fisher and I had been together, with Naomi there, but sewing beside the window, not looking up. She sat dragging forward her work into the daylight, peering at the small stitches with her eyes wrinkled up, looking as though her sewing mattered too much. Though I saw her, I only felt her there when her mother had gone out and all the energy went out of the room. Seeing how gently Naomi picked up her scissors from the floor, I remembered she was a woman. I said something, and she started and pricked her finger. I saw from the pitying way she sucked the bead of blood from her finger how much she pitied me, and saw at the same time that hers was the only pity I did not resent. I wished the blood were on my own finger. I went across to her chair and asked her to marry me: her looking up stopped any doubt in myself. When I see how the stony lines of her dress and her entirely unsurprised face moved me, I see now that it was the madonna trick – my nerves tricking my senses with the idea of peace, making someone to make for me an unattackable safe place. It seemed to me then that I had not acted on impulse but from some long inclination I had not known of. This was so strong that I found it hard to remember that I, in fact, stood above her, beside her chair and looking down at her face, and was not standing looking up from below at a more than life-sized figure, lit as far as the knees, then rising into the dark. I have never passed a figure like that un-moved; I am not rational: there is too much force in a figure of stone pity. The force of the moment seemed to have no end; its deception lasted, twisting my senses till I found her bountiful because she was thin, beautiful in being ugly – '

' – Must you say that?'

'It is against myself. Do you suppose that I cannot see I victimized her? Stripped of what I saw she is ugly for the first time. Those first weeks of false calm were intoxicating –

unenmity with myself, the silence of any doubt. I put my entire nature under her feet, and my unresistance to pity exalted me. A fatigue I had not admitted made her my pillow. Desire of what she gave seemed to be desire of her. The wish for the marriage began to dominate me, not less her aunt's death made what had appeared fantastic suddenly possible. My lack of a home, of any place to return to, had not only deprived me, it chagrined me constantly. In France to have no family can be more humbling than poverty. The ambition for some other, some advantageous marriage that I had had, the ambition with which her mother credited me, fell away. To be unambitiously with her became peace.'

'That was when I met you together. I saw. You were not dreaming.'

'It had the actuality of any other dream.'

'But I saw you together. Last night I thought of Naomi coming across the lawn with the kettle, and saw you smile at the window. You and I are the dream: go back to her.'

'She is not there.'

'You'll find her when you go back.'

'I cannot want to find her. I do not want peace, I do not want a pillow. Now *you* are tricking yourself with the idea of the more than life-sized figure. She has thought of our coming marriage for weeks; she is more than stone; she desires to be desired. Since we returned from London she has never stopped watching me: I have never once felt her eyes leave my face. Imagine the statue's face on your own level, spoilt with anxiousness, following where you go. Her eyes snatch at me and she cannot do things calmly. I had felt her refuse to be fully happy till you and I met again: since we have met and she has seen, though God knows how, that I love you, her love of me is love of her own pain. Her mother watches her watching, and misses nothing. I cannot live with them both.'

'Take Naomi away to live with you somewhere else.'

'I will not live with a woman who lives with her own pain.'

'I liked your gentleness to her.'

'Then it was her lover you came to meet?'

'No. The you in the train. The voice on the telephone – remember, she was waiting to be quite happy till you and I *had* met again. Remember how well she knew me that year in Paris without being told anything. And she must have known your nature well enough, too, not to be satisfied till this was tried out.'

'This?'

'You and I.'

'I see. Do you regret coming?'

'No, there is nothing *to* regret. I mean, there is nothing left now, is there, nothing? – Must we walk here? I've always hated canals.'

Max looked round, but there seemed to be nowhere else. So he opened a gate across the path and they walked on, at the edge of a new field but beside the same gloomy, rain-spotted water. Karen suddenly, but with intense calm, took Max's letter to Naomi from her pocket, read the address then tore it across four times. Then she hesitated with the torn scraps in her hand, looking at the unrelated French words. 'You two have another language, too,' she said. She glanced once at the water, but scattered the scraps on the wet grass, where they lay like the broken trail of a paper chase. Max, making no movement, watched her with irony. 'What was the good of that?' he said finally.

'It did me good.'

'Yes, I see. But my letter was in your charge. I see you are sick of honour.'

'I will not have her hurt.'

'Then we are back where we started. Will you understand nothing?'

'Don't be so – unloving.'

'You compel me to be. That is all you want.'

'Oh yes – you said just now that Naomi saw you loved me. But *that's* not true, is it?'

Max said nothing. Turning, she saw in a moment what was in his eyes. It made her look blindly down at the scraps of letter, now blurring with rain, saying: 'I didn't know . . .'

'You force me to hide myself.'

'You force me to hide *myself*.'

'Karen, you made me feel this was pleasure between enemies.'

'We have been people darting across the sea to each other; there has been no time yet to be anything else. There has been no time to feel anything but compulsion. If I had known you loved me I would not have dared come. That goodbye in the train only happened because those people jammed us face to face. When you touched my hand, I knew one kind of meeting was possible, but I still thought you loved Naomi. When you were asleep last night, I thought you should be beside her. I didn't ask what *I* felt; I wanted not to know.'

'Would you marry me?'

'You said that was not possible: after that I never let myself think.'

'Possible?' he said more calmly. 'In what way do you mean? If your parents would give money. I have not enough for you.'

'Is *that* all that – ?'

'It is serious.'

'Yes, I know. But – I want to so much. It is not simply being happy. Should we be happy? That doesn't seem to come in.'

'That would rest with you.'

'Me? – I can't see anything. Should we live in Paris?'

'Not in any Paris you know. You would not like it much.'

'You mean, you want me to marry you?'

'Yes. I ask a great deal.'

'I'm not much. You used to see that. You used hardly to see me. What made you see me at all?'

'How can I know? Your beauty, first. What you are.'

'You make me ashamed,' she said. 'But I didn't understand anything. Did you not really want us to come here, then?'

'Karen, I don't know.'

'Has this not spoilt me?'

'Karen – '

She looked at him and was unable to speak. Last night seemed to be undone, so that they kissed with unfamiliar gentleness, tasting rain on each other's lips. Drawing apart like a pair of very young people, they stared at each other, and at what had happened now. Her heart stood still, as when she first thought of Leopold: she felt the same shock of tenderness and life opening. The face she found was the face she had failed to find on the dark pillow. This beginning of love, wanting new hands, lips and eyes, made them stand apart patiently, looking at the trodden grass between them and hearing cars rush past on the wet Romney road. Later, they turned and began to walk back to Hythe, the canal on their left now, the trees on its far side turning other flanks. Karen, feeling how wet her own feet were, suddenly thought, had he dry shoes to travel in? Once she turned, looking back at the scraps of letter diminishing on the grass. 'Even so – I was right in one way,' she said. 'You cannot simply tell her you do not love her. It would be better to tell her you love me, that we love each other.'

'She knows. But – shall I not write, but go and see her?'

'Write first – write from here. Oughtn't she to know everything? If she wants to see you after that, go. After all, we are her friends.'

The darkness of the sky, the unfriendliness of the land-scape – grass, canal, trees, barracks – seemed to them less. Karen saw one lost seagull swing inland.

The bridge coming near, the chimneys behind it, again made a small town picture, like the view from the hill. But as they approached the bridge their figures entered the frame. Lighter even in body with happiness, Karen ran on up the slope to the road beside the parapet. She looked back and saw Max coming more slowly after her, looking back for the last time at the canal.

11

At the terminus of the Hythe bus in Folkestone they said good-bye; he went to the harbour, she to the Central station to wait for her train home. Where they both went, immediately, did not seem to matter much. So their parting had been voluntary and busy: the great thing had been for him to balance her suitcase so that, when her taxi started, it should not fall on her feet. She drove to the station along tree-planted roads of mansion villas, alight early, for this time of year, because of the thick dusk. Tips of shrubs glittered under the big windows. Karen saw quick pictures, upstairs and down: a girl parting her hair in a cool hurry; a family at a Sunday supper gathered round silver dishes; four people at bridge under a lamp. A car pulled up at a kerb and a couple in evening dress went eagerly in at a gate: you could see how occupied you could be without love. Herself, Karen felt like a shut book, glad to sit back with an empty place beside her and let Sunday finish itself. It was true, to think of the chestnut, the churchyard wall, the Ram's Head door with its brass bar made her share the dumb sorrow of objects at being left. Like rain on the taxi windows, soft affections and melancholies blurred her mind; she saw inanimate things as being friendly to love.

Rain *had* been disaster to many people; in the train you saw how hard it had come on them by the way they all sat, knees apart dejectedly, reading the notices or staring up unblinkingly at the carriage lights. You hope so much of a summer Folkestone week-end: they had been made fools of through no fault of their own. 'It costs money, too,' someone said, as the train quickened on the embankment over the churchyard: now there was nothing ahead but the week's work. To foresee pleasure makes anybody a poet – all sorts of intense fancies must have quickened during the journey down – to seek pleasure makes a hero of anyone: you open yourself so entirely to fate. Spoilt pleasure is a sad, unseemly thing; you can only bury it. The sea not having been blue

had made everyone meaner: for some time they would not
think of the sea again. A pall of disappointment hung in the
carriage. Karen, seeing that general threat to life that is
ever-present but seldom quite fulfils itself, saw why the
clouds lying darkly over the harbour when she met Max's
boat had filled her with dismay. I was right: we *were* being
threatened.

The dark, becoming complete, stood immovable at the
windows: only when there were lights did anything fly past.
The train made a noise of tunnelling through air. The girl
opposite with the splashed stockings crossed her legs and
began to smoke; the man she was with spread a newspaper
over both of them, glanced primly round then began to feel
for her under it: you could see he was certain of one thing.
Their intently vacant faces unnerved Karen; shutting her
eyes she thought once more of Leopold. When Max spoke of
marriage, no child of theirs had been present. What he wants
is that I should be tender to him, know him and not go away.
Which is what I want. But his life will stay *his* life, as it was
before. Leopold belongs to when I thought of Max going,
when I thought I must stay alone.

London was beginning; you could not mistake the train's
roar between walls, or the glare on the sky: everyone in the
carriage felt it and moved their shoulders, as though being
forced to shoulder something again. The newspaper slipped
off the couple's knees; they moved apart, their faces filling
up with Monday morning concern. The girl looked ruefully
at her splashed stockings; the man said: 'Well, well,' reaching up for his hat. Everyone waited for the train to impale
them on London. Karen stared at her suitcase on the opposite rack. Past midnight, that other train would crash into
the Gare du Nord; Max getting out would be carrying *his*
suitcase and the Folkestone mackintosh through the angry
steam a French train makes. She thought suddenly: I don't
know his address.

A wave of silence out of the park trees washed the steps of
the Chester Terrace houses. But for the fanlight and one
basement window, the Michaelis's house appeared desert-

edly dark: the night sky picked out its pale parapet. It had stopped raining here, but the steps were wet. Karen's key turned soundlessly in the slick lock: when she let herself in the whole house stood above her in unsuspicious peace. The light inside the fanlight fell on the hall chest, on which waited a letter from Ray and the telephone message pad with something written on it. So as not to have to approach Ray's letter, Karen avoided the chest, going on upstairs. The first landing was dark, but the drawing-room door stood ajar; inside she saw a lamp, the Chinese lamp, throw light up a curtain: she stood still, gripping her suitcase. Someone moved and got up; she heard her mother's step on the carpet. Mrs Michaelis came to the door of the drawing-room. She wore a black, full-falling dress, with lace from the elbows, a 'picture' dress that made her belong to no time. Her figure stood in dark outline against the lamplit curtain, the silk shadows and darkish glow of the room. She held her head like Aunt Violet. Karen heard a log fall in the fire as her mother, one hand on the door, stood waiting for her to speak. Feeling light on her face, she could say nothing.

'You came in so quietly,' said her mother at last.

'Because it's late – isn't it?'

'Yes, it is late.'

'I'm sorry, darling; I didn't think you'd sit up.'

Mrs Michaelis by pausing made Karen pause. Then she said: 'Did you find Ray's letter?'

'On the chest? No. I came straight up.'

'Straight up? Oh, then you didn't – ' Mrs Michaelis, with a curious dip of the head, broke off, looking away from her daughter. Her hand dropped from the door and buried itself in a fold of her black silk skirt. She turned and walked out of sight, back to the fire. Her voice, sounding unfamiliar, came from in there: 'Karen . . .' Karen put down her suitcase and followed her mother in, with a false ease. She found Mrs Michaelis standing facing the fire, staring at the reflection of the room in the tall mirror above it. Something made her impossible to approach.

'Has it been raining all the time here?' said Karen.

'I think it has. Yes, it has.'

'Mother?'

'Yes?'

'Aren't you well tonight?'

Her mother paused again. 'I've been missing you,' she said in the same unreal voice.

'I'm sorry, darling. I'd no idea – I wish – '

'Yes?' said Mrs Michaelis. She was not of the generation that fingers things on a mantelpiece, but Karen could see her eyes in the mirror, uncertainly moving from object to object in the reflected room. A yellow rose on the mantelpiece suddenly shed its petals, but did not make her start.

Karen said: 'I've been with Evelyn, you know. Evelyn Derrick' (naming a studio friend her mother had not met and who was out of London). 'We went through Kent in her car. I told you, didn't I?'

Mrs Michaelis's hands made the folds of her dress rustle. She said: 'Yes, I think you did. I – I wasn't sure of the name. Your friends have so many names.'

Karen saw reflected a smile she did not quite know, as though someone else were imitating her mother's smile. She came up, ignoring the barrier defiantly, and put an arm round her mother's waist, as she used to when she was small. Mrs Michaelis turned inside the arm, like a statue moving, to look at her daughter closely but from a distance. Karen smiled at her, and they stood there rooted in the deep white hearthrug till her mother said: 'Well kiss me and go to bed.'

They kissed. Karen breathed the familiar lilac scent and set free a strand of her own hair, smiling, from her mother's paste ear-ring. Mrs Michaelis turned to go to the door. 'I *am* tired tonight,' she said, 'I think it must be the rain. Will you put the lamps out and put the guard on the fire? Your father has gone to bed.' She went out, unexpectedly shutting the door. Karen, on her way to put out the first lamp, stopped to take a cigarette from the box: her hand shook. With eyes fixed on the lamp she intently listened – she heard her mother going *downstairs,* not up, with unknown cautious steps: a thief in her own house. After a minute down there

Mrs Michaelis came up again; re-passing the drawing-room door she went on up, with calm firm steps and a swishing of stiff silk. When she heard her mother's door shut, Karen put the drawing-room lamps out, crossed the landing and looked down into the hall. She must take Ray's letter tonight, or they would wonder. She went down, flicking on, to support herself, the stairs lights. Ray's letter was there, alone. Why did it look alone? The telephone pad had gone. Why had her mother gone down to move the pad?

Going into the morning-room, Karen found the pad back on the bureau, where it lived. But it was blank: the message had been torn off – and torn off unprecisely, leaving an edge jagged. The blank pad was scored with curves where writing had dug through; the sheets were thin, her mother's pencil emphatic. Karen stared at it; then, bringing the pad nearer to the light, she took the pencil and traced her mother's dinted writing. What she read was: Karen. 6-30 Saturday. Evelyn Derrick rang you up to talk plans for next week-end. She says will you ring her up on Monday when you are home, before she leaves London?

Nothing was said. On Monday there was no rain but it was a vapoury, close day. Mrs Michaelis had breakfast in bed quite often; on Monday morning she did. Karen did not go out that day; she did not dare to take her eyes off the house. Mrs Michaelis came down in a hat and went straight out. The telephone and the doorbell went on ringing: when Mrs Michaelis came in three guests arrived for lunch. Then a hamper of white peonies arrived from the country, and Karen settled these in bowls in the drawing-room while her mother sat writing note after note. Uncle Bill Bent came to tea half an hour too early: he was staying at his club, which was what he preferred, he said, but Mrs Michaelis felt anxious about him. He sat rigidly in his chair with eyes glued unconsciously to the mantelpiece, while his sister-in-law told him about the Flower Show; once or twice he glanced at her hand moving among the tea-cups; his lids were red, you could see that he often cried. When he left at six o'clock

Karen walked with him to the bus. When she came in, Mrs Michaelis called over the banisters, asking her to help to go through some things for a gift sale – lace, fans, Indian jewellery. This they did in Mrs Michaelis's bedroom: the tea-coloured lace gave out an orissy smell, the white, silver bangles were sent down to be polished. Painted fans fell open, lovely and rotten. Karen and her mother, lace and fans on their knees, talked over Uncle Bill and what there was to be done for him. Mr Michaelis came up with the evening paper, which he had brought to read Karen the cricket news from. He was glad to hear that his daughter was not going out, for once, and that they were to be alone for dinner. Over the soup, he was just beginning to ask Karen whether her week-end had been enjoyable when Mrs Michaelis suddenly brought out a long letter she had had from their son Robin. So that went no further. Karen felt like a wound-up toy running perfectly, till her father asked why she looked pale. Mrs Michaelis said: 'Nonsense, Robert, that is only the light.' An unnatural reflection did, in fact, come from the park trees. 'It makes *you* look pale, for instance, but I know you are not.' Mr Michaelis asked to have the candles lit. It was some time since they had all spent an evening together, and Mr Michaelis said it was pleasant being unpopular. He looked at his wife's arms reflected in the table, and at his daughter, shining now the candles were lit. Braithwaite brought in, for dessert, the first dish of English strawberries; they observed that it would soon be the longest day. Upstairs, the drawing-room was full of damp after-glow. Mr Michaelis and Karen played piquet; Mrs Michaelis opened the piano. Her touch was surer than Aunt Violet's, but less disturbing. Later, she left the piano and sat down beside her husband to watch the game. Once or twice her mute eyes rested on Karen: they kissed good night on the stairs. Nothing was said.

Nothing was to be said. This was like being a dog in a house in which they are packing up quietly, or a sick man from whom it is kept that he is going to die. If a silence rears its head, it is struck down like a snake, but with a light smile, as though you had struck the head off a grass. Life went on very fast, like a play with no intervals; actors, flagging, over-act, the trying lights are not lowered. Karen was no longer compelling the house with her eye: the house with its fixed eye was compelling Karen. She performed on in dreamlike, unreal distress. Even Braithwaite's tortoise face looked violently guarded. Karen saw what was ruthless inside her mother. Unconscious things – the doors, the curtains, guests, Mr Michaelis – lent themselves to this savage battle for peace. Sun on the hall floor, steps upstairs in the house had this same deadly intention to not know. To the studio, in the streets, this careful horror pursued her; she could not see traffic without seeing with what overruling coldness things guided themselves. After that first Monday, the week got speed up and went triumphantly over her like a train. Not a word from Max, not a cry from Naomi.

Karen ran into Evelyn Derrick, who said: 'Has your mother got anything on me? She sounded odd when I rang up.'

'Oh?' Karen said. 'No. She may have thought you were somebody else.'

Remembering how naturally Aunt Violet, sitting on the ivied parapet, had looked at her, she wished she were here now. So much has happened to both of us since then. But perhaps she foresaw that; she knew too much to be alarmed.

It was six o'clock on Friday when Uncle Bill, who never liked the telephone, rang up, spluttered and said he could not dine tomorrow; he would have to be catching the Irish mail tonight. He had decided to go home, back to Rush-brook, he said. Karen answered the telephone in the study; Mrs Michaelis was there in her husband's chair, looking through *The Spectator,* which had just come.

'What does Uncle Bill want?'

'He can't dine tomorrow; he's going back to Rush-brook.'

'What can one do? I wanted to do so much. I know it is wrong to feel this is very annoying of him. I suppose he liked coming here. But one always felt – '

'Perhaps he *did* really want to talk about Aunt Violet.'

'No, that simply upset him. When I spoke of her once he cried, then looked so wretchedly mortified.'

'But perhaps he did want that.'

'*You* might have talked to him, then, Karen. You were with them last.'

'I can't talk to anyone.'

'Don't be so silly, Karen.'

'Mother, how much do you mind about Aunt Violet?'

Mrs Michaelis sat nobly in the armchair, eyes fixed on the second page of *The Spectator,* behaving as she had behaved in August 1914. She said with unshaken innocent simplicity: 'It is the idea of her not being there, I suppose.'

She dares not look up and say: 'You transgress,' though she feels that; she won't ask why I ask. Her resistance is terrifying; she would rather feel me almost hate her than speak. The good morale of our troops won the war. Karen looked at the green lampshade that had been alight when Max rang up. She is full of love, she thought, she protects me. She tore up Evelyn's message – but was that love? Love would have made her say: 'Where *have* you been, really?' Love is obtuse and reckless; it interferes. But when mother does not speak it is not pity or kindness; it is worldliness beginning so deep down that it seems to be the heart. Max said: 'Why are you running away from home?' Now I know. She has made me lie for a week. She will hold me inside the lie till she makes me lose the power I felt I had.

'Mother – '

Mrs Michaelis looked up in such a way that Karen knew if one met her eyes one would weep. Dread of chaos filled the room, so that Karen's heart weakened; for the first time since Sunday she thought: What have I done? What has made home such a shell? After all, they were trying to keep me safe.

'On Sunday night, when – '

Mrs Michaelis put a hand to her face. 'You know I never ask you to tell me everything, Karen.'

'On Sunday night when I came in, I really did see Ray's

letter. I left it where it was because I felt bad, because I am not going to marry him.'

'I think you will want to, Karen,' said her mother.

'When I first came in, there was a telephone message beside the letter. I didn't look at it either. I left them both there.'

'Someone rang you up, perhaps.'

'I did not look at the message or see it was from Evelyn before I went upstairs. When I went down for the letter the message was gone. Why?'

'If you would not tell me the truth, I did not want you to have to.'

'Of course, I was not with Evelyn, as you could see. I met Max Ebhart.'

'I don't understand. In Paris?'

'No, at Hythe. We wanted to meet again. Now I am going to marry him.'

Mrs Michaelis thought this over a minute. Then she said: 'But then, why didn't he come here?'

Karen paused also. 'It was too far,' she said.

'So you went more than half-way to meet him,' said Mrs Michaelis in a strange voice, as though she were half asleep. 'Apart from anything else – isn't he marrying Naomi?'

'I haven't thought of her.'

'Then perhaps you have thought of Ray – Karen, *what has become of you*?'

'What did you think had become of me when you tore off that message?'

'Have you written to Ray?'

'No.'

'I'm glad. Then don't write; wait till he comes home.'

'You mean, you think this will pass?'

'It's some kind of dream, Karen darling.'

'This is not a dream. But I've been asleep for years.'

'Sit down. You're not yourself. You are trembling.'

'Well, *say* something, Mother.'

'One cannot even discuss this.'

'You think it is horrible.'

Mrs Michaelis, turning round in her chair, looked out fixedly at the low windows of the mews. The world was unmoved. She said evenly: 'It would be horrible if it were a fact. As it is – you have had wild ideas ever since you were a child, you know; it was always odd; in some ways you were so sensible. You are younger, too, than you realize – and yet in ways older; you must have been missing Ray, and wanting to marry him more than you knew yourself. No one admits how trying long engagements are. And his not being here has made things take this form. In a year's time all this will seem unaccountable; when you are married you will want to forget it ... Has Max Ebhart written to you, then, since he was in London?'

'No.'

'But then how – ?'

'He rang me up one night; after that we met at Boulogne.'

Mrs Michaelis thought over this, too. 'You have put yourself in a false position,' she said. 'Because you are more innocent than you realize, and have grown up in a world where people behave well, I think you cannot see how you must have seemed to him. You can't see into the mind of a man like that. But apart from anything else, can you not see that a man who is treating Naomi as he is treating Naomi, and who has let you behave as you have behaved, would not be likely to make you a good husband? ... Have you heard from him since you have come home?'

'No. There are, there were – things to be done first.'

'Throwing Naomi over – yes.'

'Yes,' said Karen, without moving her eyes.

'I do not like saying this, Karen,' said Mrs Michaelis. 'But you have behaved like an infatuated woman, an "easy" woman and he is a very astute man. No Jew is unastute. Apart from being more beautiful and more ... more possible than Naomi, he can see for himself that you are very much wealthier. He knows your background; he has been to this house. His reasons for wanting Naomi may have been disinterested – though not altogether, as Mme Fisher herself says. No doubt he valued her goodness – I cannot believe he is altogether bad. But now something better offers, he naturally jumps at it.'

'You mean, I offered?'

Her mother did not speak.

'I realized when I went to meet Max,' said Karen, 'that everything that could be *said* was on your side.'

'As I said, we will not discuss this,' said Mrs Michaelis, 'you will see a year hence that there was not much to discuss. So that it must not make us enemies, Karen. Shall we leave it at this – that you promise to take no steps, not to write to Ray or – or this other man for a month?'

There was a pause. Karen glanced at the telephone. Then she said: 'Very well.'

Her mother let out a little quick sigh. She sat back in her chair, facing the shady study as she had faced the window, the afternoon she heard of Aunt Violet's death, eyes closed, but closed so calmly that it was startling to see tears escape from under the lids. Tears coursed their erratic way down her cheeks. In her face, old for the first time, a stubborn majesty showed.

Calm tears do not ask for pity. Karen said: 'Is this the worst you could possibly hear, Mother? Is this what you dreaded when you tore up the message?'

Mrs Michaelis, not liking the damp inconvenience of tears, patted them off with her handkerchief, unembarrassedly. 'I suppose so,' she said. 'I was foolish. I have not been sleeping so well. I suppose Aunt Violet's death was bad for me. You see, once one thing has happened – If I had had more courage, this week might have been different. But it seemed to me that a thing that made you not speak the truth – This week has been so unlike us.'

'It made me not feel I lived here.'

'Karen – I mean, you can't mean to be as . . . as unkind as that sounds. Have you wanted to tell me, then?'

'You know you made that not possible.'

Her mother looked at the handkerchief with the tears on it; a whiff of lilac drifted across the room. She said: 'Then tell me, have you seen Evelyn Derrick? How did you know she had rung up?'

'I saw her, yes, and she said you sounded surprised. But I knew before that. On Sunday night when I got home, I found the pad with the message – that I had noticed but not read when I first came in – gone when I went down later for Ray's letter. I naturally wondered why. I found the pad in the morning-room. Your writing had dinted through and I was so puzzled, I traced the dents with the pencil to see what the message was.'

'That does not seem like you, either. Don't you – do you not trust me any more?'

'I broke up our being silent, didn't I? Otherwise –'

Her mother paused again. 'Yes. And so – that was what had happened?'

'Yes,' Karen said, 'that was all.'

12

Naomi's telegram came late that same night. When it was brought in Karen thought it might be from Max. It was not.

At the end of her telegram, Naomi had added that she would be coming to London tomorrow. She had not understood that the inquest and police investigations might keep her; next day she wired to say that this had been so. After that there was silence for some time. Karen bought French newspapers, which gave short accounts of the tragedy. Max had been only beginning to be important; passion did not appear to figure; elections were coming on and two big scandals in progress, so the French papers did not give him much space.

It was not till the end of July that Naomi got to London; she arrived at Chester Terrace late one afternoon. Mr and Mrs Michaelis had left London; Karen stayed on in the house to see Naomi. Mrs Michaelis had been unwilling to leave Karen; in these weeks since the telegram she had, as a mother, risen to her full height, wrapping up in gentleness and in a comprehension that sometimes came too close. Mr Michaelis had been told that Karen had lost a very dear friend – perhaps told even more, now they were safe again. His charming blue eyes softened whenever he looked at his daughter; he and she went about London together, as they used to do when she was a little girl. A frightening harmony set up in her home, more frightening than the tension of the week after Hythe ... Mrs Michaelis had certainly not wanted to leave Karen, dreading for her the ordeal of this meeting with Naomi. But she realized they had to meet – and better, she thought, in the quiet of Karen's home.

Naomi was still in black for her aunt. Today, she was shown up to the drawing-room, where Karen stood waiting, looking out at the park. As she put her arms round Karen and kissed her, Karen could feel Naomi tremble with pity.

'You have understood that I could not come before.'

'I did think,' Karen said, 'of going over to you.'

'I think that was better not; it was better here.'

'Your letter said all there really was to say? There was no – no message?'

'No.'

'I see,' said Karen.

Naomi looked round the drawing-room for which the dust sheets were waiting; small objects were already put away. 'Your mother is not here?'

'No, they are both away. Are you tired, Naomi? If so – we have all night to talk.'

Naomi, sitting down, looked movelessly for a minute at the knees of her black skirt, her hat with the black feather hiding her bent-down face. 'No, I am not tired,' she said recollecting Karen's questions. 'Will you hear now? How much do you know?'

'I found the account in some papers, then there was your letter. That is all I know.'

'Then – ?'

'Yes.'

'The Friday night before, Max had said to my mother

that he would be out of Paris over the week-end. He was not at our house that day; they talked on the telephone. Then on Monday I had his letter, written on the steamer and posted in Paris after midnight; he told me of his decision and said he would come to see me if I wished. I did not wish this, and did not know how to reply. So I did not reply. On Tuesday evening it appeared to my mother that I was ill. She came to my room; there is no lock to my door. She connected my illness with Max, whose handwriting she had seen, and pressed me for news of him. I told her that he and I would not, after all, marry; she was very kind and gave me a sleeping draught. It appears that later that night she wrote to Max, bidding him come and see her. He refused. I had observed for some time that he dreaded to be with her. But he again wrote to me, saying he had a great wish to see me again at least once. This letter my mother thought it right to intercept; she told me I was not in a state to receive letters. I do not know if I was ill, my mother declared I was; she made me keep to my room, which perhaps made me more ill. She told me that the two American girls had commented on my state. So I saw no one but her; she was with me constantly. She brought Max's second letter to me, open, and said I should do right to grant him an interview. She represented to me that he was dependent upon me; she believed him, she said, to be in a state near dementia, and said it was in my power further to injure him, if I did not grant him the interview. She said his moral need of me was unchanging, and that my love for him should make me more than myself. "He has his life to live, and you can restore him," she said. I said: "He is not alone, he is going to marry Karen." She had not known that till then; her manner changed, but then she looked at me smiling, and said: "See him for both their sakes. Do you want to poison his love for her?" She stayed by me while I wrote to Max saying yes, that I would see him, next Friday afternoon. Then she said I should rest now and gave me another draught that I did not want, but I drank it. She took my letter away.

'On Friday before six I went down to wait in the salon.

The American girls were out; I did not know Mariette was out also till Max rang and I heard my mother go to the door. She brought him immediately to the door of the salon, saying: "You must not stay long; Naomi has been ill." Then she went out, shutting the door: I did not ask where she went. Max looked ill; I tried to do what I could for him. It was evident that for nights he had hardly slept. We spoke of you and our love for you. When he began to be calmer, he told me that the difficulties of his situation with regard to you and your family had been preying on him. I said I was certain anything could be made possible. He spoke of a dread of being fatal to you.'

'Did he tell you everything that there was to tell?'

Naomi made a slight movement. 'Yes,' she said. She looked unthoughtfully, steadily at the window beside which Karen stood, and Karen again remembered Max's saying that Naomi was like furniture or the dark.

'Knowing my love for you, he expected that I would judge him. I said you, Karen, must have done as you wished; it did not seem strange to me. I reminded him how I could not have been content to marry until you and he had met again at least once. I reminded him of our happiness in the garden, we three, in the garden of my aunt's house. I believe that he took my hands. If I had been ill, I was still ill, for I felt weak, and sat down on that chair by the window where I sit to sew. He began to attack his own nature. "What she and I are," he said, "is outside life; we shall fail; we cannot live what we are." I said I believed love to make any life possible. "She does not know me, she does not know me," he said.

'All the time he spoke, I could be conscious of nothing outside him. But then he started, listened, turned white, then stepped to the door and suddenly opened it. My mother stood outside. She must have crept back or never gone away. She would have heard everything. You know our hall is dark and she wears black; I only saw her face, which seemed to be hanging there. When he opened the door she smiled and came in calmly, with the quiet manner she has when there is no more to know.

'I saw then that Max did not belong to himself. He could do nothing that she had not expected; my mother was at the root of him. I saw that what she had learnt about you and him pleased her, that she had pleasure in it in some terrible way. Her eyes were bright, she was smiling. She said: "This has been enough, Naomi, you must rest now. Go, now." Max looked at me like someone through bars in a death cell; to part is to leave him to what must be. The law takes you away. First, his eyes would not let me go; I stood by the door. Then my mother said to Max: "So with Karen you have already secured your position." He looked at me and said: "Go!" He stood with his back to the mantelpiece; after that I saw that my presence martyrized him. So I went. They were silent till I had shut the door. I went upstairs: the door of the room that used to be yours was open; the American girl who had it had left dresses about and I remember that I put them away.

'I do not know how long I was in her room. Wherever I looked, I saw Max's face as he stood opposite my mother, after his love for you had fallen into her hands. When I went to the head of the stairs I could hear her voice. Because I was ill, I began to tremble and sweat, and went back to your room. I saw then, that evil dominated our house, and that the girls who were with us should not be here. By the bed I saw a photograph of a house with white pillars, and of the young man the girl who slept here was to marry. Either my eyes suffered or it began to be dark: there was darkness on the photographs. Then I heard the salon door open and Max go out through the hall; the step was not like his own. It seemed to me that he fumbled with the street door; I heard the street door open and strike the wall, but I did not hear it shut. After that it was strange that I heard no movement anywhere in the house. I do not know what I feared. I began to go down. Our street door was wide open and three or four people stood out there in the daylight, staring at our doorstep. I felt they had come to attack my mother. When they saw me on the stairs their voices stopped. Not facing them, I went in at the salon door.

'My mother was there. She was as though she had fallen across the sofa, with eyes half shut and no colour in her face, but I looked at her with no pity.

'If she had not been conscious, my standing there made her so, and she looked at me. I saw then that all her life her power had never properly used itself, and that now it had used itself she was like the dead, like someone killed in a victory. Her lips were stiff and she could not speak at first; then she said: "Go after him," and when I still stood there she said: "You fool, he is dying." I thought she meant in the spirit. But she moved herself on the sofa and, with a frown like she has when someone spills wine or ink, made me look at the mantelpiece. The room is not light, and till then I had looked only at her. But then I saw his blood splashed on the marble, on the parquet where he had stood and in a trail to the door, smeared where I had trodden without knowing. I saw his penknife with the long blade open, fallen between where he had stood and where my mother sat. She said: "He cut his wrist across, through the artery, to hurt me." Her eyes turned up, going white, and I then ran to the street door. I saw then why they all stared at our step. Then a police agent pushed through the crowd quickly, to question me. A taxi stopped outside the crowd and the American girl who had your room then ran to me. When she saw our step she became faint. I said: "He is somewhere: quick, you must let me go." What you read in the papers is all the rest, Karen. When Max came out our street must have been empty; you know, for minutes together sometimes it is: so few people pass. He must have stood a minute on our door-step; then, holding his wrist and muffling it, for there was no trace of blood in the street, crossed the street to the mouth of that alley between the two studio walls. At the end of that he fell down. As no trace led us there, when we came to him it was too late, which was as he wished.

'That evening I sent the American girls away. When that was arranged, I went back to my mother. She was not easy to be with. But even if the police had not delayed me, I could not have left her to come to you, as I had wished, next day.

183

That first night, she was more than herself, she was made of iron again; she made me go to bed but walked in my room all night. She kept stopping by my bed saying: "Weep – why don't you weep?" I had sent you the telegram, dreading (though I see now that this was foolish) the English papers next day. She had seen the telegram go; she said "Karen will weep." When I had lain some time I said: "Why did you reproach him?" She said: "It was commendation he could not bear. I was commending him when he took his knife out. He struck myself, himself, my knowledge of him." She said his attack on himself had been, however, so quiet that when it happened she did not understand. She had seen the knife in his hand but thought he was playing with it; he had been weighing it on his hand deliberately while he had been listening to what she said. The force he used took so little movement; she said: she only saw him frowning, then blood flowing. When she had told me this she stopped and smiled and said: "He needed so much to escape." After that she was calmer; she put out the light and lay down on the sofa at the foot of my bed. She said: "Weep if you can, sleep if you can; I will not leave you alone." But next day she was ill. She made me stay close to her, saying that till I could weep I ought not to be alone. For some days after that we did not go out, because of the people who came to stare. Since then, when we go out we walk together. My mother cannot be left but says, always, that it is I who must not be alone. The police inquiries were not too difficult for us. Max was found to be much in debt, and pressure of his work, since we had returned from London, had been like fever with him: I remember that when he came from work to see me his eyes used to be like a night-bird's forced into the light. They attributed what had happened to debt and strain. In the court, two colleagues of his said they believed his brain, though brilliant, to be unsound. A friend of his who was called said he believed Max incapable of repose and had for long anticipated a breaking-point. Pleasure itself fatigued him, his friend said. A woman who had at one time been his friend said she too often found him nervous and desolate.

She said one had hoped much for him from a marriage. Directed beforehand by my mother, I admitted anxiety as to his nervous health, but said there had been no trouble between us two. For the inquiry, I remained his fiancée. My mother said his nervous crisis had been precipitated by her pressing questions – with regard to my welfare in the approaching marriage – as to the exact state of his money affairs. She added that, though one could hardly reproach oneself for a mother's anxiety, she regretted not having seen he was already overwrought. Nothing found among his papers cast doubt on what we had all said. The police, satisfied, closed the inquiry.'

'Were you ill then, Naomi?'

'No; my mother was ill, which occupied me. All the time I had on my mind that I must get to you, and I could not.'

'I was all right,' said Karen – 'unless you were wanting me, too?'

'Yes, I was. That was it.'

'I have never helped you . . . I see why there was no message, he did not expect . . .'

'No. It was not his will; it was a passionate act.'

'Yes, I see now.'

'Till he found her outside the door, he had foreseen nothing.'

'Even if he had foreseen, even if you had been with him – there would have been no message.'

'Surely, surely – for you?'

'Not after that. Whatever your mother said, it must have turned me to dust for him. *You* she couldn't have touched, but he had given you up. She turned everything he had left to dust; then, I expect, said: "You have done as you pleased." It may have killed him to see his love for me in her hands; but he had given you up by his own will. That was where she had him. I told Max once that she loved him; her age can only have made that more terrible for her, and made her more relentless. She saw him love you, then me: she only had her own power – No, I am wrong, though: it was her power she loved. That time it overreached itself; that was all

185

'. . . I did want you to tell me everything – but I wish you had not. Some of it, but not all. After all, it was lived through once: that is enough.'

'It all happened; I still cannot divide one part of it from another. Have I told you too much? I cannot tell where to stop, now I have become, myself, familiar with this.'

'If you bore it, I cannot see why I shouldn't. But, you see, I am going to have a child.'

Though Naomi stared at Karen, her already dilated eyes altered so little that Karen thought at first that she did not understand. This was not so – but Naomi's calm had, since her story began, been pitched so high that nothing more could affect her. The fatal house in Paris still so possessed her that nothing was real that happened outside that. If she saw Karen changed or pale, she saw this in a dream. Karen, who in these last weeks had fainted twice, saw that frightening edge of blackness begin to close round the room, and put a hand to her head. Naomi, with a quiet look, went past to open the window. 'Let us be quiet then; you must not be upset.' She instinctively looked round the room for something to offer Karen, but everything was dismantled, everything said: Gone, gone.

Karen said: 'No, I'm all right.'

Naomi paused for a minute to make certain. Then: 'What shall you do?' she said.

Karen said in a dry, matter-of-fact voice (already knowing her plans), 'Travel with you as far as Paris tomorrow. Then go on somewhere else, I am not quite sure where, yet; I think somewhere in Germany. I drew money out of the bank this morning, and can get more when I know where I shall be. From wherever I am, I shall write to mother, telling her I shall stay abroad for a year. I shall ask her not to ask why; if she does ask I shall tell her. I ought to feel more than I do, but I cannot feel. If there is anybody I cannot bear this for, it is my father. If mother knows she may help, so that he need not know. After all, she *is* my mother: surely one cannot have children without seeing that anything in the world may happen to them? Nothing makes life safe – I don't think this need hurt her from the outside; people she knows are not suspicious or prying; they take for granted everyone is all right. "Such things do not happen." They can think my engagement being off has upset me, and that I am travelling, or working abroad, to distract myself. Girls often do that. Or else ill – no, that would not do: love has never made anyone in our family ill . . . When I say this, it all sounds ordinary, doesn't it? In ways, you know, Naomi, I should like very much to be ordinary again. But I cannot remember myself before this happened . . . I am glad not to have to be here when Ray comes home.'

'I had been thinking you might marry him.'

'I began to think so, too, some days after your telegram. It began to be what I wanted most. But finding this is to happen makes that impossible. So I must not think of that any more: apart from anything else, with his future, Ray has to have an irreproachable wife. When he hears nothing more, and comes back to find me gone, he will have to see, I suppose, that my letter breaking things off did really mean what it said.'

'Does he not agree to "No"?'

'No,' Karen said wearily. 'Since I wrote last, his letters have been from a different man. He sees what he wants now. He used to force me to reason; now he won't let me, he refuses to listen. If he had made me feel *that* Ray from the first, what happened might not – Why do we talk about him? We might not have been happy.'

'I think you should tell him.'

'My dear Naomi . . .'

'I think you should tell him.'

'Oh, you talk like a mystic: try and understand people! I want help so much. All we have been discussing is so immediate, just the next few months. I can see myself through that. But after that? This child, don't you see, may live seventy years. I want him to be born: if not, I suppose one could stop it. Now, his birth is what I want most: why should Max leave nothing? But I must see some way for him to live. I could go off and live with him somewhere, I suppose. Somewhere where no one knew us – I cannot even imagine such a place. But if he is like Max and me he would hate that – hate exile, hate being nowhere, hate being unexplained, hate having no place of his own. Hate me too, because of all that. He would be better without me, in any place he could believe was his.'

'Have you at all thought *how* you should like him to live?'

'Yes, with you.'

'That is impossible.'

'Why?'

'Because of my mother.'

'Must you live with her always?'

'I was not going to leave her even for Max, you know.'

'Oh, Naomi! What is the good of saying you make me humble, when you know I cannot feel anything now? When feeling does come back, I shall begin to dread you. I have expected and taken everything from you. But everyone has, always – Why should your mother come first, though? She doesn't love you.'

'If she does not love me more, that is because she needs me. She does not care to need anyone so much. She is all mind and will, but she cannot make a *tisane* without flames running round the spirit stove. In the same way, when I am not there she burns herself out for nothing. If I could ever have left her – which, even for Max, I did not ask myself – the shock she has had from Max's death now makes it impossible ... She and your child must not live in the same house.'

'No ... What shall we do then?'

'We will think. Do you sleep well?'

'Only, I have bad dreams – Braithwaite is coming up; dinner must be ready. Mother told me to tell you that she is so sorry, only the kitchenmaid's left to cook for us.' Karen looked round the room, with its empty half-moon tables, in which the furniture sat so queerly on the floor. 'Doesn't the room look funny without flowers?' she said.

'I do not know it well.'

'I don't feel I do either.'

Karen picked up Naomi's dusty black overcoat from a chair and took her upstairs to wash. Naomi had been put to sleep in the spare room dressing-room, next door to Karen: a high press overhung the conventual narrow bed. As Karen left her to go to her own door, the idea of the night to come – darkness, comfort with Naomi in the echoing house – flooded her with peace for the first time.

On their way down, they passed Mrs Michaelis's door, open, and saw sheets on the mirror and on the bed.

Part 3

The Present

I

'YOUR mother is not coming; she cannot come.'

Leopold looked with his dark eyes searchingly at Miss Fisher who with her arms round him still knelt on the floor. He stood stone still inside her embrace. After a moment more, having felt him offer, simply by staying still, violent resistance to her – she let him go. He stood with his chin up, disengaging himself from her and from everyone. Miss Fisher sat back on her heels, then slowly got up. But she did not, even to Henrietta, look foolish, as women disregarded so often do. She did not know she was she; her body moved itself – till, all at once, the glance she cast round the salon seemed to be torn from her.

As for Henrietta, she went flat. She would grow up to date her belief that nothing real ever happens from Leopold's mother's not coming this afternoon. In spite of having been told she was to be taken out to look at the Trocadéro, so as not to be there when Mrs Forrestier came, she had been certain she *would* come in on all this somehow. Leopold would mention her name, his mother would say: 'But do tell me, who is Henrietta?' . . . When Miss Fisher had let Leopold go, Henrietta dared hardly look at him. This will not make him like me any better, she thought. She felt it was like Miss Fisher to have been so incontinent with bad news.

Looking down at his feet as they took each step on the parquet, Leopold walked to the mantelpiece. With his back to it, he suddenly faced Miss Fisher. 'I suppose,' he said coldly, 'that *you* are sorry.'

'I had hoped to see her, yes.'

'But you had been going to take Henrietta out.'

'We should have come in again.'

191

'Oh. Then what would you have done with Henrietta?'

'Leopold, Leopold *darling*, be more natural!'

'Why should I?'

Miss Fisher's exclamation made Henrietta burn. Leopold, however, was not embarrassed; she saw his mind gripping some kind of argument. There need be no question of saving Leopold's face; he did not think of his face, he thought of himself: he *thought*. Miss Fisher's emotion therefore did not offend him; in his own cold way he enjoyed dealing with it. Henrietta had not realized till this moment that two races, in feeling, go to make up the world, or how nonplussing it is when both meet in a room. No wonder today with Leopold had been difficult. If I had cried when he upset my dispatch case, he would have liked me much better, she thought. Picking up Charles she went to sit on the sofa, where she examined his ears to see if more stitches had come out in a manner that said: 'This is no place for you or me.'

Henrietta's resigned manner and retreat to the sofa made Miss Fisher remember, and look anxiously at her. Miss Fisher had been standing against the table, her hands hanging down, trembling, against her skirt; Henrietta's annoyed face must have made her, also, remember that there is more than one race, and quickly reproach herself. Those Chambéry carriage-drives with Mrs Arbuthnot and those sympathetic talks beside the lake must have passed through her mind, like traffic outside a silent room. So she said: 'Henrietta, where shall you and I and Leopold go to this afternoon?'

'I don't want to go anywhere, thank you,' Leopold said, surprised.

'I don't want to go anywhere, either,' said Henrietta at once.

'But your grandmother will be disappointed if you do not see Paris.'

'I shall probably see it some time.'

'I don't want to see it ever,' said Leopold.

'Oh, Leopold, what a pity!'

'I've seen Rome.'

'But – '

'No one wants me to see Paris. I only want to see important places. I want to see Moscow.'

'Some other day, I *know* you will see your mother!'

'I don't see why,' said Leopold.

'Something unforeseen must have happened. You know, even grown-up people cannot always do what they want most.'

'Oh! Then why grow up?'

Miss Fisher replied simply, '*I* never could answer any questions, Leopold.'

At this, Leopold looked mutely at Miss Fisher: for the first time Henrietta saw despair in his eye. She thought: If we stop arguing, he will weep. He wants some kind of fuss to keep going on. While she wondered what to say next, for Leopold to contradict or that should bother Miss Fisher, Leopold stooped to pull up one of his black socks. The dignity of his looks was all he had. Then he said: 'But didn't you know my father?'

'But he was older than you are when he came to this house.'

'You mean, he thought he knew everything,' said Leopold scoffingly.

His eyes, looking round the prim, vacant, crowded salon, showed that involuntary contempt for the dead – for their ignorance of the present, their impotence now – that nothing in Leopold softened to pity yet; asking: 'Who wanting really to know would have come *here*?' His small dark-coloured figure, solitary before the mantelpiece, swelled with content at his own ignorance of the past. Today was his own. To stay fully himself, he no longer needed argument; he could stop putting pressure on Miss Fisher. His dark eyes darkened, their pupils expanding. Yes, his mother refused to come; she would not lend herself to him. He had cast her, but she refused her part. She was not, then, the creature of thought. Her will, her act, her thought spoke in the telegram. Her refusal became *her*, became her coming in suddenly, breaking down, by this one act of being herself only, his imagination in which he had bound her up. So she lived outside himself; she was alive truly. She set up that opposition that is love. 'Yes,' he said, 'I shall see her some other day.'

'You know – ' began Miss Fisher.

'Only she was afraid – '

– Three sharp taps on the ceiling made Miss Fisher and Henrietta anxiously look up. (Henrietta, seeing the twist of incense, grey twilight across the foot of the bed.) 'My mother,' said Miss Fisher. 'She is impatient. She has been expecting your mother to come.' Through the ceiling, silent after the tapping, came the impatience of Mme Fisher lying up there. Some sort of alarm must sound in her senses the moment she was forgotten – which happened so seldom – sound, and start angry anguish, making her strike the floor. Miss Fisher looked at Henrietta confidentially, earnestly, as much as to say: 'In this house we have two implacable people: you, Henrietta, must do what you can down here.' Aloud she said to Henrietta and Leopold: 'I must go up to my mother.' She left the room, shut the door and they heard her going upstairs. Henrietta was left with Leopold.

'She doesn't sound like anyone ill,' she said.

'I had only imagined her.'

'Madame Fisher?'

'My mother.'

'Oh . . . But you must be disappointed; I'm awfully sorry, Leopold,' said Henrietta firmly.

'Are you? Why? I'm not, I'm excited.'

'I don't see why.'

'No, I didn't expect you would.'

'Then why say so?'

'Oh . . . Because you are somebody here.'

'Oh,' said Henrietta, looking at Charles again.

'Do you think *Miss Fisher's* natural?'

'Well, I suppose she must be.'

'Yes, I suppose she must be . . . She knew them both.'

'Leopold, I think you ought to stop being excited. It was all very well this morning, when something was going to happen, but now it hasn't happened I think you might calm down. I know you are being brave, but I think you are showing off rather. If me being here makes you show off I'll go and sit on the stairs.'

She got up from the sofa. Leopold said nothing but watched her till she had got as far as the door and put her hand on the knob. Then he said sharply: 'No. Don't.'

'I will: you give me the creeps.'

'Then I shall come and sit on the stairs too.'

'I do think you are beastly,' said Henrietta.

'Why didn't you go and see Paris? She said you could.'

'Because I was feeling sympathetic with you.'

'I don't call you sympathetic,' he said coldly. 'You get upset whenever I say a thing.'

'It's the things you say.'

'Well, I don't say them to you.'

'Then, my goodness, why – '

'I want to hear what they're like.'

'Well, I really did want to look at the Trocadéro, only Miss Fisher gave me the creeps too. I'm sure she is quite different from everyone else in Paris. I'd much rather look at Paris with somebody ordinary – if it comes to that, though, why wouldn't you go out?'

Leopold looked at her.

Henrietta pursued: 'You might just as well.'

'Because my mother is not here.'

Leopold, having said this in an experimental voice, stopped to hear it echoed, looking, meanwhile, self-compellingly at and through Henrietta, as though '*My mother is not here*', were written all over her – face, dress, hair – and he were forcing himself to read it again and again and again. Henrietta *became* the fact that he could not escape or bear. Her eyes, her chin, the brooch joining her collar, the red buttons down her stomach, her belt-buckle and her shoes each added pain of knowing to Leopold's eyes, which travelled down her steadily. But when Henrietta's hand, making another nervous move to the door-knob, reminded him that she was in fact, *Henrietta*, animosity made him more frightening still. You are here, she is not. Pressed tightly together, his lips went white. This collapse of his pride in his isolation left him without one ally. His hands went behind his back and she saw his shoulders shake. He became like a boy who is the butt of a dancing class. 'Well, *say* something!' he said.

She only clutched the door-knob.

When she could not speak, Leopold turned round facing the mantelpiece and suddenly ground his forehead against the marble. One shoulder up dragged his sailor collar crooked; his arms were crushed between his chest and the mantelpiece. After a minute, one leg writhed round the other like ivy killing a tree. The clock ticked away calmly above his head.

If it were just crying . . . thought Henrietta. The first sound torn from him frightened her so much that she began to count the white lines round his collar. At first each sob was like some terrible accident, then they began to come faster. He wept like someone alone against his will, someone shut up alone for a punishment: you only weep like that when only a room hears. She thought: But none of us are punished like that now. His undeniable tears were more than his own, they seemed to be all the tears that ever had been denied, that dryness of body, age, ungreatness or anger ever had made impossible – for the man standing beside his own crashed plane, the woman tearing up somebody's fatal letter and dropping pieces dryly into the grate, people watching their family house burn, the general giving his sword up – arrears of tears starting up at one moment's unobscured view of grief.

She could not know how sharply Leopold realized everything that at this moment perished for him – landscapes, his own moments, hands approaching making him unsuspicious. She had seen the country he had thought he would inherit – her certainty of it made it little, his passionate ignorance made it great – trees rounded, standing in their own shadow, spires glittering, lakes of land in light, white puffs from the little train travelling a long way. He is weeping because he is not going to England; his mother is not coming to take him there. He is weeping because he has been adopted; he is weeping because he has got nowhere to go. He is weeping because this is the end of imagination – imagination fails when there is no *now*. Disappointment tears the bearable film off life.

Leopold's solitary despair made Henrietta no more than the walls or table. This was not contempt for her presence: no one was there. Being not there disembodied her, so she fearlessly crossed the parquet to stand beside him. She watched his head, the back of his thin neck, the square blue collar shaken between his shoulders, wondering without diffidence where to put her hand. Finally, she leant her body against his, pressing her ribs to his elbow so that his sobs began to go through her too. Leopold rolled his face further away from her, so that one cheek and temple now pressed the marble, but did not withdraw his body from her touch. After a minute like this, his elbow undoubled itself against her and his left arm went round her with unfeeling tightness, as though he were gripping the bole of a tree. Held close like this to the mantelpiece he leant on, Henrietta let her forehead rest on the marble too: her face bent forward, so that the tears she began shedding fell on the front of her dress. An angel stood up inside her with its hands to its lips, and Henrietta did not attempt to speak.

Now that she cried, he could rest. His cheek no longer hurt itself on the marble. Reposing between two friends, the mantelpiece and her body, Leopold, she could feel, was looking out of the window, seeing the courtyard and the one bare tree swim into view again and patiently stand. His breathing steadied itself; each breath came sooner and was less painfully deep. Henrietta, meanwhile, felt tears, from her own eyes but not from a self she knew of, rain on to the serge dress, each side of the buttons that were pulled a little crooked by Leopold's hand. They stayed like this some time.

'Leopold . . .'

'What?' he said.

'Nothing.'

Leopold touched her belt and followed it round a little; for the first time his fingers had a reasoning touch. Then he turned, his eyes that had reflected the plane tree now reflecting her face flushed with tears. He looked at her with no thoughts. A strand of dark hair from the crest above his forehead had fallen down and lay on his white skin; he looked drowned, as though sea had been washing for some time over his unstruggling face and eyes unchangingly open between the matted lashes, ceasing to see. But then she saw consciousness march back into his eyes, which became Leopold's looking at Henrietta. Like a grown-up hand coming between their bodies, something outside put them gently apart. Leopold's arm round her loosened and fell away. Still unalarmed, they stood as they had been standing, but Leopold slid his hands into his pockets; she stared at the clock and the striped paper behind.

Miss Fisher must have stood by Mme Fisher, telling her what was not going to happen, but now they heard her once more above the ceiling, moving about busy with something else. Grown-up people seem to be busy by clockwork: even when someone is not ill, when there has been no telegram, they run their unswerving course from object to object, directed by some mysterious inner needle that points all the time to what they must do next. You can only marvel at such misuse of time. In this carpetless, sounding French house the rustle, patter and click of people being alive became, only, more audible: Henrietta knew it was everywhere. Leopold was more happy than Henrietta in having learnt already to keep this outside himself, more happy in having intellect. So he stood no more than noting the steps to which she listened, fatalistic but with a sinking heart, waiting for Miss Fisher to make inroads on her again. Soon the upstairs door did open; Miss Fisher was on the stairs.

Henrietta walked back defensively to the sofa. Picking up Charles, she acted the self she had been before. Miss Fisher came in, her face extremely perplexed.

'I hope Madame Fisher is better?' said Henrietta at once.

'Thank you – oh really, yes. She is wonderfully herself: nothing today has tired her . . . Leopold?'

'Yes, Miss Fisher.'

'My mother insists – my mother would like very much to see you for a few minutes. That is, if you wish, she says . . .?'

'I don't mind,' said Leopold. 'Shall I go up now?'

2

Mme Fisher's hand was lying outside the bedclothes, ready for Leopold's. He came to the head of the bed, on the wall, not the window side, and they shook hands. She stayed with her head screwed round his way on the pillows, and in the red half-dark they looked at each other gravely: one shutter was shut. Leopold had brushed back the strand of hair from his forehead and straightened his square collar before coming up.

'Well, Leopold,' she said, 'this is hard, I am afraid.'

'My mother being delayed?'

'Your long journey for nothing.'

'I liked the journey.'

'You have been long enough in Italy, I expect?'

'It depends where in Italy,' said Leopold.

Mme Fisher smiled and, raising her hand a little, looked at it reflectively, as though glad life should have been renewed, for a moment even, by its meeting with Leopold's for this old friend that had nothing to do now but lie on a counterpane. Then regretfully she drew the hand back under the bedclothes, to signify that the forgotten old are chilly and must seek warmth above any other food.

So she lay rigid, sheets up to her chin, turning a little on one side to the red wall against which Leopold stood. 'Well, we meet,' she said.

Leopold said nothing.

'Will you sit down, Leopold?' said Mme Fisher. He looked at Miss Fisher's chair, moved the knitting off it and drew the chair closer to the head of the bed. Here he sat hands pressed palms down on the chair-arms, chin up and bare knees crossed, his attitude saying: 'Well?'

'You must not, of course, judge your mother,' said Mme Fisher. 'She always had courage, but could not always command what courage she had.'

'People change their minds,' said Leopold.

'My daughter says you ask curious questions: do you?'

Leopold thought over this with his eyes turned down. 'It depends who I ask.'

'You may ask me curious questions, but not plain ones. We – my daughter and I – are not to answer questions: that was made the condition of your coming here. So you must not embarrass me,' said Mme Fisher, smiling. 'No doubt you do not care for fairy-tales, Leopold? An enchanted wood full of dumb people would offend you; you are not the young man with the sword who goes jumping his way through. Fairy-tales always made me impatient also. But unfortunately there is no doubt that in life such things exist: we are all very much bound up in what happens. So you must be content to see me as so much gingerbread, or whatever you wish ... It is not easy for me to talk to you naturally, for fear of perhaps inadvertently telling you something you do not know and they mean you never to know.'

'Who are "they"?'

'Your good friends in Italy, my daughter, your mother.'

'But those people in Italy – *do* they know anything?'

'That is the point; they cannot wish you to learn in this house more than they know themselves.'

'People who knew me must not know I was born, and people who knew I was born must not know me?'

'Exactly,' she said, in the dry avid quick voice she kept for exact talk.

'No one except you here and, of course, my mother, knows I *was* born, then, do they?'

'And your mother's husband – or so I am told.'

'Oh ... Mr Forrestier?'

'This Mr Forrestier may have urged her to see you. He has an incalculably romantic mind.'

'But then why – '

' – Will you take Naomi's knitting off the foot of my bed?

On the table, perhaps: yes. I do not care for things on the foot of my bed.'

'I'm sorry,' said Leopold, moving the knitting. He sat down again and said: 'Did you know my father, too?'

'Fairly well,' Mme Fisher said. 'But you do not know of him.'

'I know one must have a father to have been born.'

'Oh, your American friends have told you so much have they?'

'I suppose so,' he said, indifferent. 'They told me once he was dead. That is true, I suppose?'

'Perfectly,' she said, nodding on the pillow.

'Then he must have known I was born.'

Mme Fisher deliberately shut her eyes, which till the moment before had been burning at Leopold like an old lion's out of their caves of bone. As though the strength she was saving by not looking had all gone with her voice, she said with energy: 'Never. He was at the time he died still more ignorant of you than it is generally wished you should be of him. In one thing, you have the advantage of him, Leopold: you know it is necessary to have a father, he did not know it was necessary to have a son.'

Leopold looked at the stretches of sheet between them, dyed grey by afternoon dusk. 'Then why did nobody tell him?'

'He was not there; he was dead.'

'But –'

'I think you must not ask me any more questions; your questions are curious in being so plain.'

'There aren't any more –'

Mme Fisher's chin moved on the sheet, derisive.

'To ask *you*,' he ended up with polite distinctness.

'Good,' she said. 'Then we shall not waste more time.' So, inside her tabernacle of bed-curtains, she relaxed to a hardly human flatness and stillness, in which to lie steadily watching Leopold – his fine eyebrows and narrow pale-skinned forehead tense with thought, his lashes cast on his cheeks, his unchildish deliberate and tactile fingers feeling their way over the padded arms of the chair, sounding creaks in the stuffing, stopping at every button. His blouse-cuffs fell away from his wrists, which she glanced at. Not an object in this unknown room had, since he came in, distracted his eyes a moment, but, sitting still, he knew of everything there. Everything, to the last whorl of each shell on the bracket, would stay sealed up, immortal, in an inner room in his consciousness. That her presence ran against him like restless water showed only in the unmovingness of his face. She re-read a known map of thought and passion in miniature.

She said: 'Have they told you downstairs that I am dying?'

'Henrietta said you might be.'

'But I have not been alive for nearly ten years.'

'Have you been in bed?' said Leopold.

'That does not matter. Wherever I am now, I do not feel and am not felt.'

'Do you not feel anything?'

'I am fortunate in being as ill as I am.'

Searching consideration of what she said, not awe or timidity, kept Leopold silent. He turned once to glance at the right chair-arm, to see for the first time what he had been touching so long. Then he said, in the exact voice that had a ring of her own in it: 'How do you mean, not been felt?'

'What would you mean?'

Leopold's eyes narrowed between their lashes; he looked towards Mme Fisher cautiously, penetratingly. 'People not knowing I'm there.'

'Then all you want, Leopold, is the exercise of a vulgar power, simply.'

Leopold's mind checked at the knotted sentence, like a horse refusing a blind jump. He thought his way round to the far side of it, calmly, then said: 'But till they do know, I cannot do anything.'

'Yes, you are quite right. But to have been born is to be present – though I find one may cease to be present before dying. For you or me, Leopold, to have been born at all is an opportunity. For you or me, to think may be to be angry, but remember, we can surmount the anger we feel. To find one-self like a young tree inside a tomb is to discover the power to crack the tomb and grow up to any height.'

'Does a tree do that?'

'They need not stay ignorant of you. That is in your hands. But you must grow faster, more strongly than other people. There is no question, for you, of having someone to cherish you. For the man it may be you may be, that your father was not, the father and mother have only been instruments. Their faces and names do not matter. By deluding themselves with each other, they served you without knowing.'

'Must I go back to Italy?'

'Why should it matter where you go immediately?'

'It does matter,' he said, raising his eyes.

Under the blankets, Mme Fisher's hands moved with muffled force at her sides. Pressing back among the pillows, arching herself weakly, she stared up at the canopy that was her sky now. Rapidly, she exclaimed under her breath.

'What did you say?' said Leopold, relentless.

'I said: "My God, it is terrible that you are still a child." '

'In French?'

She nodded, her eyes darkening inside their caves.

'Which you do not speak?' she said. 'Naturally.'

'No. Hardly. Only some words.'

'They have clipped your wings for you nicely, then,' said she.

'What made you say it was terrible, me being a child?'

Mme Fisher kept her smile and, with it, a frightening lightness of humour, like someone pretending she has not looked through a door. 'You overheard me,' she said, 'addressing myself to God, who for all I know may be sitting on top of my canopy, if Naomi has not already dislodged Him, dusting along the cornice with her feather broom. From what I hear of Him from friends who are *croyantes,* He takes an exaggerated view of things: one would naturally speak to Him in His own terms. In your and my terms, Leopold, your childishness is simply a pity for me – for me, solely: naturally I regret it. If you were less a child, I could enjoy more fully my short time of being alive again. As it is – yes, I may still say to you frankly: rather you as you are than some grown-up sot. But it is a pity for me: I am dying too early.'

'It is more a pity for me, if I must go back to Italy!'

'If you have to, you will go. As I say, it is not important.'

Leopold drew his head back; he looked at Mme Fisher like a child prisoner, not knowing whom to turn to, a cup of something doubtful being held to his lips. He stared; he seemed to suspect for the first time that she might be either mad or laughing at him. Then, pushing hard with both hands against Naomi's chair-arms, he broke out suddenly: 'Why?

'Why should I have iodine stung on my knees when I fall down, and see one of them on a rock the whole time I'm on the shore, and be weighed every Saturday like something to eat, and be asked about my ideas when their friends come, and have them whispering round when I shut my eyes in bed, and be taken away from Rome and not let drink wine even with water and told about Shelley the whole time? I'm glad he was drowned; I wish he had never been born. The servants laugh at them because they never had children, so they never let me alone, which is like finding ants in everything. When I am angry they whisper in other rooms and when I use dirty words they look away from each other. They show off to other people to make them think I am theirs. They keep trying to make me be things. Have they bought me, or what? Why should I have to kiss them when I wish every time I have to that their faces would fall off, like the outsides of onions.' When they walk about in the sunset not saying anything because of the sunset, or look poetically at things, their bodies look so silly. You can't say, "I don't love you" any more than you could say that to a sheep. They make me feel like a place with sheep eating on it the whole time. They are so pleased because I cannot remember anything else but them.'

'You see this all very plainly,' said Mme Fisher.

'Since my mother's letter came, I – '

'It might have been better if she had never written. When one has to live among sheep, exaltations are dangerous. I have lived among sheep, they have been my life; I have found that. How many times have I heard the door of this house shutting behind my friend – and each time it seemed the last time – then gone back to my sheep! Do you think I could not have struck the faces I saw then?'

Leopold only said: 'But you weren't theirs.'

Mme Fisher said in an open, reasonable voice: 'But look: they have been very good to you. What you say does not shock me, but, you know, it is shocking.'

'Why must I go back?'

'You and I,' said Mme Fisher, 'must not waste too much time rebelling.'

'Shelley was a rebel,' Leopold remarked bitterly.

She said decidedly: 'Shelley went beyond that. But to be quite oneself one must first waste a little time. It is that phase, no doubt, in a young dead man that your friends would enjoy. Let them like to cry for Shelley; it does no harm.'

'Because Shelley's dead. But *me*? I was never asked.'

'No, you were never asked: that is true. The unwilling helplessness that you had as a baby offered you to their hearts, before you knew. Until you were two, since not long after your birth, you lived by your mother's wish with a German friend of Naomi's, a lady with a family of her own. How you might have grown up there one cannot say. The lady died. Her sudden death made a crisis for Naomi: what was to become of you? Stress was laid on the fact that you must never come here. Your mother was not able to be consulted: that year, the second after her marriage, she was very ill from the birth of a dead child. Naomi, whose right to act in the matter you and I must not question, therefore acted alone. These three Americans whom you call sheep were relatives of a young American lady who had been for some time with us in this house. During her stay they had sometimes visited us, and so, happening to pass through Paris, they visited us again, at a time when my daughter's anxiety as to your future was at its height. She recalled having heard from their young relative that, being childless and disappointed, they had expressed the wish to adopt a child. So her thoughts flew to a plan. She knew their affairs were secure and their characters amiable, and she satisfied herself in the course of one interview as to their highly natural cravings of heart. Optimism, and a regard, which I do not share, for certain qualities, made my daughter fix upon the Grant Moodys as proper parents for you. For their part, they did not put out many inquiries; they appear to have been content to know nothing must be known. I have no doubt, myself, that they took the child to be Naomi's, but what she thought fit to tell them later I do not know. My daughter, as always, acted incontinently but, again as always, as she thought for the best. I played no part in the matter: if she appeared impulsive it was not for me to say – '

Mme Fisher broke off, moved on the pillows with wasting impatience, and slid one hand outside the sheet again. Downstairs, the street doorbell rang, somebody was admitted, but she and Leopold, eyeing each other closely, did not for a moment turn from the past. Her breathing was laborious; in her face, for a minute, appeared despair at having to go on. Then she pushed back the fatigue falling over her.

'As the result of her choice, you were brought up from Germany, made the appeal she hoped and soon after left for Italy with the Americans' baggage, like any puppy or kitten that has changed hands. No doubt the idea of Italy tempted Naomi for you. Your father and she (who at one time proposed to marry) used, I understand, often to talk of Italy, planning to travel there. She does not dread the friends of Shelley as you do. Also, no doubt, they promised her access to you, a promise of which – having been since then unable to leave Paris for longer than her little visit to Chambéry, where she met your friend Henrietta's grandmother – she could not avail herself. At all events, the arrangements she had concluded left my daughter Naomi in an exalted fervour. With fervour she must have written of it to your mother, as soon as health let your mother receive news.

Everyone being satisfied, it was not for me to question. Your mother, convinced by Naomi, whom she had always trusted, permitted the formalities of adoption, which made you these people's property, to go through. You and I must not judge her, then or today. Courage as much as passion made her your mother. Dread of the past and nervous weakness of body must have made her, later, grasp at what appeared to be peace. Dread must have made her shrink, on her own account or her husband's – whom she dared not wrong further – from knowing you. That must still be so, since she has not come today. That she must not love you was written on her heart. Since she loved your father she has changed very much, they say. Also, the death of her husband's child must have closed what heart she had against you, in panic. No doubt, too, she hoped to have other children. But I have heard lately that this may not be so.'

'So now my mother has no one?'

'No other child, no.'

He exclaimed: 'But how could she have? I never thought of another child.'

Mme Fisher did not reply. This last part of the story had laboured out in jerks, with agonized flaggings, and pauses that seemed not to know how they could end. That the halts were weakness of body, not overmastering feeling, was made plain to Leopold by her manner, which, by sustaining above the physical tussle its level of irony, made the story coldly continuous. That physical tussle was itself an emotion, behind which her purpose stayed as calm as his own. Only purpose could flog along a sick body or weight precarious breath with so many exact words. While she spoke, her eyelids slipped down with irresistible weakness; when she paused, only the sheet supported her dropping chin. Before the story was done, her face was a flaccid mask, the lips worked by some other agency. Her words showered slowly on to Leopold, like cold slow drops detached by their own weight from a tree standing passive, exhausted after rain.

Leopold, while she spoke, had sat with his eyes fixed on

her, defying every fact that came from her lips. When she
stopped and her face rolled away, blue-white on the pillow,
he thought she saw what had been in its full shame. He had
not, like Henrietta, seen this room as a sick-room since
coming in here: guarded from natural light, with fumey air.
Perhaps, since his own crisis in the salon, his senses were still
absent, or shut off. The sweep of the dark curtains framed
only her eyes as she lay, a magnet to him. Her being ill had
been simply part of her presence, her personality, something
put on by choice like a certain dress. If he now became conscious of her distress of body, with dismay seeing her ham-
pered for the first time, if he could *feel* now, beyond simply
knowing, how ill she was, and how illness martyrized her –
he diagnosed her as prey to one creeping growth, the Past,
septic with what had happened. Knowing this, how should
she not be ill? He saw life as a concerted attack on himself,
but noted she had been struck by one arrow too. After the
exclamation that she did not reply to, he said no more, but
sat with eyes reflecting the dull-white bed and the outline of
her body shaken by rasping breaths. If she still knows I am
here, she is not able to show it. At one time he was glad ...
His eyes went anxiously to the clock. I have been here a long
time, almost an hour; everyone has forgotten. Suppose they
take me away?

To leave her became unbearable. He looked at the veined
eyelids: her eyes stayed shut. If she is asleep she must wake,
if she is dead she must live again! You make my thoughts
boil: listen! Now *I* have more to say –

He heard voices through the floor, in the salon. A man's
down there; perhaps that is the doctor. Oh, Madame Fisher,
if that is the doctor they will bring him up and take me
away. He may say you have died of talking. Oh quickly,
quickly, quickly, before he comes! Do not seal me up again,
listen, listen! At Spezia when I am angry I go full of smoke
inside, but when you make me angry I see everything. If *this*
is what men come to women for, what is love, then?
Madame Fisher, listen – I could not help being helpless.
Nothing makes me belong to them. Open your eyes again;

make me see what I saw. You said I was not the young man with the sword, but –

Mme Fisher, as though assailed by Leopold's silent clamour, rolled her head his way, twitching her eyelids up. One curtain, coming untucked from behind the bolster, swept forward, cutting off what was left of daylight, making her pillow now entirely dark. She said: 'This is too late!'

'But let me stay!'

'However, do what you can – '

They were coming. The salon door opened; Miss Fisher came running agitatedly up. She came in, fixed her eyes on the bed immediately, then put her hand up to her lips. Then she signalled to Leopold, who stared stonily past her. 'Come along, dear,' she said in an urgent whisper. 'You must come now, at once. I have left you here too long.'

3

Once on the landing outside her mother's door, Miss Fisher's manner changed; she looked at Leopold collectedly.

'Listen,' she went on in a decided whisper. 'I must stay with my mother; she has made herself terribly unwell. You are not to blame; I was detained downstairs. I was detained unexpectedly – '

Leopold, looking past her through the banisters, said: 'Henrietta is sitting on the stairs again.'

'Well, I cannot help that: it is naughty of Henrietta, I told her to go and play in the dining-room. Listen – '

'Why can't she stay in the salon?'

'Someone else is in there – '

He immediately said: 'My mother?'

Miss Fisher, unnerved again, said sharply: 'Allow me to finish. No, it is not your mother. There is a gentleman there with whom I wish you to talk while – '

'Can't Henrietta talk to him? What's his name?'

'No name you would know. Henrietta has talked to him. Now will you please go down? Stop – ' She ran her eye over

Leopold, straightened his collar and gave an unnecessary touch to his crest of hair.

'Leave my hair alone!' exclaimed Leopold, backing. 'You've interfered quite enough.'

Miss Fisher's hand at once dropped to her side. She glanced at her mother's door: no explanation was needed. 'You must not accept all you hear,' she said steadily. 'Now go down. Quietly, please.' Leopold, starting contemptuously downstairs, looked back once to see her still facing the door, composing herself, preparing to go back again. He went on down, sliding his hand on the banisters. His head sang and he wanted to be alone.

He reached Henrietta, who looked up and said: 'Hullo?'

'Who *is* in there?' The salon door was shut.

'They said I wasn't to say.'

'Santa Claus, perhaps,' said Leopold bitterly.

'This is February,' said Henrietta, unmoved. 'Leopold, what did you think of Mme Fisher?'

'I don't know,' said Leopold, pushing past.

'Did she make jokes?'

'I don't know. I've got to talk to this man.'

'Yes,' she agreed primly, 'you ought to go on down.' He went on down.

Ray Forrestier had Naomi's leave to smoke. She had taken the lid off a white alabaster crock and, putting it upside down near the edge of the salon table, left it to be an ash-tray; they had no other now. He connected resourcefulness with Naomi, who had been resourceful the other time they had met.

When she had gone upstairs, he stood half-way across the room, wishing the room were likely to be empty for longer. He looked at the plush monkey propped up on the sofa, asking himself if this hideous toy could be Leopold's. The other child in the house, the unexplained Henrietta, had been turned out by Naomi after he had been shown in, and told to play in the dining-room: he strongly wished to believe the monkey hers. But if it is, she may come back for it, he thought.

Ray stood smoking his cigarette incisively, pinching the butt with his lips, sipping the smoke, turning to knock ash off into the marble lid. He felt as dry as cuttlefish all through. He had not met Naomi for nearly ten years, but it was not surprising that she had not changed. He remembered her as being calm and decisive, so the way she took his just walking in just now had been what you would expect. By not telegraphing to say he would be coming, he might, had Naomi been any other woman, have been saving his balance at the expense of hers. He had wanted to feel free. He had wanted to feel, till he came to this very door, that he was not *bound* in any way. He had stayed free up to the moment when he walked in. He stayed as free as he had been when he had picked up his hat and walked, without another glance at Karen, out of the Versailles door. He stayed free all the way here. So free, he had walked in. If this walking in *was* a shock, Naomi's nerves had rallied to it well. Was there so much, though, to rally to? He was here, that was all. The world had come to an end.

It seemed so likely that Leopold would be in the salon that the walking in and the seeing him had appeared one act, for which act he was keyed up when he rang the bell. Expectation of this had been so knit up with walking behind the fat French maid down the hall that when the salon door opened – 'When the pie was opened, the birds began to sing' – and *Henrietta* had started up, staring at him inside her falling fair hair, he thought they had all been mad: Leopold was a girl.

Yes, Naomi had taken his walking in calmly, making him feel how natural it was, as indeed it was. Had he not the right to present himself at their door like an inspector, saying: 'You have a boy here, my wife's son?' In fact, he had had only to say compactly: 'I've come instead of Karen,' for her to stare expectantly back with those eyes that would have been extraordinary if he had not been certain how calm she was, he was, they both were.

She had said next: 'Karen is where?'

He said: 'Versailles: didn't you see on the telegram?' Naomi then said: 'Oh, Versailles? Oh, I didn't look.' He said: 'She's not well – ' just that, not 'Not well in mind,' because that was not cogent, also because the staring girl Henrietta had not yet been ordered out of the room. By being not well in mind in the Versailles bedroom, Karen had done him one good turn – drained him into herself, so that nothing in him resounding or fluid was left, no nerves left and no blood, so that when he had had to come here, as he saw he had had to come here, he came as brittle and dry as dried cuttlefish. What else had been him stayed resisting, suffering with her in the hotel bedroom, or was perhaps now walking away among the trees in the park.

When Ray ground out his cigarette in the white lid, the lid skidded off the table to smash on the waxed floor. That is very odd, he thought, I must have pressed very hard. Going down on one knee to pick up the broken pieces, he thought: I behave like a man under a strain. The pieces of alabaster shook his hand. He thought: I am still free, I can still get out. I can go back alone and take up the old fight that makes us three all the time.

Henrietta, apparently, had not stayed in the dining-room. But the children's mutters he heard on the stairs stopped. Ray stood up and looked about for another ash-tray. His eye lit on the lid of one more alabaster crock, but the door opened and Leopold came in.

Ray was made conscious of his own height by the angle at which Leopold's eyes looked up. Leopold stayed with the door at an open angle behind him, crooking his arm round to hold the outside handle, spine pressed to the edge of the door, swinging a little with it nonchalantly. His eyes measured Ray with no kind of expression. But his nonchalance was, still, faintly polite: he had the resigned air of a child sent down to see someone.

Ray saw Leopold thinking: Oh yes, an Englishman! (It should be clear that Ray looked like any of these tall Englishmen who stand back in train corridors unobtrusively to let foreigners pass to meals or the lavatory, in a dark grey suit with a just visible stripe, light blue shirt, deep blue tie with a just visible stripe, a signet ring of some dull stone, trimmed spade-shaped nails, a composed unclear romantic evenly coloured face with structure behind it, a slight moustache two tones darker – and, if you look down, deeply polished brown shoes. He was the Englishman's age: about thirty-six. To make marriage with Karen entirely possible he had exchanged the career he had once projected for business, which makes for a more private private life. In business he had done well.)

Ray still held the pieces of alabaster, so Leopold looked to see what he had in his hand, then glanced at one piece Ray had overlooked on the floor, and at the ash scattered round it.

'I've just broken the lid of something,' Ray said.

Leopold's eyes of unsmiling intelligence travelled to the chiffonier on which the lidless crock stood. 'How did the lid come off?'

'I had it for an ash-tray.'

Leopold, with the smile so naturally like Karen's, said, 'It's marble, too.'

'You are Leopold?'

'Yes,' said Leopold vaguely.

'I'd better put these pieces . . .?'

'If you shake them, you'll drop them.'

Ray frowned at his own hand. He tipped the pieces quickly on to the table, then looked round to see where he could least unnaturally sit. Every line of the room, like a convent parlour, suggested an interview. So he sat on the sofa, budging Charles from its head with a quiet savageness. 'That's not yours,' he said, 'is it?'

'No, Henrietta brought it.'

Leopold, who had let go the outer door handle, now shut the door and advanced into the room. The same lack of reason to sit anywhere seemed to present itself to him also; he pulled out a chair from the wall beside the window and sat on it, crossing his black-socked legs. Looking across with his father's dark, unknown eyes he said detachedly: 'Have you come to tea?'

'Yes. I suppose so. Yes.'

Leopold leaned forward to study his knees attentively. Every movement he made underlined Ray's oddness of manner by making Leopold's consciousness of it clear; he behaved from now on with unnerving tact. The effect he had seen his eyes, and before that his smile, make had been so remarkable that his leaning forward said as clearly as possible: 'Of course, if you'd rather I didn't look –' He behaved as an actor might who, deprived of the lead for no reason, comes impassively round in front to watch someone else play his part, but then, at one or two moments, gravely lowers his eyes. Today was no longer his, but even as a spectator he could not yet become entirely cold. He said in the same detached voice: 'Miss Fisher didn't say what your name was.'

Ray, taking a cigarette, paused. 'I don't think you'd know it.'

'I don't know anybody in Paris,' said Leopold – 'Will you want another tray for your ash?'

Ray, with his thumb on his lighter but not pressing the cog, looked intently into the air between them, deciding whether to speak. He did not answer the question about the ash-tray; Leopold having waited, got up, went to the chiffonier and took the lid off the second crock. Coming across the room, with princely politeness he placed the lid on the sofa beside Ray, who was busy making his lighter kick. Instead of 'Thank you,' Ray turned his haggard direct eyes on the Karen-like small cleft chin, and said: 'Stop – stay where you are.' The reach of wax floor was gone for the first time. 'I was wrong,' he said, 'perhaps you may know my name. Forrestier . . .' His eyes fell to the knot on the front of Leopold's sailor blouse.

'Do you know my mother, then?'

'I –'

'Are you Mr Forrestier?'

Ray nodded. Leopold, seeing Ray's eyes transfix the knot

of his blouse, put up a hand to cover the knot, defensively. Staying close to the sofa, he shifted his balance on to his other foot with a creak on the parquet. 'Is that why you came?' he said.

'Yes. This seemed a chance to –'

'I came to Paris to see my mother, you know.'

'I know.' Ray leaned further back, letting his arm drop across the head of the sofa, to look straight at Leopold, with whom he was now on terms. His hand with the cigarette hung down forgotten; the cigarette presently burnt out.

'Madame Fisher said she was coming to please you.'

'Madame Fisher was wrong, then.'

'Then you wanted her not to?' said Leopold swiftly.

'I wanted her to decide.'

'Well, she did decide. Then, you see, she didn't come.'

'She's not well today.'

Leopold, without any change of expression, said, 'She dreads the past.'

Quotation marks were apparent: 'Who said – ?' began Ray, then stopped, feeling the charnel convent parlour contract round him. This little brittle Jewish boy with the thin neck, putting a hand at once wherever you looked, was the enemy: she was right. No wonder she shuddered on the Versailles bed, with the gloves she had put on to go to Paris, then pulled off, dropped on the floor, and the violets she had pinned on for Leopold pressed dead between her breast and the bed. When she suddenly would not go, she saw Leopold. 'You can't not go, now,' Ray had said, standing desperate beside her. But she only drove her knuckles into the pillow, deadly quietly: 'You don't know,' she had said. 'He is more than a little boy. He is Leopold. You don't know what he is.'

He did not know; she was right. His intense feeling for Leopold had used his inner energy, without letting, all these years, any picture form. Out of known and unknown he had not tried to compound the child. 'Our child would have lived if you'd wanted him,' she said once. 'But you wanted your own ideas more. All you wanted was Leopold.'

His and her life together was an unspoken dialogue.

SHE: I want to be back where we started.

HE: But that is not possible.

SHE: But I loved you the way you were.

HE: But I never was like that.

SHE: Yes, you were, you have changed. Why should what happened to me change you? It should be me that has changed, but I stay the same: you have changed.

HE: If I have, it is in loving you more than I did.

SHE: Because Max loved me?

HE: That may be.

SHE: Because I loved Max.

HE: That may be, too.

SHE: How much Naomi knew when she said: 'Tell him,' when she sent you to find me. But I did not agree to marry a mystic, a martyr. You feed your complicated emotion on what happened to me. For God's sake, is there no plain man?

HE: Was Max a plain man?

SHE: No; that is just the point.

HE: Perhaps you did not know him?

SHE: Yes. No. I don't remember. I never remember. It's time you stopped.

HE: I only remembered your coming back.

SHE: No, what you remember is taking me back. Kissing me with that unborn child there. That emotion you had.

HE: Did you want me to hate the child?

SHE: No, but – you know your kind of love appals me: mysticalness, charity. All I wanted then was to come back and be with you. I have been frightened ever since I stood with Max on the front and saw the lighthouse out there, that night.

HE: Did you want me to hate Max?

SHE: No, but – I came back to be with you. I want to be alone with you. Stop remembering.

HE: It is you who remember.

SHE: All I want is for us to be alone.

HE: We are not alone: there is Leopold.

SHE: Leave my child alone.

HE: I can't, because he *is* your child.

SHE: Because you love me?

HE: Yes.

SHE: Then why can't we be alone?

HE: Because he is always somewhere. Why should he miss you?

SHE: He doesn't know.

HE: But we never are alone, while you're dreading him. It is you who remember. If he were here with us, he'd be simply a child, either in or out of the room. While he is a dread of yours, he is everywhere.

SHE: Simply a child! He is more to you than that.

HE: Well, if he is?

SHE: Stop feeding on my experience.

HE: But I love the whole of you.

SHE: If you loved me as you used to, not complicated emotion, not mystical ideas, I could be natural again. I could be a natural mother.

HE: What it comes to is: you would want him if I didn't?

SHE: Yes, no, yes. The you I wanted wouldn't have wanted Leopold.

HE: Simply put up with him?

SHE: But he has been adopted.

HE: You gave me no chance there. You shouldn't have done that.

SHE: I was desperate after our baby. I saw nothing but failures. I couldn't face things.

HE: You should have told me, before you did that.

SHE: I liked him to go to Italy.

HE: You should have told me.

SHE: Am I not enough?

HE: You know that is not the matter.

SHE: Then what is the matter?

HE: We should have Leopold here.

SHE: I want to be back where we started.

HE: But that's not possible.

SHE: But I loved you the way you were.

217

HE: But I never was like that.

SHE: Yes, you were: you have changed. Why should what happened to me change you?

Such dialogue, being circular, has no end. Under silences it can be heard by the heart pursuing its round, and, though it goes on deep down, any phrase from it may swim up to cut the surface of talk when you least expect, like a shark's fin. Karen's resistance to Leopold and Ray's idea of Leopold hardened each time the shark's fin showed. Feverishly, she simulated the married peace women seemed to inherit, wanting most of all to live like her mother. In nothing spoken did he and she disagree. She could not do enough for him. Their life in London, their house in the country, their travels, were pictures with each detail deliberate and intense; their peace was a work of art. She was more beautiful, kinder and less exacting than the young girl he had first asked to marry him. If Ray in melancholy were ever detectable, it was taken to be the melancholy of a successful man. There is a touch of queasiness in many Englishmen's noble and honest eyes.

The happiness of the Forrestiers' marriage surpassed the hopes of those friends who had received the engagement with so much pleasure, that spring in London many years ago. As a couple, they were delightful to meet. They were a little envied, also sometimes held up to heady younger people as not having rushed into marriage: had they not suspended matters a year? No wonder it worked; they had been sure of themselves. It was understood that their childlessness, though an infinite pity, kept their companionship uninterrupted and close; when Ray went abroad on business she travelled with him. Karen's critics found her a little passive, but thought all the more of Ray for staying in love with her. The intimates of her youth saw Ray becoming prosaic and were impatient with her for deferring to him. They often wondered why she had given up painting, she might have done something – no one specified what. Not a soul in England knowing about Leopold, there was no one to take what would have been the middle view: 'He has been more than good, really superhuman. She is right to make any sacrifice, the child should never have been and not a breath of his name ought to trouble their marriage. It is hard on her, as things are, but it was much harder on him. One cannot expect everything of the best of men. As things are, the child is better off where he is.'

No one knew about Leopold. The husk of silence round him was complete. Even outside England, not a soul whose discretion was not absolute knew the facts of his birth. For Mrs Michaelis – with whom, after the terrible weeks in Germany, it had become difficult for her daughter to be – had died more or less peacefully not long after Karen's marriage to Ray. It was seen that the shock of her sister's death must have been greater than she herself had realized; doctors dated her break-up in health from this. After his wife's death Mr Michaelis, who knew nothing – not even the height of her greatness in passing anything off – came to live at the Forrestiers' country house, devoting himself to the garden when they were away. They were sometimes visited, also, by Colonel Bent, but he stuck on the whole obstinately to Ireland. Mr Michaelis's presence, when they were in the country, drove in deeper the vital silence between Karen and Ray – though at the same time, often, in the constraint of his company their unspoken dialogue most loudly marched its round, Karen's and Ray's eyes meeting, urgent with trouble, across the placid old man who so plainly regretted their childlessness. Karen's eyes would say: 'Look how he loved my mother. That is the love I wanted. *He* is the plain man.'

When, travelling, they might have been most together objects would clash meaningly upon those open senses one has abroad. That third chair left pushed in at a table set for a couple. After-dark fountains playing in coloured light, for no grown-up eye. The transcontinental engine, triumphant, with flanks steaming, that men and boys stop to look at when they get out at the terminus, while the woman hurries ahead thinking: Here I am. Cranes and fortifications. Someone being arrested, a good street fight. The third bed in their room at the simple inn. France being France at nights, with lights under trees, over tables, a band, an outdoor cinema. (But, after all, he has Italy.) A tale of blood in a guide-book. The quickening steamer-paddle churning the lake. The woman sitting unmoving, smiling at cramp, with a child's head on her shoulder. The man explaining how something works. Venice, New York, places seen too often, their marvel faded, crying out to be seen for the first time. Children's eyes excited and dark from sitting up so late.

Their dialogue was not entirely unspoken. Phrases from it made quarrels leave them trembling. When Karen lay awake beside Ray sleeping, she thought: Where is he? Who is with him now? When they both lay awake she thought: Is that what he wants so much? When they made love she thought: We are not alone, so this is not love; or else: He is pitying me. When she thought, she thought: Forgiveness should be an act, but this is a state with him. So he has not forgiven. He forgives me for wanting Max while there is my not wanting Leopold not to forgive me for. If I gave in to wanting Leopold, Ray would bring Max back. He won't let us be alone. He does not forgive.

But one afternoon in Berlin she stopped at a street corner, pulling her furs round her and staring at a tram. She said, 'Ray, I should like to see Leopold somehow. For an afternoon, even. If it could be arranged? I should like to see him alone, if you don't mind. Not where he lives: perhaps at Naomi's house. Do you think it could be arranged?'

– Leopold, who, looking at Ray, so defiantly and acutely, chin up, had said: 'She dreads the past.' That the phrase he had picked up and was using meant nothing to Leopold, meant nothing to Ray. A child knows what is fatal. The child at the back of the gun accident – is he always so ignorant? I simply point this thing, it goes off: *sauve qui peut*. No one could be less merely impish than Leopold. Behind the childish *méchanceté* Ray saw grown-up avengingness pick up what arms it could ... Karen's unalarmed smile appeared in Leopold's lips when he had said this, but his deliberate look was from someone else's eyes. Ray saw for the moment what he was up against: the force of a foreign cold personality.

'What do you mean?' Ray said bluntly.

'If I don't mean anything, why should you mind?' said Leopold.

'It wastes time saying things you don't understand.'

'Well, I've got to do something till I go back to Italy.'

'You waste my time. I didn't see why you should go back.'

'I belong to them. They adopted me. She said they might,' said Leopold implacably.

'Who said all that?'

'Madame Fisher.'

'So you swallowed it, did you?'

'Do you mean she tells lies?'

'When people are ill alone they think things crooked, you know. She's been ill ten years, on and off, and she's pretty old. She counts much less than you think.'

Leopold said calmly: 'Have you *met* Madame Fisher – '

Ray admitted he hadn't; upon which Leopold, shrugging, wheeled round on his heel to look at the mantelpiece, against which he had wept. He saw not the mantelpiece but a woman with long hair being propped up in bed to sign away Leopold, then his own head helplessly bobbing and rolling on that journey to Italy, like a kitten's or puppy's. Nothing said undid that. He understood that this Mr Forrestier had begun by wooing him, but now liked him less. This left Leopold cold; he wanted not just one ally but everybody's submission. Twitching a shoulder under his square collar he said, without turning around: 'Didn't you *know* my mother gave me away?'

'Not at the time. Later.'

'Then were you angry with her?' said Leopold, curious.

'Yes,' Ray said, without hesitation.

'But you love her, don't you?'

'Yes; that was why I was.'

'Oh . . . Did you say just now I needn't go back to Italy?'

'I said I didn't see why you should.'

'But don't I belong to them?'

'Turn round,' Ray exclaimed. 'I won't talk to your back.'

Leopold turned round. In the February afternoon dusk beginning to fill the room, the two eyed each other intently, but so impersonally that each might have been a photograph. Leopold thought wordlessly, like his mother: This grey man is a fanatic. Ray thought: It can still be done. Their immaterial closeness up to each other, the silence after Leopold had turned round, made their sudden common demand for an understanding tower outside this afternoon and this room. There was not a sound over the ceiling: Mme Fisher lay in rigid silence upstairs.

Leopold said: 'But, look – '

'I think that could be got round.'

'Then where should we be tomorrow?'

'We might stay somewhere here, somewhere in Paris.'

Leopold said: 'But you don't like what I say ... Had my *mother* been meaning I shouldn't go back?'

'I've no idea, I tell you.'

'What should we do in Paris?'

'Walk about, I suppose.'

'For how long?'

'I tell you, I've no idea.'

'And she'd be with us?' Leopold said, casual.

'I haven't – I don't know. Yes. Sometime. Of course.'

'She's where now?'

'Versailles.'

'Where the king lived – But then what?'

'It's no good keeping on asking me. I don't know myself.'

Ray, getting up, abruptly for such a big man, walked to the mantelpiece. Here he discovered the dead cigarette between his fingers, dropped it and lit another. His dropping the charred cigarette on to the speckless parquet startled Leopold more than anything yet. Ray moved again – to the window, where he stood behind the curtain, looking out at the tree. From now on it was Leopold who watched Ray, first each step he took, then that fanatic immobility. He was made conscious of someone's being consciously other than

Leopold. (He had felt other people *as* other only in opposition.) He had never seen a decision come at before, or been there when a mind went round like machinery in the dark. He had recognized impulse in grown-up people, never yet its adoption by the entire will. Vacillating outside his own iron scheme of things, grown-up dictatorship, therefore, had seemed to Leopold arbitrary and purposeless; his idea was: They dispose of but do not affect me. But *this* present decision being come at was vital. This man affects me; I cannot affect him. He is he, but not his, hers. My mother, my mother, always my mother. I must not speak while he wonders what she will say. Watching Ray's cigarette being held between his fingers, fuming, watching smoke being puffed out sharply against the light, Leopold contemplated this theft of his own body that was being proposed, rejected, decided upon. Ray, still looking out of the window, said: 'I am taking it that you *don't* want to go back to Italy?'

'No.'

'And that that's not just an idea someone just put into your head?'

'Mme Fisher said I was wrong to mind where I go.'

'She did? . . . But you've been all right there?'

'I didn't think, till – '

' – Till your mother wrote? You know, till things get fixed up – if they ever do get fixed up – this amounts to stealing you?'

'I don't mind.'

'There's no doubt, you know, that I ought to have kept out of this.'

'Doesn't my mother know you – ?'

'I daresay she guesses. Because when I went out, I – '

'Are you afraid?' said Leopold.

'We can put in time somewhere,' his mother's husband went on. 'Across the river from here. At the hotel we always – '

'Put in time? You mean, wait till – '

'Yes, I mean wait.'

'For her. Oh. Yes.'

223

Turning round from the window, Ray looked at the boy in the dark blouse who sat gripping the wooden kerb of the sofa on which he sat. For how long, Ray thought, have I thought? For how long has he not stopped gripping the sofa? All he has to say is: 'Oh. Yes.' Ray stared at the child's outline against the wallpaper. But after the outside light behind the branches the salon was so dark that he hardly saw what he saw.

A door shut over their heads and Miss Fisher came downstairs. She looked in and said it was five o'clock.

4

The significance of its being five o'clock was that Henrietta's train left the Gare de Lyon at half-past six, so Miss Fisher wanted to know where she was. She was not still on the stairs, so must have crept either up or down. Miss Fisher feared she might have returned to the salon, breaking in on the conversation there.

Naturally, Henrietta would not have done this. She turned out to be in the dining-room; she sat at the table re-reading *The Strand Magazine,* which she had brought in here from the salon when Miss Fisher sent her to go and play. When Miss Fisher looked in she did not look up, pointedly. She had switched on the hanging light, which shone on the glazed pages and her fair falling hair. The room, still smelling of *blanquette de veau* at lunch and packed with bracketed furniture of a dull reddish grain, like pencilwood, had not from the first pleased her; by now she was bored, too, with looking through the tight blind at a street with so little animation and telling herself that this was a street in Paris. She had hitched her heels on to the rung under her chair.

'Oh, dear,' said Miss Fisher, 'you haven't had any tea.'

'No, I suppose I haven't,' said Henrietta remotely.

'You shall have tea now, at once – or would you prefer chocolate?'

'Do you think I ought to, before a journey?'

'Perhaps not, no: tea, perhaps. You know, Henrietta, your train goes at half-past six? So soon we must . . .' She put her hand to her forehead. 'I reproach myself,' she said, 'that you have not seen more of Paris.'

'I shall some day, I suppose.'

'And that there has been no tea yet. I have attended to nothing. Just now, my mother is not at all well.'

'Isn't Leopold going to have tea?'

'I shall go and see,' said Miss Fisher. She darted back to the salon, went right in, shut the door. This did not seem the way to order anyone's tea. Henrietta's inside rumbled politely; she pressed her hand to her belt and returned to *The Strand Magazine*. It had been waste being wise with Miss Fisher too much agitated to notice; she wished now she *had* said chocolate inside of tea. After several minutes the salon door opened, let out the gentleman's voice saying – 'full responsibility – ' and, apparently, Leopold, who appeared in the dining-room.

Hands clasped behind his back, electrically silent, he stood looking at Henrietta, who thought: Heavens, what has been happening now?

Aloud she said: 'Did they send you in here, too?'

'No, I just came.'

'We're supposed to be having tea now.'

'Oh, I shan't want any tea; I'll have mine out.'

'Why?' Henrietta said with a sinking heart.

'I'm going away in a minute with Mr Forrestier. He's telling her now. I shan't come back.'

'Neither shall I,' she said quickly. 'My train goes at half-past six.'

'I haven't got to catch any damned train now.'

'I don't see why you should show off, even if you haven't.'

'He says I needn't go back to Italy.'

'Aren't you sorry *at all*, when you've lived with them all your life?'

Leopold looked embarrassed, and then angry.

'Besides,' pursued Henrietta, 'why should *he* interfere?'

225

'He's married to my mother.'

'Then he's your step-father?'

Leopold hesitated, he said quickly, 'Yes.'

'Well, I hope you will like him,' said Henrietta. She was beginning to say: 'But look at Mr Murdstone – ' when she found tears of mortification pricking her eyes, bent over *The Strand Magazine* and said nothing more. The matter might simply be that she wanted her tea so much.

When she looked up, Leopold still stood by the sideboard; having taken an orange from the dessert basket he rolled and squeezed the orange between both hands, smiling down at it in a secret way. His eyes were darker than ever, his face whiter, his nostrils distended like her rocking-horse's. She did not like to look at him with the orange. She steadied her voice and said: 'You do have your ups and downs.'

'I knew this would happen somehow.'

'Tomorrow I shall be seeing the south of France,' Henrietta said, as though to herself.

'Have you seen a tree growing out of a crack in a grave?'

'They don't.'

'Yes, they do; Madame Fisher says so.'

'To begin with, no one would plant a tree in a grave ... *She* says Madame Fisher's worse tonight.'

'Is she?' said Leopold, looking at the orange.

'Poor thing,' said Henrietta. She added: 'I shall see oranges growing, and, of course, palms.'

Leopold held the orange up to the light at arm's length, against the dark dusk showing over the blind. His demoniac pride, his remorseless egotism made Henrietta lower her shocked eyes. She heard Miss Fisher hurry out of the salon, open the kitchen door and give an order in French. 'That sounds more like tea,' she said. As Leopold stayed like a statue, looking up at the orange, she decided to go to the bathroom before tea, and left the room without saying another word. On the landing she thought: He has forgotten crying ... There was dead silence behind Mme Fisher's door.

In the salon Naomi, who had come back to find Ray still standing as she had left him, repeated for the last time: 'Yes, I agree. Well? But you *are* forcing her hand.'

For the last time he said: 'I cannot help that.'

They had both said what they had to say. Naomi had given in. She was tired, clearly in pain of mind; he saw he would never know what she really felt. Dropping her head and looking for the first time at the broken alabaster on the table, she said: 'My dear Karen . . . My dear poor Karen.'

He saw what she saw. 'Yes, I broke that,' he said. 'I'm very sorry. It skidded off the table and broke. I'll get you another somehow. I hope this one wasn't precious?'

'Only, my mother liked it – Then I am not to write to Spezia, only to send the telegram?'

'Just that. We – I – we will write.'

'You understand that it all may be difficult?'

'We'll keep you out of it, naturally.'

'They have good hearts, too good, perhaps. But this is much to expect.'

'Naturally. It's preposterous.'

'I think it is sometimes simpler to do preposterous things,' she said, looking across at him.

Seeing her dark-circled eyes with pity, he said: 'This has been a hard day. *Is* there anything I can do?'

'No, no,' she said quickly. 'Up to now it has all been perfectly possible. The two children have both been quiet and good; one would have hardly known they were in the house. The accident of Henrietta's crossing Paris today has, of course, made things more difficult, but that could not be helped. And without her there I should have been more anxious about Leopold; they played together with cards and her magazine. But about Henrietta – yes: I *have* one favour to ask.' She stopped, smiling, then said: 'And it is not a small one, either. Henrietta must be accompanied to the Gare de Lyon to meet her escort for the Mentone train. The train goes at half-past six, and she must be there early. I have expected all day to take her myself. But since I last saw my mother I am in a predicament. I find my mother is worse;

she has agitated herself. She has not been so unwell for a long time. It has not been possible to keep what has been going on in the house away from her, as I should have wished. In consequence, she is restless and very weak; in some pain and demanding me constantly by her side. I blame my own negligence, leaving Leopold with her for so long: I had meant him, originally, not to enter her room. It was not good for him, either ... At such times, my mother cannot sleep but lies constantly watching one. Her state tonight has made me send for the doctor, though I do not think he can do much. This makes it impossible for me to leave the house. All this I could not foresee when I promised Mrs Arbuthnot – '

'In fact, we have all made her ill.'

'No, she is always ill. Tonight she makes herself more ill.'

'So you would like me to see off Henrietta?'

'That was what I wanted to ask.'

'I wish I could do more.'

'I know you are very kind. But we can only help ourselves.'

'I think that is true of you. Look how you helped Karen.'

'I helped myself; at that time we needed each other – If you will really do this, I shall be greatly helped. With Henrietta in your charge, I can feel confident. Look, I must give you Mrs Arbuthnot's letter; this makes it all clear, I think. Also I have a letter from Miss Watson confirming everything. It is carefully worked out – Then when you come back I will have Leopold's clothes packed; he has not much here, you know.'

'Just as well,' said Ray. He looked at Naomi oddly. 'I somehow stick at making off with his clothes, on top of everything else. Can't he do with what he stands up in?'

'Only luggage for three days. Yes, a little boy must have that – pyjamas, vests, a clean blouse. You will not want to waste time buying him clothes in Paris.'

'I suppose it will all square up. Look, need they take long

to pack? If you could pack them now I think we might make one job of it – all leave at once, I mean.'

'You would prefer that?'

'Yes,' Ray said, nervy and definite.

'Perhaps you are right.'

'We'd leave your house quiet sooner.'

'Yes,' she said. 'That is true.'

At half-past five Henrietta came quietly downstairs, ready to start at once. But nobody was about, so she had to wait in the hall. Like smoke coming under a door the dead silence of Mme Fisher seemed to pervade everywhere. She peeped into the salon, but Mr Forrestier, writing, did not look up. Her hat was put on straight, her hair brushed smooth hung over her overcoat, her gloves were firmly buttoned at each wrist. Of a crumb of *brioche* on one cheek she was unconscious; her morale was better since she had had tea. She was holding her dispatch case and had Charles the monkey under the other arm. On the right lapel of her coat was pinned the cerise cockade. The taxi had been ordered and should be here soon.

She looked upstairs, anxious. Could they all have forgotten? No, she believed Mr Forrestier to be truly dependable; she was glad of the change that sent him to see her off. She had felt at home with him from the first.

There were muted steps upstairs, then Leopold came down, followed by Miss Fisher with an admonishing finger on her lips. The departure became still more like a conspiracy. Leopold was buttoned into a bulky overcoat, below which his black-socked legs looked spindly thin. His crest of hair stood up from having been brushed, and he carried his sailor cap in his hand. His coming down made the staircase a grand staircase; he came down like a personage. (It is absurd, the silence, thought Henrietta, she must be lying and listening, she knows perfectly well.) Mariette the servant followed Miss Fisher, carrying Leopold's suitcase; she dumped the suitcase at the foot of the stairs, embraced Leopold with emotion, Henrietta with less emotion, heaved a big busty sigh and was sent away, regretting something in French. Miss Fisher, who had a half sheet in her hand, darted into the salon. 'Please listen,' she could be heard saying to Mr Forrestier. 'This is my telegram:

'Grant Moody Villa Fioretta Spezia. Leopold wishes remain in Paris few days longer full explanation follows trust no inconvenience all well Fisher.

'I think that is well put? I think that starts no hostility.'

He said, inside the salon: 'That sounds all right.'

Leopold had paused to hear the telegram being read out. Now he came up to Henrietta marvelling at the cockade. 'What are you wearing *that* for?'

'For Miss Watson to know me.'

'Who's Miss Watson?'

'The lady I have to meet to go to Mentone with. She will be wearing one too,' Henrietta said patiently.

'You will both look funny!'

'We'll take them off in the train.'

'Take yours off before you get in. I'd like to have it, rather: I like the colour.'

'Then perhaps you can have it for a memento, Leopold.'

But as she spoke the taxi drew up outside. 'Hi!' yelled Leopold. '*Taxi!* Here's our *taxi*, Miss Fisher!'

'*Sssh, ssh!*' she said, running out in despair. Ray from the door behind her said: 'Shut *up*, Leopold!'

'Oh,' she said at once, 'he did not mean any harm.' Then her eye, more happily, lit on Henrietta's cockade. 'Look,' she said to Ray, 'that's her cockade, you see. And Miss Watson will be wearing one just the same.'

'I see. Yes, it all seems very neat.'

Leopold ran down the hall, fought with the latch a moment; then swung open the street door with a bang. Fresh damp air came in. Outside stood the taxi, clicking away in the dark street, impatient as a new world at their door. The hall light fell on it, through the light fell fine rain. 'Come on,' he said, as quietly as he could. 'Come on everyone.'

'Leopold,' said Henrietta, 'aren't you going to say good-bye to Miss Fisher?'

Miss Fisher stood at the foot of the stairs, under the hanging light with its crimped white bell. She stared down the hall at the dark where the taxi stood, as though seeing something not happening today. When Leopold walked into view, politely holding his hand out, she started and looked down at him. Instead of shaking hands or bending down to kiss him, she put out her right hand gently to touch his face. The act seemed so natural that he stood with his face up, as though her expected fingers were so much rain. Her touch passed delicately across his forehead, down the line of one cheek. She looked into his eyes that were still to see so much, and at his lips, consideringly and gently, as though she could be no enemy of anything they could say. Leopold's upturned face remained during these moments thoughtless and pure. Then her hand drooped and, as though recalling what she must do, she stooped to kiss his cheek gently. 'Goodbye, Leopold.'

'Goodbye, Miss Fisher.'

Leopold turned and walked out into the taxi.

Henrietta approached with *her* face up to be kissed. 'Goodbye, Miss Fisher,' she said, 'and thank you so very much. Please say goodbye for me to Madame Fisher; I do hope she will be better tomorrow. Shall I give your love to my grandmother?'

'Yes, indeed. Remember to tell her, too, that I shall be writing tomorrow. You must have a happy journey. Goodbye, my dear Henrietta, goodbye.' She kissed Henrietta more warmly, more regretfully than she had kissed Leopold; Henrietta was startled to feel Miss Fisher's arms round her so close. You would think she was sorry for me. Picking up the dispatch case she had put down, she walked down the small lit hall, with its red stripes, into the taxi, through the cold fine rain.

She looked back to see Mr Forrestier take both Miss Fisher's hands, say something, drop them, then turn away hurriedly to pick up Leopold's case. He came heavily down

231

the hall with his hat in his other hand, told the driver Gare de Lyon, heaved the case into the taxi, got in and slammed the door without once looking back. Miss Fisher came uncertainly down the hall as though she were going to wave. But the taxi ground into motion and moved off; they left her still standing there, staring out at the patch of dark where they had been.

There now, thought Henrietta, I have forgotten my *Strand*.

Ray had moved Leopold on to the small seat opposite. They drove past the dark gardens into the bright boulevard, downhill. Wet pavements reflected the cafés; it must have been raining softly for some time. Lights wheeled in the artificial dusk. Henrietta thought: How much I should like to get out and have some fun. She looked through her window with heartbroken animation. What a party to miss! How fastidiously the French run through the rain, picking their way like cats. Once or twice she leaned forward to see out of Ray's window, stealing a look at his face, across which street lights ran. But as he did not speak she felt she had better not. Opposite, Leopold sat like a young idol, tottering once or twice when the taxi swerved. Not looking left or right, he appeared to Henrietta to be holding off Paris almost violently. If Paris happened to him on top of everything else, he would burst, she thought; I am very glad *I* do not take things like that. He was attacked on all sides by bright noises; lights wheeled across his small set exalted face.

She shifted Charles on her arm and his head bumped Ray's shoulder. 'Sorry,' said Henrietta.

Apparently glad to speak, Ray said: 'That's a large monkey.'

'His ears have come very loose.'

'Has he travelled much?'

'No, not much. I haven't, you see.'

'Have you seen much today?'

'No. There was no one to take me out.'

'That seems bad luck.'

'Of course, I envy Leopold, having seen Italy.'

'You will some day, I'm sure.'

'And staying on in Paris: that will be marvellous for him. What I had been wanting to see was the Trocadéro. Leopold will see everything, I suppose.'

'How possibly could I?' Leopold said, unmoved.

'Oh, Leopold, remind me to give you that cockade!'

'What cockade?'

Henrietta tightened her arm round Charles. 'Mr Forrestier, what is a *couchette*?'

'Er – not quite a berth. Why?'

'Miss Watson and I have got them. How I look forward to waking up tomorrow!'

'Yes, I'm sure you do.'

'I mean, seeing orange trees and the bright blue sky ... What is *apéritif*?'

'Something to drink.' Ray re-crossed his legs. ('Sorry,' he said to Leopold. 'That your foot?')

'The worst of it is,' she said, 'I get so thirsty in trains.'

'We'll get a bottle of something.'

The taxi stuck in blocks, jarred, swerved clear, darted between lit buses solid with heads. On kerbs people watched it come and drew back suspiciously. I have not met the French, Henrietta thought. It was funny to stare into their unseeing eyes. The taxi pumped itself through wet-evening Paris in jerks.

'Oh, look at the lights in the *river*! Oh, Leopold, look, look!'

'I saw that last night.'

'Leopold's been in Paris a night longer than me. – You'll be here tonight, too, when I'm in the *couchette*. – I envy Leopold, staying in a hotel.'

'There'll be a hotel for you at Mentone.'

'Oh no; my grandmother has a flat.'

'Have I got a grandmother?' said Leopold.

'Yes, Mr Forrestier, *has* he?'

'He's got a grandfather.'

'Oh, I wish I had!'

'Where?' said Leopold.

'In England,' Ray said, not adding: 'Your grandmother died of you.'

'Oh, England,' said Leopold. 'Yes, of course.'

Silence sat in the taxi as though a stranger had got in. Leopold now began casting glances at Paris, turning his head aloofly from side to side. The taxi got too tight. Ray's knees, jammed sideways by Leopold's suitcase, which had been moved to let down the flap seat, bulked between the children; it was inevitable that Leopold, turning, should kick him and Henrietta's monkey keep lurching against his thigh. The free flow of lit objects made being boxed up crucial: Henrietta had a throe of the fidgets; she routed about with her toe for her dispatch case, took off her gloves and, heaving, scrammed one into each pocket. Ray was boxed up with two restless octopi. A taxi can hold two men, not sitting on tails and wearing opera hats, and two women in crushable gowns, with fans; they can laugh and talk. But sense of space is emotional: *this* taxi, bursting, seemed to groan on its springs. What was inconvenient could, now, only be said. ' – Leopold, try turning right round and putting your feet on the suitcase. Henrietta; look here – '

'Would you rather I had Charles on the far side?'

'Well, I would, yes. But what I wanted to say, was – You've had a funny day, not at all what you bargained for or your grandmother bargained for, or the Fishers either, when they took you on. You seem to have had a thin time; no Trocadéros or anything. In a roundabout way that's my fault; we won't go into all that. The point is, that you've happened, entirely by accident, to come in on a good deal that's not your affair at all. You will regard it as that? As not your affair, I mean?'

'How?' she said, very anxious. 'How do you mean?'

'You or I would never discuss other people's affairs, would we? Naturally not. Besides wasting one's own time, it might be a nuisance to them. Of course you would see that.'

Henrietta glanced at Leopold nervously: he showed no

sign of interest. 'Oh *no*,' she said. 'I mean, oh *yes*; of course.'

'So you will not discuss this with your grandmother, your girl friends, your relations in England, in fact with anyone? Best of all, quite forget it; it's not interesting.'

But she peered at him doubtfully.

'That's how you feel, of course. One can't forget things to order. I'm taking it, then, that as what has gone on today regards Leopold, me, the Fishers and someone else you don't know, you will not talk about it ever, to anyone.'

She took a deep earnest breath. 'No, I never, never will.'

'Thank you,' said Ray. 'I thought we'd see eye to eye. What do you like in the train: lemonade, Vichy?'

'Anything not gassy, if you know what I mean.'

'Have you got all your things? We shall be there in a minute. Gloves? Handbag? Dropped anything down the seat?'

She was too much uplifted to tell him she had no handbag yet.

Ray, Henrietta and Leopold now approached the barrier of the Ventimille train. This station is more daunting than the Gare du Nord: golder, grander. Henrietta discovered that half-past six is 18.30 in Paris: clocks must be larger, she thought. She walked by Ray like a lady. Supposing, supposing, supposing Miss Watson is not here! ... Ray carried her dispatch case and a bottle of Vichy in a twist of pink paper. Henrietta carried, in addition to Charles, three outsize packets of Suchard, a carton of grapes, and two rolls with ham clapped inside them that she had fancied the look of and Ray had bought for her at the buffet here. When they were already half-way to the barrier, Ray had plunged back to a kiosk and bought her an armful of American picture papers, and a bronze paper-weight, with the Eiffel Tower on it. 'That was a mistake,' he said. 'I'm afraid it was the Trocadéro you wanted. Now, that will just be heavy.'

'No, I love it,' she said, scarlet with pleasure.

Henrietta still had her happy flush when they perceived

235

what was unmistakably Miss Watson, standing beside the barrier. A cerise cockade was pulled out under her fur and she eyed everyone closely, almost suspiciously. The moment she saw the cockade on Henrietta, her chaperonage snapped on her like a trap. 'You are Henrietta Mountjoy?' Henrietta's hand, which had crept through Ray's arm, loosened sadly. 'Yes. Are you Miss Watson?' she said.

'But where is Miss Fisher?' asked Miss Watson in a challenging voice. Henrietta feared she was going to be difficult, as the other lady had been at the Gare du Nord.

Ray, who had raised his hat, said: 'I am Miss Fisher, virtually. Her mother is unwell, so she asked me to take her place.'

Miss Watson gave him a look, but his appearance was calming. He sympathized with her wish to get into the train quickly to see nobody else took their *couchettes*, which would mean a fight, and how disagreeable that was. Then she said she hoped she had not been abrupt, but somebody else's child was a responsibility and one did not know where one was these days. 'Thank you,' she said, 'you have been really most kind. Henrietta, thank Mr – thank your friend. Now that's *your* dispatch case, is it? Oh yes, and the monkey. And come along now; now we must come along.'

Henrietta looked up at Ray with sad grey eyes. Leopold stood by, silent, looking at her. Suddenly, she put down her dispatch case and, pell-mell, all the parcels, unpinned her cockade and gave it to Leopold. 'Here,' she said, 'this was the cockade I meant.'

'Oh, what are you doing?' said Miss Watson. 'Ought you to give that cockade to that little boy?'

'The person I'm meeting next is my own grandmother, and if she doesn't know me without it I might as well be dead.'

Miss Watson feared Henrietta was going to be difficult; snatching the parcels up from the dusty, spitty platform, she blew them over reproachfully. 'Well, come along,' she said.

'You said you liked the colour,' said Henrietta, hurriedly, to Leopold.

'Yes, I like it; it reminds me of you.'

Miss Watson said: 'Now, say goodbye.'

Henrietta and Leopold shook hands for the first time, like people attempting some savage rite. His hand was nervy and dry. Their eyes dropped and they edged away from each other. Henrietta looked lost. Ray held his hand out and she put hers into it gratefully. His overwrought eyes held no reflection of her, but, bending, he said: 'Henrietta, good luck.'

Miss Watson, who had possession of Henrietta's ticket, presented it at the barrier, and they both walked away alongside the long high train ... Ray and Leopold stood watching Henrietta, long fair despondent hair down her back, walk away down the platform with Miss Watson. Charles's rump hung out under one arm; she grew smaller and smaller.

She turned round, waved, and held up the paperweight.

Ray, watching Henrietta walking away, thought: And so now ... 'Come on,' he said, 'she won't look round again.'

'All right,' said Leopold. 'Where are we going now?'

Where are we going now? The station is sounding, resounding, full of steam caught on light and arches of dark air: a temple to the intention to go somewhere. Sustained sound in the shell of stone and steel, racket and running, impatience and purpose, make the soul stand still like a refugee, clutching all it has got, asking: 'I am where?' You could live at a station, eating at the buffet, sleeping on the benches, buying your cigarettes, going nowhere next. The tramp inside Ray's clothes wanted to lie down here, put his cheek in his rolled coat, let trains keep on crashing out to Spain, Switzerland, Italy, let Paris wash like the sea at the foot of the ramp. And a boy ought to sleep anywhere, like a dog. But the stolen boy is too delicate. Standing there on thin legs, he keeps his eyes on your face. Where are we going? Where are we going now?

Henrietta is gone, importantly silent, for ever. That straight talk – or was it straight? – that public school talk when the taxi got too tight has settled Henrietta. Now peace rests on girders of clever honour, like that glass roof on clever girders of steel. I think like a drunk man. What *about* that drink? But here's Leopold; here will always be Leopold —

– What have I done?

What will *she* do?

Leopold repeated: 'Where are we going?'

Ray said: 'I've got to telephone.'

But a train went out and the hollow station thundered. Leopold shouted: 'What?'

'Telephone. I've got to telephone.'

'Oh, to my mother?'

'What?'

'To my mother?'

'– For God's sake, come out of here!'

So they walked across the big space between the barriers and the buffet staircase, the exits: Ray head down, Leopold looking round him, twirling like a camellia Henrietta's cockade. Leopold took a step and a half to each of Ray's, when anyone barged their way he swerved in to Ray instinctively. Ray strode like a robber with one babe through a wood. Their inappropriateness to each other made people stare. Leopold had in blazing gold round his cap the fierce name of a battleship. His silence fell in with Ray's as imperfectly as his step – he seemed to be buoyed along.

In the hall outside the turnstile it was quieter. Ray slowed up. 'I'm sorry,' he said, 'I can't stand the noise in there.'

'I rather liked it,' said Leopold.

(The devil you did. You will notice, we talk where I can talk. You will not quote Mme Fisher, you will not kick me in taxis, you will not shout in houses where they are ill. You will wear a civilian cap, not snub little girls and not get under my feet. There will be many things that you will not like. There are many things that I do not like about you.)

'What I was trying to say,' Ray went on aloud, 'was: I must telephone – yes, to Versailles, to your mother. She may be beginning to wonder why I am not back. Then I shall get a drink. Then we might get something to eat.'

238

'What, at the hotel?'

'I'll see; we'll check in these first, anyway.'

'Then?'

'Come on,' Ray said, quickening his steps again.

'Will my mother come tonight?'

'Come on,' Ray repeated.

'Where to?'

'A taxi out here.'

They left the hall, which was quiet enough to echo, through an open arch, and stood outside the station. Fine rain still fell outside the projecting roof. No taxi came immediately; here they stood, under the strong arc lamps, watching the rain falling against the dark. The air tasted of night and Leopold shivered once. 'Cold?' 'No.' No, he was not cold; he had been someone drawing a first breath. Ray had not seen Karen's child in bright light before; now he saw light strike the dilated pupils of Leopold's eyes. Egotism and panic, knowing mistrust of what was to be, died in Ray as he waited beside Leopold for their taxi to come: the child commanded tonight, I have acted on his scale.

Here, at the head of the ramp, they stood at a commanding, heroic height above the level of Paris, which they saw. Leopold said: 'Is it illuminated?' The copper-dark night sky went glassy over the city crowned with signs and starting alight with windows, the wet square like a lake at the foot of the station ramp.